SAVANNAH 1.0

The Quest for Love

Terry R. Lacy

For Ada Mae, whom I dearly love, yet hardly know.

CONTENTS

FOREWORD

No one does this sort of thing alone, and I need to thank many people for their help along the way. To Charlie Martin, who read every word of every draft until I'm sure he grew sick of it, thank you for giving me a place to write this, and allowing me to bring a dog into your house of cats. To Andy Solomon, editor, teacher, and friend. Thanks for teaching me how to do this, and for always being there, even after you retired. Thank you to every student who gave me input on not only this series, but also the Jackal series. Your help is invaluable. The cover art was professionally done by Randy Smith. I think he does great work, and you can find him on Facebook. You can also find me on Facebook. Look for the Jackal's Galley room for infrequent updates and junk I find funny. As always, feel free to drop a line at Terry-.R.Lacy@yahoo.com. (Don't forget the middle R. There's another Terry Lacy out there who gets pissed when he gets my emails.) Thanks for reading.

SAVANNAH 1.0

The Quest for Love

CHAPTER 1

Dan Mitchell stood, straightened the crease in his trousers, then sat again.

He placed his hands back in his lap, fingers against his thighs, flat and straight and perfectly parallel to the aforementioned crease, which was fine on the right side, but askew on the left. He stood and tried it once more. The two police officers who had testified against Savannah and him sat across the hall from them. They wore suits and ties instead of their blue uniforms, looking more like bankers with badges than Hamilton, Ohio's Finest. The white one hunched forward, elbows resting on his splayed thighs, while the Black one leaned back with his arms crossed over his chest, ankle resting on his knee, and when he looked at Dan or Savannah it was without expression. Neither seemed to mind that sitting that way wrinkled their suits. Dan could still feel the cold metal cuffs closing tight around his wrists as though it happened yesterday, the white one yanking him to his feet, leading him to the back of the cruiser while the Black one escorted Savannah as though they were common criminals. Neither had missed a single day of the trial, which struck Dan as odd. He assumed they would testify then go back to work. They had been here for every minute, as if they had a personal stake in it. Perhaps in a way they did. It wasn't every day that an arrest made national news after all. Maybe they saw a movie-of-the-week deal in it for them, or at least an episode of *Cops*. He wished he could stop glancing at them every few seconds, but that didn't seem to be optional.

He looked straight ahead at the blank wall in front of him,

over the heads of the officers. This wasn't like the movies, where courthouses were made from dark stained wood, polished to a high gleam, with rump-worn wooden benches lining the corridors. Those were the days of craftsmen, showing off their skills in the county's most respected place, when people took pride in their work. This was modern—drywall long ago painted a dull, flat green now gouged in places, leaving long white scars of not-so-fresh plaster, as if someone had scored them with a jagged knife, but since everyone had to pass through a metal detector to enter, he doubted that was the cause.

Savannah took his hand and gave it a mild squeeze, and he turned to her and smiled, trying his best to look stoic, but it was fake. He didn't feel brave at all. In fact, he was terrified. In his entire life, he would have never guessed that he of all people would wind up here, waiting to be adjudicated on not one, but seven felony charges, each carrying a sentence recommendation of seven years, which, if they ran consecutively, totaled longer than he had been alive. His lawyer, Ms. April Gatherwright, who stood just over six-feet in her platform heels and was dressed in a plain yet expensive business suit that made her look like a lawyer from one of Dan's favorite TV shows, (coupled with her raven-black hair, olive complexion, and smoky voice, she and the actress could have been sisters), said he shouldn't worry. She didn't seem to be. She was currently standing next to the door that led back into the courtroom, chatting with Greenley, the prosecuting attorney, as if they were old friends, and Dan glanced over Savannah's shoulder and watched the woman smile as she stroked her long black hair away from her face then leaned in and touched Greenley's arm as they chatted. No—she didn't seem concerned at all. But then, win or lose, she wasn't the one facing five decades behind bars.

He realized that this was the worst part—not the arrest—not the fall from grace in the eyes of his neighbors, not that he believed they held him in high esteem to begin with—not even the trial itself—it was the waiting for twelve people whom the State of Ohio, County of Butler, City of Hamilton, had determined were his peers, to decide whether he deserved to spend the next half-century in a six-by-eight foot cell with someone named Bubba. Dan had seen the movies—he had watched *Oz*—so he knew what went on in prison. On the tough-guy scale, he knew his ass would be traded for a pack of Ramen.

Savannah smiled for him again, and he forced one in return. She had a wisp of blonde hair that had fallen forward and he brushed it back, fearing his OCD would kick into full-blown overdrive if he left it hang. He could manage it for the most part —it had been months since it had ruled him—but it grew worse when he was stressed, at times so bad he called himself crazy, and this was probably as stressed as he had ever been. She caught his hand as it brushed the hair away, and kissed his palm, soft and warm. The odds were better than average that this would be one of the last kisses he ever got from her, regardless of what his expensive lawyer said. That thought frightened him almost as much as prison.

The courtroom doors opened, and the prosecutor entered first, but April Gatherwright paused and waited for Savannah and him to enter before her. She smiled as they passed, confident and reassuring enough that he wondered if she practiced it in a mirror for the benefit of all her clients.

They moved to the defendant's table together. He and Savannah were being tried under the same charges for the same incident—might as well be tried together. The only difference would be the sentencing for each would be completely different. Even if his sentences ran concurrent, and he was facing only seven years, he knew he wasn't the type of person who would survive prison, not because he had one of those souls that couldn't be pent up, but because he had a personality that seemed to attract life's bullies, and what was prison if not a collection of them? With the knowledge that he would die at the end of a homemade shank either in the shower or the yard, it meant their sentences wouldn't be that different at all.

He looked down at the legal pads in front of them. His own had a few simple lines scribbled on it, things he had written to his attorney to counter some of the statements the people testifying against them were making. "She was just saying hello," and "It wasn't assault, I barely touched him," were the first two, but the others were variations on the theme. Savannah's had no words at all, but was an ink-on-yellow-legal-paper rendition of the courtroom with Dan in every position, as if he were the prosecuting attorney who questioned Dan on the stand in front of a jury of twelve Dans, each in a different pose, while a Dan in black robes sat in judgment of a coat-and-tie wearing Dan at the defense table. He found the artwork itself quite beautiful, but the idea seemed profound, a not-so-thinly-veiled statement on society, as if each person committed crimes against himself— accused himself—sat in judgment upon himself. It was a subject matter he had never before seen. When he considered that she had taken up drawing only about a month ago, it seemed doubly impressive.

Greenley looked smug. Dan didn't blame him. The jury had been out less than two hours. It meant that these peers who weren't smart enough to get out of jury duty had reached a quick and easy decision. Either they agreed they were both guilty, or that the law itself was unconstitutional, and since none of them struck Dan as enlightened, he didn't like his odds.

Everyone rose when The Honorable Margaret Mason entered, and she gaveled them back into session. She was an elderly Black lady—her silvery-white hair making her appear old enough to have retired if she'd worked a job that required labor of the hands and not the mind. She asked the bailiff to bring in the jury and when they entered, Dan searched their faces for any hint of what they had decided—perhaps a reassuring nod from one of the men, or maybe even a look of disgust from one of the women, but he got nothing from any of them. No one made eye contact. He didn't take that as a good sign.

When the judge asked the foreman—forewoman to be precise, and Dan liked being precise—if they had reached a unanimous verdict, the lady, a whip-thin white woman who looked as if she had watched a lot of daytime court TV shows and was now

5

happy to be a part of one, rose and said they had. The bailiff took the piece of paper that held Dan and Savannah's fate from her and carried it to the judge. Mason read it, nodded, and returned it to the man, who took it back to the forewoman. Dan, who normally enjoyed things like pomp and circumstance and procedure, and believed he would have made a fine military man if he had only been required to perform drill and ceremony, had to fight to not scream for them to just get on with it.

"On the first charge of lewd and lascivious acts in front of a child, how do you find?"

"We find the defendants—"

CHAPTER 2

Three months doesn't seem like a long time. Three months is barely long enough to do much of anything, short of maybe travel, but even then, it's not long enough to really get to know a place. Three months is good if someone wants to play tourist—not enough to become a local.

Three months was a death sentence. The doctor would come into his office where he had asked you to wait, looking grave in his white lab coat and say, "I'm sorry Mr. Mitchell, but you have only three months to live." Three months would be barely enough time to get his head around the concept of his own mortality, much less come to terms with it.

Three months is a season. Any season, pick a favorite. Three months is Spring, with its promise of new life—blooming flowers and baby bunnies. Three months is Summer, filled with heat and bikinis and trips to amusement parks. Autumn has pretty leaves, Halloween and Thanksgiving, and even Winter boasts Christmas and new-fallen snow. Three months is a blink, a whisper, the flash of a moment when cast against a lifetime.

Three months ago was when this began. Three months ago, Savannah arrived on his doorstep, and it soon became three months of accusations and disgusted leers from his neighbors —three months of being in the news every night—of the incessant ringing of the phone and barrage of emails—of reporters camped in his yard like paparazzi, hoping to get even more footage of Savannah, as if she were a movie star. Three months of that was an eternity. He'd often wondered what it must be like to be famous. He'd never wondered what it would be like to be infamous.

* * *

The day she arrived was the happiest in Dan Mitchell's life.

He sat on his immaculate couch, in his immaculate living room, the television on for background noise. He wanted to check the weather again, to make sure it was to be a pretty Easter Weekend. The forecaster had said it was supposed to be, but now that the actual weekend was approaching, the predictions would firm up, and he wanted to check it again. Perhaps it had changed since this morning.

"This is the Ohio News Network with your Weather on the Tens, and now for our latest look at your Ohio Legislature," the news anchor said. The anchor was a clean cut man, with one of those faces that didn't give away his age on camera. If someone had told Dan the news anchor was thirty, he would have believed it just as easily as he would a claim of fifty. Dan found it odd that people were expected to trust a man whose face was so easily deceptive about his age.

"The latest on Ohio's new 'Sex Bot' laws, yesterday Governor Richard Tubman signing into law what many have called the strictest of all regulations governing Sex Bots, that's robots manufactured specifically for sexual gratification. Governor Tubman, a long-time supporter of the bill, had this to say—"

"It is the responsibility of the state to protect its citizens, especially our children, against these acts of sexual perversion. We're not trying to legislate what someone does in the privacy of their own homes, or in their own bedrooms, but we must band together—"

Dan turned the volume down and waited for the weather to come on. The new laws were necessary, he agreed. They were to stop sexual deviants from fornicating with dolls in public parks and playgrounds. Who would do such a thing? Acts of sexual gratification should take place in the privacy of one's home, preferably in the bedroom with the lights out.

His nervous fingers picked a dark blue piece of lint from his tan trousers—where had that come from?—which he rolled into a ball and placed in the glass ashtray that had never held a cigarette. Smoking was a vile habit, but he found ashtrays useful for holding life's tiny messes until he could find the time to properly clean them. The lone lint ball was the only thing in the ashtray, no larger than the head of a pin.

It taunted him. "Look at the mess, look at the mess." For some reason, the lint ball had his mother's voice. Look at it? He couldn't look away from it.

What if she arrived now? Not Mother of course, but her. Her, her. What if the doorbell rang and she was here? She would see this mess in the ashtray and believe him a slob—a total and utter pig, living in a sty. Was that the first impression he wanted her to have of his home? Worse yet, of him? He checked his watch, and the clock on the mantel. Both were synced electronically to the Department of Defense master clock in Washington, D.C., so both said 1:04pm—she was due between 1:00 and 3:00. What if she arrived and he was cleaning? Wouldn't that mean he didn't care enough that she was coming to have cleaned beforehand, or that he hadn't planned ahead for such an event? "I should have planned ahead," he said to himself, not out loud, because crazy people talked to themselves out loud. He wasn't crazy. Of that, he felt certain.

He would leave the lint ball. There—that was settled. It was just a lint ball. He would ignore it. He placed his hands, palms down on his thighs after adjusting the crease in his pants to be straight, and waited, content in his decision. If she arrived and saw it and was offended by it, he would find a way to make it up to her, perhaps with a movie and a nice dinner, or a pleasant drive. She had never taken a drive through the countryside, the windows down, warm air blowing in as he drove a consistent 30 mph, both hands on the steering wheel of course, on the winding back roads, past the bright painted barns and fresh-mown fields, the aroma of honeysuckle filling the car, the fragrance of Spring—the smell of life.

"Look at the mess—mess—mess."

He would pack a lunch, and they could picnic beside a babbling brook, the gentle sound of the water as it rambled through the stones on its way to the mighty Ohio River, then on to the Mississippi, then the Gulf of Mexico, then on, and on, and on... He would have to buy a picnic basket, of course— "I should have planned ahead," he said again—and a tablecloth so they would have a place to sit, which he would have to throw away afterwards, because no one wants a tablecloth that has been on the ground, especially after someone sat on it, so he would have to remember to take trash bags—two white ones like he used in the kitchen, one for the mess ("look at the mess, mess, mess") of the picnic, and one for the tablecloth, then a large black garbage bag from the outside cans so he would have a place to dispose of the two white ones. It would be a perfect day—a beautiful day, with a blue sky untainted by clouds, except for maybe one or two cumulus clouds—the white puffy ones that held no rain—off in the distance for ambiance. Songbirds would sing in the trees, but none of those wretched crows with their cawing. There would be no ants, either. No flies while we're at it. No mosquitoes, no grasshoppers, no snakes, bunnies or bears. Okay, maybe a bunny and a butterfly or two, but not too close—over there by the creek is fine.

He checked the time again. 1:07. The lint ball quivered in the light breeze created by the central air. What if it blew away? What if it blew away and landed on the carpet and he couldn't find it? What would he do then?

He breathed a heavy sign of frustration and stood straight and tall, then bent at the waist and picked up the glass ashtray, carrying it to the kitchen, hand cupped over the top so the lint ball wouldn't blow away. The kitchen trash can was one of those with the electronic sensor which opened when he waved his hand over it. What had taken them so long to invent such a wonderful contraption? You could open a trash can without having to touch it? They had the ones you could open with your foot, of course, but then you had to change your socks every time you used it, and that meant you also had to wash your feet. Who would put on clean socks without washing their feet? This electronic gadget had saved him a fortune in laundry and foot powder. He was on a waitlist to buy one for the outside cans as soon as it was released. He shook the lint ball out of the ashtray and into the white plastic bag inside the can. It landed, a tiny blue spec on a field of white that reminded him of the hardest jigsaw puzzle he had ever worked, a lone blueberry on a solid white background. At 5000 pieces, it had taken him over a week of his summer vacation to complete when he was fifteen. He'd glued it to a piece of poster board and had it framed, and it hung in his home office to this day.

And now he had a miniature replica of it in the bottom of his kitchen trash can, staring back at him, almost mocking. The trash can had been empty—pristine—but no longer. He stared at it until the automatic lid closed, then he washed the ashtray with his scrubby brush, dried it on a dishtowel which he folded with precision and hung it back on the drying rack and took the ashtray back to the living room and placed it on the coffee table. There. That's done. He took his seat on the couch and resumed his wait. It was 1:12. He had missed the weather thanks to that stupid lint ball which was now defiling the pristine garbage bag and he should really take that to the outside cans, but it would just have to wait. He would take it out later, after dinner. After dinner would be fine. He straightened the crease in his trousers as he fought the urge to pick another lint ball.

The Cincinnati Reds logo was on the screen behind the commentator. Dan wasn't a sports guy, so didn't turn up the volume. He didn't understand people's preoccupation with what person put what ball through what apparatus, as if they, the spectators, had personal stakes in it. He was aware of gambling, but surely not everyone who watched sporting events wagered on the outcomes, did they?

He refused to think about the lint ball in the garbage can. He wouldn't allow himself to dwell on it. It was in the trash can and it was fine. It was no big deal. He could ignore it. He just needed to think of other things—that's all. Easy enough.

He wondered what she would be like. Not what she looked

like—he knew that already, in theory of course, but he knew looks were a tiny fraction of the entire package. Someone could be pretty, but if they weren't nice, their looks ceased to matter—take Sheila for example. When she had been nice, he'd been attracted to her. When she'd stopped being nice, he was less attracted to her. That was the way it worked for him—he wasn't sure about anyone else. Or a person could seem fine—almost perfect, but they could have that one serious flaw you couldn't stand, like smoking, or making smacking noises with their lips while eating. That one lone flaw could stick out like a lone blueberry on a field of white, (or a lint ball in a pristine garbage can?)

"Dammit," he said aloud, not caring that he was alone. "Not now. Not today." He clenched his fists tight against his thighs and tried to force the thought of the lint ball away. His breath turned deep, as if he were in an actual physical altercation, and he felt his heart beat harder—not faster, just harder—he could feel it thumping in his chest, and that wasn't normal, was it? "Not today," he said again, and it worked—he was able to ignore the lint ball—for ten seconds at least. "Dammit." This time he stood up and went to the trash can.

He stood over it, staring down at the closed lid, not wanting to open it. That would be the line—the point of no return—he knew it would be. If he could just not open it, he could forget about it. He could wait and take it out later. "Later," he said aloud. "I'll take you out later." Any dog owner would have recognized that commanding tone, leaving no negotiations for the dog. The dog would understand that they would go on their walk later. The dog would obey.

A little red LED light on the can's sensor flashed periodically. He'd never timed it, but it felt like ten seconds. Every ten seconds or so, it would blink, then nothing. He had no idea what purpose that light served, and it didn't do it all the time. It did it for about fifteen minutes after the can was used, then stopped. He had not noticed any delay in the response time between when the light was flashing and when it wasn't. He'd read the enclosed manual, curious about the light's purpose, but the can was manufactured in China, and the manual a poor translation. It said there was a light, but it said nothing about why it had a light. He counted the flashes as he stared at the lid, trying to not think of the lint ball in the down time. He made it to ten.

"Dammit," he said again. He couldn't remember ever having cursed so much in a single day, and what made it worse was he wasn't cursing the lint ball—he was cursing himself—cursing his failure. He went to the cabinet under the kitchen sink, put on the rubber gloves he kept just for this purpose, the can of Clorox wipes, and a fresh trash bag. He removed the inner plastic liner from the can's outer metal shell, and put it on the floor, then removed the lint-ball-filled trash bag. It only took two Clorox wipes to clean the inner liner because it wasn't that dirty, and he put those into the bag with the offensive lint ball that he was about to take outside, put the new bag in the liner, then the liner back into the can. He left his gloves on as he went to the back door and slipped his outdoor slippers on, then carried the bag to the outside receptacle. He washed the gloves before he returned them to the shelf under the sink, then washed his hands for the ninth time that day. Nine wasn't good. It was odd, and it wasn't prime. Good numbers were either even or prime. Of course, only the number two could be both, which made it the best number.

He swept the floor where the liner had sat while he changed the bag, then mixed hot water and bleach to mop that spot, but didn't stop there. He mopped the entire kitchen for the second time since breakfast, then dumped the dirty mop water in the sink in the mud room by the back door, and put the mop and bucket back in the garage, in the corner where they belonged. He washed his hands again. Number Ten. That was good. Ten was a good number. He would say ten was a lucky number, if he believed in things like lucky numbers. He went back to the couch and sat, upset with himself for not being able to let the lint ball go, but glad he'd dealt with it. It was behind him. He could relax. He looked at his watch. It was 1:48.

He was quiet, a true introvert, uninterested in after-work drinks with after-work friends. In reality, he had no friends, only acquaintances, colleagues he could share a friendly nod with as they passed in the halls. There was Jeffrey Donovan, the guy who was always forgetting his password—well, not always, Dan scolded himself. "Always" wasn't the correct word, and Dan liked using correct words. "Always" meant "all the time," and Jeffrey didn't forget his password all the time, but he forgot it more often than everyone else in the office. "Frequently," was a better fit. Jeffery frequently forgot his password and needed a reset —that was better. When Jeffery mused that perhaps he should write it down, Dan turned serious. "Oh no. You mustn't. Someone might find it. That would be a breach of security." He liked educating people about policy and procedure, especially when security was an issue. As the head of IT, it was the one part of his job he was fussy about.

There was Alice, the heavy set lady who always wanted to talk about her grandchildren when Dan needed to install updates to her system—for that he was comfortable saying always. He couldn't think of a single time he had updated her system when she hadn't wanted to talk about these children Dan had never met—Darla the dancer, Jennifer the gymnast, and Robert who played rugby. Dan wanted to ask if they chose their hobbies through alliteration, until she had announced that her youngest, Stevie, was a swimmer, and while that was close, it wasn't close enough. When Dan remarked that Stevie should have become a stamp collector or a storm chaser, Alice had laughed politely, but looked confused.

There was Sheila, the lady who had only recently crossed that mental threshold from "girl" to "woman" in Dan's mind, and had spilled more than one cup of coffee into her keyboard, even though beverages were strictly forbidden at work stations. It was company policy. He'd had to crawl under her desk to replace it—the one part of his job he loathed—and when he turned to crawl from under it, she sat in her office chair, facing him, and he could see up her skirt to her—his breath grew shallow every time he thought about it—her panties. They had been pink and trimmed with white lace, and he had stopped and stared, a deer caught in headlights, unable to move or swallow or even breathe.

It's not that he hadn't seen women's panties before. He had watched pornography. Really—who hadn't? It was 2028. Thanks to the Internet, pornography piped into people's homes like water. But pornography seemed silly to Dan. All that moaning and groaning, with girls willing to do it with any random person who walked through the door, male or female, as if they waited all day for a warm body to show up. If pornography was real, pizza delivery guys got all the action. Cable installers did pretty well, too.

And it wasn't as if he were a virgin, either. He had his share of dalliances in college—the occasional tryst with one particular girl who was also interested in computers, but she stopped seeing him and began dating another boy whom she had declared was more intelligent than Dan, although to be honest, Dan had never noticed Jason Bradshaw's intelligence. After college, when he had failed to procure a suitable mate with which to have the occasional dinner and obligatory movie, he had tried prostitution. He had taken a bus to the seedier side of Cincinnati—which was in Newport, Kentucky he'd found out—and hired a young woman whom he had met on the street—a literal street walker —but the entire encounter had been too business like for Dan's taste, and with the necessity of condoms—he would never have dared to perform such an act without one—it became almost clinical. He could have had an equally satisfying time shaking a stranger's hand. He hadn't been able to finish. He had started off okay, but realized in mid-coitus that he was bored, so had stopped, because deep down, he hadn't found her that attractive.

He had since considered using an escort service. He thought perhaps the added rapport of the aforementioned dinner and a movie might help add interest, and thereby intimacy to the experience, but then he realized that wasn't what he wanted either. If he wanted anything at all, it was someone he could share thoughts and ideas with—a conversation that went beyond, "You want a date, sugar?"

So his attempts at sex—at any human interactions, really—

had been limited because his opportunities had been limited, and the few successful ones he had acquired in his 34 years, he kept stored away in his memory—his, "spank bank," his room-mates in college had called it—the way a squirrel stores acorns. They were the bulk of his fantasies, with a few about some of the women in his office scattered in for occasional seasoning.

But when he turned and saw Sheila's panties, her smooth legs opened slightly at the knees and her staring down at him, know-ing he was looking at her there, in that place, seeing her pink panties, he'd cringed. She would go to HR and file a complaint, and he had been to HR more than once for a good scolding. Women in the office said he made them uncomfortable when he looked at them. He wasn't sure what that meant. Were we not to look at people now? When he'd asked, he'd been told it was the way he looked at the women that made them uncomfortable. That left him even more confused. Were there different ways to look at someone? If so, what were the right ways? What were the wrong?

But Sheila had smiled at him when she caught him looking, her green eyes sparkling emeralds in an Irish meadow, her red hair—she was a redhead—God, he loved redheads—there was something magical about redheads. They were breathtaking or hideous—there was no in between. Sheila was in the breath-taking category. When she had smiled at him even though she had caught him looking—and he knew this was a bad look—there was no way Kristy McCullen, the raven-haired woman—God he loved black hair—and head of HR and the star of a few late-night fantasies herself that always seemed to involve black leather cat suits—perhaps because it would match her hair—there was no way she would believe it was an accidental look at Sheila's panties, even though it was, and she would fire him over an innocent look—a glance—a peek, really—nothing more. But Sheila smiled when he turned to crawl out. So he had looked at her knees—so what? It was perfectly harmless to look at some-one's knees, wasn't it? When she was standing, her skirt barely covered her knees, as if they cried out to be looked at. And when he'd glimpsed—that's really all it was, a glimpse, the way one might glimpse a girl on the street out of the bus window on the ride home, just a casual, non-threatening glimpse, nothing to go to HR about—her knees had been open. That wasn't his fault, was it? And he had seen her pink panties with the white lacy trim, just the hint of a triangle of fabric that reminded him of an arrowhead pointing the way to—he felt goose bumps rise on his arm. She had smiled. Demure. Innocent. Dare he say sexy? A small smile of secrets, something that passed between conspirators, a smile that had flipped her out of the "woman" category and back to the "girl" one, young and fresh and vulnerable. "You won't tell on me, will you?" she'd asked.

He blinked, his face showing no expression, because all he felt was confusion. Him tell on her? Was this another joke he didn't understand? Often his colleagues told jokes and he had learned to laugh politely at them to fit in better. This didn't seem like a joke, though. People laughed when they joked, and Sheila wasn't laughing. She looked concerned. Was it maybe a role reversal, the way therapists on TV used puppets when they wanted people to act out the other person's point of view? He had played with puppets as a child—had even considered becoming a ventriloquist at one time, until he realized he didn't like the way the doll made his hand sweat. He was silent for a few seconds while he tried to figure out what she meant. Finally he asked, "Excuse me?" in a confused tone. "Why?"

Her smile became a grin and she leaned forward and shoved his shoulder, light and playful—friendly, and he smelled her perfume, delicate and sweet and flowery— captivating— that was the right word— captivating. "For having coffee at my desk, silly." She leaned back again, but this time she crossed her legs, one calf resting lightly over her other shin, forcing her knees together, cutting off the chance at another peek, not that he would have taken one. She leaned forward again and spoke in a low voice so no one could hear. "It's not allowed anymore. I'm afraid they'll fire me if they find out."

Silly? She had called him silly? No one had ever called him

silly before, and he decided he liked it. He could be silly—he had a silly side. Not pornography silly, of course, but still playful. How astute it was of her to notice. He had once tossed out the silica pack in a Tylenol bottle, and that was silly. What if the medicine got damp? It would be ruined. Sometimes, on Sunday mornings, not every Sunday morning, mind you, not even most Sunday mornings, but on occasion, he would fix breakfast and not do the dishes until after lunch, and what was that if not silliness?

"Oh," he said as he realized the balance of power between them had shifted. She was right. They probably would fire her because she was the reason there was a policy against beverages at work stations to begin with. If he wrote up why she needed a new keyboard, she would be called to Mr. Levitt's office and fired. It was almost certain. She had broken company policy, after all, and Mr. Levitt held no truck with silliness. "Oh," Dan said again. If he didn't tell, it meant he would have to lie on the official company form, something he had never considered doing before. But maybe he wouldn't write it up at all. They kept extra keyboards on hand for emergencies like this one. The last time Dan had needed to replace a keyboard, he had suggested to Mr. Levitt that they buy a few extra, just in case something like this happened again, and Mr. Levitt had agreed. Mr. Levitt was all about efficiency, something that Dan could admire. He believed that was what made Mr. Levitt a good manager. Dan could take Sheila's damaged keyboard and put it back in the new box then place that box at the bottom of the stack of fresh keyboards. It could be months before anyone found out—maybe even years unless they suffered a rash of keyboard malfunctions. There was a good chance it would be him who pulled the damaged one out of the box, and he could always say they had gotten a bad one from the factory. He doubted anyone would question him. The thought seemed diabolical in Dan's eyes, but he deemed it an acceptable risk. She was a redhead, after all. "I suppose not."

"Thanks," she said, as relief seemed to wash over her. He was still on all fours, under her desk when she leaned over and scratched his head as if he were a puppy who had remembered to not pee on the rug. She kept her legs crossed, though.

"Not a problem," he said as he climbed from under her desk and stood beside it. The power balance was completely in his favor now. The lecherous side of him, the one that controlled those late night fantasies of Kristy McCullen in black leather, and blonde haired Janelle Hederman— God he loved blonde hair — in a bikini top and shorts, the way she was dressed in the vacation photo she kept on her desk, that side of him, the fantasy side, which would soon have to make room for Sheila Reid's arrow-shaped, pink panties, that side of him wanted to offer a quid-pro-quo. He was washing her back, she could now wash his. But he wasn't that type of person. At least not outside of his darkest fantasies. Instead, he looked for common ground, something they might share between them other than a conspiracy of broken keyboards. Comicon was next weekend—maybe they could go together. He could probably still get another ticket. He looked at the personal items she kept scattered around her desk. There was a ceramic kitty that held pencils, but it was sleeping, curled around a ceramic ball of blue yarn, the pencils sticking out of individual holes in its back, and in no way Neko, the Japanese kitten fetish that some girls were into. Girls in Neko outfits loved the conventions. If the pencil holder had been Neko, or even that dreadful Hello Kitty, he could have used that to invite her to come with him, but it wasn't. He searched for something else, anything that might fit—a Wonder Woman magnet, perhaps—or something Batgirl related—or Batman himself for that matter. Some girls were into Batman. Anything would do, but he saw nothing.

Okay, so the convention was out. What about coffee? She liked coffee—he liked coffee— maybe they could get together and enjoy a nice cup of coffee. It didn't have to be coffee, of course. It could be any beverage. The choice of beverage didn't matter. It could be milkshakes, or malteds, or even a soda. He reached out and touched one of the pencils that stuck out of the cat's back the way knives must have once stuck out of Julius Caesar's, and moved it back and forth, as if he were trying to grind it deeper into the ceramic figurine. They could go Dutch treat, or, if she felt obligated to him for not writing up the keyboard incident, he would allow her to pay in order to restore the balance between them. He would remember to refuse any offer of compensation the first time, but if she insisted, he would acquiesce, perhaps with a slight bow. Did girls like bows in the real world, or was that just the movies?

He opened his mouth to ask her out when her phone rang. She rolled her chair a few inches forward. "Sorry," she said. "I have to take this."

"Oh sure," he said, resigning to wait until the call finished. This was company time, after all. Business came first.

She looked at him, her eyebrows raised as the phone rang again, and that's when he realized his body was blocking her access. He chuckled at his own silliness and stepped to the side. She wheeled herself into place and answered as it began its third ring. "Thank you for calling USX Advertising, this is Sheila, how may I help you?"

Dan stood to one side, leaning against the flimsy cubicle wall. It was covered in a light beige fabric that he picked at, pinching little pieces of lint between his finger and thumb, then balled them up but he realized he had no place to put the ball. Sheila had a small trash receptacle under her desk—everyone did—and hers now held the empty Styrofoam cup from the coffee she had spilled. He leaned forward, over her shoulder and dropped the lint ball in it, catching another whiff of her scent. "One second, please," Sheila said. She turned to him, her hand over the receiver so the other person couldn't hear, her eyebrows raised. "Was there something else?"

And he couldn't ask while she was on the phone—that would be unprofessional and awkward. "No," he said. He held the ruined keyboard up as if it were a small trophy he had just won. "That should just about do it." The lecherous side of him screamed that he was an idiot and he told it to be quiet. If he were to have anything with Sheila, he didn't want to acquire it in an unseemly manner. Nothing long-term could come from that.

"Daddy, how did you meet Mommy?"

"Well, Son, I blackmailed her into having coffee with me and we fell in love over the creamer."

"It was a malted, Dear," she would say, correcting his bad memory.

"Oh yes, of course," and then the whole family would laugh. No—it wouldn't work that way. If he were to ask Sheila out on a date, it had to be on the up-and-up.

She smiled, but it wasn't the same smile as before. This one seemed dismissive and impatient. "Okay then." She took her hand off of the receiver as she turned back to her desk to resume her call.

He stepped toward the hall, then thought he needed to say something else. He had seen other people say more before they stepped away from someone's desk. He should as well. He stopped and put his hand on the corner of the cubicle entrance, and leaned, trying to appear casual. "Catch you later." It was something he'd heard others say.

She turned back, her hand over the receiver again, and this time the look she gave him, he did recognize. It was a combination of pity and revulsion he had seen many times before. "Bye," she said with a slight eye-roll. She turned away again. He decided that maybe now wasn't the best time to ask her out. Later would be better. That had been over a year ago. Other than polite nods in the hallway, they hadn't spoken.

CHAPTER 3

The doorbell jarred him out of these thoughts of prostitutes and panties, shocking and sudden enough to startle him. He snapped back to reality with a small jump, and he felt the slight trip-hammering of his heart racing from anticipation. He fought the urge to run to the front door and fling it wide, because he didn't want to appear too eager. Girls didn't like men who were too eager. He'd read that somewhere, perhaps in the waiting room at his doctor's office, or maybe the dentist's, in one of those relationship magazines found in the checkout aisle of every grocery store with the slim-hipped women on the covers wearing low cut clothing and pouty looks that reminded him of the girls in the pornographic movies. That would have had to be in the days before electronic tablets, because he had stopped reading doctor's office magazines once he'd gotten his first Kindle. He couldn't believe he had read those magazines to begin with. Everyone in the waiting room was sick—some probably dying, and they all touched the same magazines with their death-germs. What idiot thought shared magazines would be a good idea? They were nothing more than gloss-paper Petri dishes. The thought disgusted him.

He stood and straightened the crease in his pants again, wanting everything to be perfect for her. He took a deep breath to steady his nerves before he went to the door, and when he opened it, he smiled, big and wide.

It was a woman. He wasn't expecting a woman, and it surprised him. She wore the brown sexless uniform he had expected, though, the short sleeved shirt and matching shorts that showed her knees. See? There was nothing wrong with looking at a woman's knees. Her brown hair—God he loved brown hair—was in a ponytail that she had pulled through the gap created in her hat by the plastic tabs that adjusted the size. She was young —about Sheila's age—and thin muscled. She held a hand truck with a single box on it that was almost as tall as she. "Dan Mitchell?" she asked.

He nodded before he spoke, still not sure he was comfortable with a woman standing there. "Yes," he said.

"Delivery for you," she said. "Two boxes, and you'll have to sign." She spun the hand truck and began to back her way in. "Where do you want them?" She had a distinct Boston accent, and it felt out of place to his mid-western ear. Who would move from Boston to Cincinnati? Boston had history and culture—Cincinnati had winged pigs on its bridges.

Dan held the door wider so she wouldn't bump it. "The living room is fine," he said. "In front of the fireplace."

She wheeled the cart over the carpet—he would have to remember to vacuum that later—and went to the fireplace. "Wow," she said. "Nice place. Retro. You live alone?" She set the box down and moved the truck from under it, then placed it long ways, so that the "This side up" arrows were pointed toward the ceiling before she took the electronic pad from her hip and handed it to him. "Just sign on the line," she said.

"Yes," he said. "I live alone." He held the pad in one hand and the plastic stylus in the other, about to sign in the place he was supposed to, but then he stopped. "I'll need to see the other box," he said. "To make sure there isn't any damage."

"Oh, sure," she said. She headed to the door with her hand truck. "I need you to show my boyfriend how to clean," she said. "He's a total slob." When she left, she let the wood-framed screen door bang closed behind her. She shouldn't allow the door to bang closed like that. It was both rude and hard on the door.

Dan went to the box and ran his fingers over it, gentle, a lover's touch. He read his name and address printed on the white label, along with the return address—RWR Enterprises, then the street address, Anaheim, CA and the zip code. The box was stamped "2 of 2." That was wrong. She should have brought the first box in first. This was backwards. It should have been "1 of 2" then "2 of 2." Didn't she go to kindergarten? He considered asking her to take the box back out and bring in the first one, the way it should have been done to begin with, but decided he would just have to live with it being incorrect or he would risk getting that look from her. He didn't care enough about her to be concerned over what she thought of him, but he didn't want to get that look—not today—not if he could help it. That look would turn the blame back on him, when this wasn't his fault. It was hers. Not everyone had his attention to detail, nor did they take pride in their work the way they should.

She came in without knocking this time, and he heard her wrestling with the door as she entered. If she had knocked, he would have held the door open for her and made the job easier. She wheeled the box into the living room and plopped it down beside the other one, but she put it on the right side, not the left, so now, not only had they been delivered in the wrong order, they were placed in the wrong order. The first box should be on the left. "Whew," she said, wiping the sweat from her face with her shirt sleeve. "Those are heavy." There was a white salt ring on her sleeve that meant this wasn't the first time she had wiped the sweat away. Dan decided he hated her, brown hair or not. She was as disgusting as a doctor's office magazine with her sweaty face and sloppy work ethic. "Any chance I could trouble you for a bottle of water?"

Dan stared at her for a second, not believing she had the audacity to ask. It would have been fine to accept if he had offered, but he hadn't offered—he just wanted her to leave so he could straighten out the mess of these boxes. "They're backward," he said.

She took a deep breath, as if the exertion had winded her and leaned on her handcart. "What's that?"

"The boxes—they're backward. The first one should be on the left, and it should have come in first."

"Oh yeah," she said with a chuckle that consisted of nothing but air. "That's funny."

Dan didn't smile because he wasn't joking. "I'll get your water," he said. He went to the kitchen and opened the refrigerator where exactly six bottles of Fiji stood in two rows, like soldiers in rank and file. He wasn't particularly fond of Fiji over any other brand, except for the square bottles. That made them more efficient to store in the refrigerator. He took a bottle out and put it on the counter, then went to the cupboard and got a fresh one from there. He moved the row in the refrigerator which now had two bottles forward and placed the new one behind them, so the coldest would be at the front. He closed the refrigerator and took the cold bottle to her.

She opened it and drained half without stopping, the gurgling of the water the only sound beside her noisy swallows. She stopped with an, "Ahh," and held onto the bottle without replacing the lid. What sort of idiot didn't replace the lid? She must have been raised by monkeys. "That's good. Cold too. Thanks." She took another drink still not replacing the cap.

"Sure," he said. He didn't want to say she was welcome because that would imply it hadn't been an imposition.

He signed her electronic tablet to verify there was no damage to the packages, but she still talked to him while she waited. "Some weather, huh? Hot. Too hot for this early in the year. Summer is going to be a scorcher. But hey, it means we'll have a nice warm Easter, am I right?"

"That's what they're saying," Dan said, or at least that's what they said this morning. He had missed the afternoon forecast thanks to the lint ball.

"Well, thanks again," she said as she stepped through the door, toasting him with the near-empty bottle and the water sloshed inside, threatening to spill. "We'll be seeing you." She pronounced it, "ya."

"Yeah," Dan said as he closed the door behind her. He might have added a, "Catch you later," if he hadn't loathed her.

CHAPTER 4

It had taken the better part of ten minutes to put the boxes in the correct order, because she was right—they were heavy. They were also rather large and bulky and together took up most of the living room. When he had them lined up side by side, the tops straight and even, he went to the garage through the door in the kitchen. He retrieved his utility knife from the peg board, and checked to make sure the blade was fresh, even though he knew it would be. He replaced the blade every time he used it —he wasn't some Neanderthal banging on a deer carcass with a rock. He closed the blade again for safety and walked back to the living room. There, he opened the blade again, this time to the smallest notch because he didn't want to risk cutting too deep, and slid the knife along the taped top of the first box. Then he cut the sides, closed the knife and put it on the coffee table.

His fingers trembled as he stood over the box. This was a moment for which he had waited over a year, that began exactly three days after the incident with Sheila and her panties, where he had failed to ask her out. It had been that failed attempt that had been the last straw, the one that triggered his action to place the order. It wasn't that he hadn't been able to bring himself to ask her out, although in truth, that was a small part of it—it was the look she had given him—that look—the one of disgust with a hint of pity that had pushed him over the edge.

He had considered placing the order for months, and on some smaller level even years, ever since he had seen videos of the prototypes on the Internet. He'd waited because there were sure to be bugs in the beginning, as there were to be in any new technology, and while he considered himself a first-adopter of technologies like phones or tablets, the contents of these boxes were far too expensive to deal with issues, especially if there were big ones. So he had waited through the first generation and even the second, telling himself it hadn't come to that—not yet. A month before Sheila's panties, the third generation had launched, and they were received with wild success. He had looked into taking a mortgage out on the house, even though he'd owned it free and clear since his mother's passing six years ago. That had been the only thing that had stopped him then—he didn't want to go into debt, so he decided to wait and save for it. Then Sheila's look had pushed that final button and he'd placed the order the day the loan came through. And still, it had taken a year because the company handcrafted every order. They took pride in their workmanship.

He opened the box, not knowing what to expect, but he knew it wasn't what he saw. It was a piece of white Styrofoam as blank as the puzzle in his office—blanker even, because it was missing the lone blueberry in the corner. He slid his fingers down the side of the box and tried to lift the Styrofoam out, but it created a vacuum, causing it to stick. He straddled the box and squatted, making sure to lift with his legs and not his back and raised himself, clutching the packing material tight between his open palms. When he stood, the Styrofoam blocked his view of the box's contents and he moved it, peeking around it the way a small child might peek around a corner to see if Santa was the one making the noises in the living room on Christmas Eve.

The faceless skull in the box startled him enough that he dropped the Styrofoam. The deep blue eyes stared straight ahead, frozen, motionless. The teeth and red-painted gums looked hideously large, something out of a horror movie ready to bite and shred flesh and bone. It was obviously plastic molded to resemble a human skull, but not an exact copy like the plastic man they had in middle school health class with the removable organs that only he and the teacher could figure out how to get back in the right order once they were out. This had wires and electrodes instead of a hollow plastic brain. He could see them because the back part of the skull was clear. It would be hidden by a wig eventually but for now he could see the ram sticks and processors. "Ugh," he said, repulsed. "I can't believe they shipped you without a face."

A red light flickered in the middle of the skull, as if it had been waiting for the sound of a human voice to turn itself on. The blue eyes moved from side to side and the jaw worked its way up and down a few times, making the horror movie image seem all the more real. He half expected it to come out of the box and begin chasing him throughout the house. Finally, it spoke, the feminine voice silky smooth, even buttery, but with a slightly tinny tone. "Hello." The teeth and tongue moved with precision, an exact match to the words. The eyes turned and locked onto his, and it seemed as if the skull was trying to turn as well, but it couldn't because it was still encased in Styrofoam.

"Hi," he said, trying to sound confident, but realized he sounded rather weak and puny. That was unfortunate. He'd often considered his voice to be his best feature. He cleared his throat but didn't think it would help.

"What's your name?" the skull asked, light and even flirty, as if she were actually interested in his name, and it wasn't just a question built into the programming. It didn't sound robotic at all—it sounded like a real woman, right out of the movies, when she first meets a handsome stranger. There was a touch of excitement in that voice, the apprehension felt at the beginning of a new adventure, but there was also the innocence of a young girl unjaded by the ways of the world. He knew it was his imagination playing tricks on him, of course. He was reading too much into a grand total of four words. He believed it to be true because he wanted it to be true.

"Dan," he said. He sounded a little better, but not a lot. He couldn't get over how well the teeth and tongue matched with the words. The only thing that threw it off was the missing lips.

"Hi Dan. It's nice to meet you," the skull said. The tone was sincere and non-defensive, one he hadn't heard from a woman since he'd hit puberty with the exception of teachers who had to be nice to you. It was school policy that teachers be nice to students, he was sure. "Have you decided what you would like to call me?"

"No," he said, and it wasn't a complete lie. He had a few names picked out, but he wanted to meet her before he decided on a final one, to make sure it matched her. Names were like gloves—they needed to fit. "Not yet."

"That's okay," the feminine voice said. "Do you have any ideas, or would you like for me to offer some suggestions?"

"I have some ideas," he said, "but you can suggest some if you like." If he wanted this to be a partnership, choosing a name together seemed a good place to start.

"How about, until we decide, if you are speaking out loud, I will assume you are speaking to me. Will that be alright?"

"Perfect," he said. She had said "we"—until "we" decide. She wanted this to be a partnership, too. "That—that's perfect," he said. He didn't normally stammer, but he felt a little thunderstruck.

"Also, don't feel as if you have to settle on just one name for me. You ordered three faces. Why not choose three names, one for each face? I can have three distinct personalities to go with them."

That was actually a good idea. He had already narrowed his list to four names. He could pick the best three from that list, after listening to her suggestions, of course.

"Would you like to begin assembly or would you prefer to chat some more?"

"Whichever you prefer is fine," he said, then realized how stupid that sounded. Preferences? Really?

"Well, what if we do both? That way we can get to know one another while we assemble." She seemed eager to get started and she didn't wait for a reply. "First you want to open the second box." For some reason she had the tone of someone reading an instruction manual but it still sounded human.

"Okay," he said. He picked up the utility knife and again

opened it to the shallowest cutting depth.

"You're cautious. I like that." The eyes had shifted to watch him and the head had turned as much as it could, considering it was encased in Styrofoam. He found himself staring at the mouth again. It was fascinating.

"Say that again," he said. He wanted to see if he was correct in what he thought he had seen.

"Which part?"

"Say you like that again."

"I like that?" she said, but she sounded confused, as if she found it an odd thing to want repeated.

He watched closely this time, paying attention to the teeth and tongue. Sure enough, the tongue went behind the teeth for the L but danced over them for the TH. "Fascinating."

When she laughed it was light and playful like a schoolgirl without a hint of meanness. "If you say so, silly."

And there it was, that word again. He had grown disenchanted with it in the past year. He associated it with Sheila and her mean look. But now it was like hearing it again for the first time and accompanied by that brilliant laugh, it was stupendous, far greater than anything he'd felt when Sheila had said it. He smiled because for the first time since he could remember, Dan Mitchell felt happy.

"Oh no," she said. "Oh this is just awful." She sounded genuinely upset, as if she were about to cry.

"What?" he said, and he almost reached for this disembodied head to try and offer comfort, but he stopped himself. He wasn't sure it was safe to pick her up.

"This is terrible. I just realized they shipped me without a face. I must look horrendous— hideous. You ordered three faces but didn't choose which one to use for shipping, so they sent me without one. I'm so sorry."

"No," he said. "Don't be. I don't mind." And he realized that was true—as true as anything he had ever said. He didn't mind that she had no face. He didn't mind that she had no arms or legs yet, either. He didn't mind that she had no torso or hair or skin.

Dan didn't even mind that she had no soul.

CHAPTER 5

"Can you?" she asked, reaching behind her back, first over her shoulder, then from underneath, as if she had an itch she couldn't reach. "I can't quite—" she struggled more, both arms flailing, looking not unlike a turtle on its back, trying to right itself.

"What are you trying to do?" he asked. He suppressed a grin at her ridiculous flapping, worried it might hurt her feelings.

She sighed, exasperated. "I'm trying to line up the seam in the back and I can't reach it. I think it's a design flaw and I'm going to send them a nasty email about it, too."

She wore the Briana face now, secured by magnets that stuck to her skull. It was the most neutral, both in skin tone and shape, billed to look like the, "All-American Girl Next Door." Dan wanted to know next door to whom? With her long blonde hair that was now messy and hung slightly askew thanks to her recent thrashings, she didn't look like anyone who lived next door to Dan, or two houses away, or even in the whole neighborhood, for that matter. Most of Dan's neighbors were in their fifties and sixties, and he doubted any of them had been this pretty even when they were younger.

They'd assembled the skeleton first, allowing Dan to see the actual technology that went into her. A lot of her skeletal features were designed just for that, with windows built into them, so you got an idea of why she had been so expensive. She was basically a massive computer, with what he would liken to the mainframe he used at work in her chest, or at least it was comparable in processing power and memory. She had massive sticks of RAM, twelve neuromorphic processors with 1024 CPU's each, and eight solid state drives in her chest alone. Each SSD held 128 petabytes of data. There was a desktop equivalent in her head with RAM and processors and SSD's of its own to handle 90% of her input and output devices, namely her ears, eyes and mouth—a laptop equivalent in each hand and a top of the line tablet in each leg. The computer in her chest ran the big picture functions, like "Walk to the kitchen." From there, the other computers would take over, working in sync with one another as controlled by the mainframe—the computer in her head would utilize the cameras in her eyes and microphones in her ears, along with thousands of other sensors located throughout her head to insure she was heading in the right direction, there was nothing in her path, or if there were, to figure out the best way around the obstacle, move it out of the way, or find a different route. The tablet sized computers in her legs would begin the walking process, clenching and relaxing her leg "muscles," while the laptops in her arms controlled the familiar swinging motion, both to maintain balance and to appear more human.

Her "muscles" were nothing more than high-grade oil that contracted when electrical current was supplied to it, not much different than a human muscle. It flowed through carbon fiber tubes that connected at the joints, utilizing a piston inside the tube for flexing and retraction movements, so unlike human muscles that would only flex and relax, hers would flex and extend, using the same muscles to open her fist as she did to close them. The effect was a smooth, continuous, flowing motion that wasn't mechanical at all. He would describe her movement as elegant and graceful. With the sensors in her fingers and hands, she could handle a strawberry without bruising it or crush a walnut with a single finger and thumb pinch.

Her bones were carbon fiber tubes as well, with rechargeable batteries inside of them. A full charge was supposed to last 48 hours of constant movement, or longer with limited.

They had attached the face first, at her insistence. He tried his best to convince her it didn't matter to him, but she didn't seem to care. The faces were packed in the bottom of the second box, and he dug them out and held them up one at a time for her to see, and after looking at all three, stretched across his splayed fingers, they had decided to begin with Briana, use it for the assembly process, then she would model the others for him.

Deep in his heart, even though he was alone, Dan had always had a girlfriend. They did things like the picnics, held extended conversations on long drives, sometimes with his hand resting on the console so she could take it in hers if she wanted. Driving one-handed made him nervous, but she enjoyed holding hands, and he wanted to make her happy. They would go to dinners together and the occasional movie, and sometimes, in his mind, they went shopping, and afterwards, they would go home and she would model her purchases for him—even the underthings. This girlfriend wasn't real, of course. He didn't open the car door for her, or allow her to enter a building first, although he would have if she had been real. He knew she wasn't because Dan wasn't crazy—he was just tired of being so alone all the time. His mind had invented a companion the way small children invented invisible playmates. When Dan did speak aloud to an empty room, he wasn't talking to himself—he was talking to her. Her face might change—so might her name, when she had one. Oftentimes she didn't. But she was there, just as sure as an invisible playmate was there for the child.

This wasn't schizophrenia—these weren't voices in his head that gave him orders to kill the president, or blow up a school bus, nor would he listen if they had. This was a desire for something more—something he hadn't been able to find in the real world, so his mind had created a placeholder, a sort of practice girlfriend, a place to hone his skills until he found the real thing.

And perhaps that is why, when Dan held these silicone masks up, with their embedded magnets and slits for eyes and lips, and the nostrils with tiny holes that actually were for air circulation to dissipate heat, looking for all the world like something one might wear for Halloween, perhaps that is why this overwhelming feeling of *déjà vu* fell upon him, this undeniable feeling that he had done this before, that he had somehow lived this scene from his life time after time. It was more than familiar. It was greater than that. It transcended anything so mundane as that.

When Dan's mother died, a scant six years ago, something had changed.

He had met his father once. The man abandoned Dan and his mother long ago, when Dan was an infant, and Dan had never felt the need to search for him. He believed that if his father wanted nothing to do with him, he would want nothing to do with his father in return. It was from a belief—at least what he told himself—that stemmed from the idea that to seek his father out would be rude. The man had made a choice and Dan intended to honor it. He could never admit, to himself or anyone else, not even his mother, that his father's decision had hurt him deeply. Dan had Mother and together, the two of them forged a life. Dan had asked a few obligatory questions about his father when he was old enough to understand that most other children seemed to have one, but he didn't. His mother's responses had been vague and unemotional. "He's gone and he won't be returning." Mother was never sentimental. She was practical. She would buy gifts like socks and shirts for Christmas and on his birthday, which fell at the end of September, he had come to expect a small bag of school supplies for his present that were to last the entire year. In the 4th grade, days before the Thanksgiving holiday, Jackie Taylor had broken all of Dan's pencils and laughed about it. Jackie Taylor was a bully. When Miss Cassidy saw Dan writing with a broken nub, she gave him a brand new pencil and a matching eraser. When Dan asked her how much they cost so he could reimburse her, she had laughed, small and kind and patted him on the shoulder and told him they were a gift. Miss Cassidy was young and pretty with long, straight black hair and she always wore long, pretty dresses with long sleeves and floral prints, even in the summer when the other teachers wore skirts and short sleeves.

It wasn't that Mother and he were poor. Mother wasn't one of those single parents who struggled to pay the rent or buy food, the way some did in the movies. They were not rich, but they were comfortable. Her choice in gifts was not because she didn't have the money. It was because she was practical and saw toys as frivolous. If he wanted a toy, that was fine. He could use up to half of the money his grandparents gave him on special occasions to purchase a toy. Mother would permit that. The rest was to be saved in a ceramic piggy bank that was dressed as a cowboy, standing on its hindquarters, its pistols drawn as if protecting the contents in its belly. His father had brought it on the day he came to meet Dan, and it was the only gift his father had ever given him. Dan had come in after school, days after he had asked the obligatory questions, a week before classes were released for Christmas break, and found a man sitting on the couch sipping coffee from the good china kept only for company. "Dan, I would like for you to meet your father," his mother said. The man stuck his hand out, saying it was nice to meet him. Dan shook with him. The ceramic pig sat on the coffee table.

"It's where you keep your money," his father had told five-year-old Dan. When Dan said he didn't have any money, his father had taken a twenty dollar bill from his wallet and given it to him and told him he did now. Dan had taken both the piggy bank and the money to his room. He wrote a note on a slip of paper, clipped it to the bill, folded them neatly and inserted it into the back of the pig's head. When he'd returned to the living room, he paused in the doorway, listening to his mother and father chat. "He seems smart," his father said. "Is he smart?"

"Not particularly," Mother replied.

The pig stood sentry in the corner of his room from its place on the floor, out of sight when the closet door was opened. It had been there since Dan had put it there, and he had no idea how much it held, but his childhood mind had dreamed it must be fortunes. Instead of buying two toys, he had only purchased one. Instead of the best toy, he had settled for something smaller or not as nice. All of that sacrifice must have added up to something great, surely. He had been allowed to open the cowboy pig on his 18th birthday. It was to go into a savings account at the bank and used for his college tuition. He sat on his bed, counting change and bills, sorting them into stacks. When he reached ten dollars in quarters, he stopped and wrapped them in paper rolls, then marked the total down in a notebook and continued counting. He did the same for dimes and nickels and pennies, stacking the rolled coins one atop the other and marking it in his notebook. He unfolded the bills and stacked them as well, binding them with rubber bands when he hit fifty of any denomination, but that only happened a few times with the $1's and once with the $5's. The $10's and $20's were fewer. When he reached the twenty with the note clipped to it, he opened it and saw his own five-year-old's scrawl, two words he didn't remember writing, "Love Dad."

When he finished sorting and rolling, he added the columns. He added them again. Then he recounted everything, believing he must have made a mistake somewhere. He had a total of $2,347.76. This pig had stolen half of his money for years but now it only held $2,347.76. It was supposed to pay for college. It wouldn't even cover his textbooks. He had carried the pig to the garage, taken a worn out hammer he had purchased at a flea market for fifty cents down from the pegboard where he had hung it and smashed the pig until it was nothing but dust. He smashed and pounded the pig until there wasn't a single fragment as big as any of the coins it once held. There was no expression on his face—no anger—no disappointment. His teeth weren't clenched—his brow not furrowed. To anyone watching, he would have appeared perfectly calm. He wore a large pair of safety goggles and his eyes perspired from both the exertion and the lack of air circulation, and while he normally would have stopped because he found sweat disgusting, he kept pounding, smashing, obliterating, his face never changing.

When he finished, he took the broom and dustpan from the corner and swept, first the powder that had once been the pig which he dumped into the trash can, then the entire garage. He used the dustbuster to vacuum the workbench then emptied the contents into the can as well. Once that was finished, he swept the garage one more time, then used spray cleaner and paper towels to clean his goggles, then the hammer, then the bench, and then the dustpan. He removed the white plastic bag from the can, replaced it with a fresh one, then took the bag with the smashed pig and used paper towels to the outside receptacle, and tossed it in without ceremony. He went inside and took a long shower, washing his hair twice to make sure he got out all of the dust that might have flown into it, then scrubbed the sweat from his eyes until the skin was raw. He dried and dressed, combed his hair, then placed his dirty clothes in the laundry bin which he carried to the washing machine and put them in along with a premeasured detergent pod and started the washer. He returned to his bedroom, sat on the edge of his perfectly made bed, his palms flat against his thighs, and stared at his fortune for an hour, his eyes drawn in particular to that hand-scribbled note. He stopped when Mother had called him for dinner.

"Can you?" Savannah asked again, still trying to reach behind her.

"Can I what?" he asked, moving to sit beside her.

She was naked with most of her silicon skin attached. The holes in her nostrils were attached to a bellows in her belly, a secondary cooling system that imitated breathing. The primary cooling system was water filled tubes that ran like veins through the skin and gave off body heat. Each section of skin had dozens of small tubes that had to be attached to the cooling system one at a time, and electrical wires that connected to the embedded skin sensors, so they had been at this for the better part of four hours. He said "they" because once he had installed her arms and covered her hands with the skin, she had helped with her own assembly.

"See the way I aligned the skin on my legs?" She ran a finger up the top of her bare thigh. It appeared seamless, and if he hadn't watched as she'd put it on, he would have never known there was a seam there at all. "You have to do that with the seam in my back. Run your fingers over it. It has to line up exactly, or we'll have to cut it and do it over again." Once she had put on her face, which also covered her throat, her voice had changed, no longer tinny at all, but it was still silky smooth.

He sat behind her and saw what she was talking about. The skin wasn't perfect, the right side sticking up about a millimeter or two higher than the left. He ran his finger over it and felt the bump better than he could see it. "Won't it just pull apart again?"

"No," she said. "It will bond with itself once I heat it. You didn't know that?"

But he did know that—he had read the specs, after all. Who would buy something this elaborate without reading the specs? He just didn't realize they had reached the point of heating her skin yet. He pushed the flap down to line it up, but went too far, so pushed the other side, trying to make them match.

Her skin was smooth, but with fine, bleach blonde, almost white hair at the small of her back. He had paid an extra $2500 for that and the same wispy hair on her forearms and thighs. He didn't know what the hairs were made of, but he ran his fingers over them as he stared, barely touching them. Where they entered her skin, they left tiny indentations that looked like pores. She shivered. "That tickles."

"Really?" he asked. "You can feel that?"

"Sure," she said as if it was no big deal. "Do you have it?" She tried to look over her shoulder, holding her long blonde hair back with one hand.

"I think so," he said. He ran his finger back and forth again and felt a tiny, miniscule ridge, but was afraid if he tried to fix it, he would only make it worse. "Yeah."

"May I have some water?" she asked.

"Water?" he asked. While the request echoed the delivery girl's, this one didn't bother him at all. He would have asked, but it never occurred to him that she might want or need any.

She nodded. "Please. There will be air bubbles in my primary cooling system that need to be flushed, and the heating process to seal my skin will have to be regulated. I'll need about five liters."

"Of course," he said. He stood and went to the kitchen and

took all of the bottles out of the refrigerator, not bothering to re-place them. He cradled them in his arms and carried them back, placing them on the coffee table in front of her. He opened one and tried to figure out how or where to pour it in. "How do I—?"

She giggled. "You don't, silly. I do." She took the bottle from him, her finger brushing lightly against his. She held it to her lips and poured it down, the bottle making the same gurgling sound as the one the delivery girl had drained, and her throat moved up and down, but he wasn't sure if it was some sort of pump forcing the fluids in or if it was just a simulation to make it look as if she were swallowing. She didn't stop until the bottle was empty. It didn't bother him this time. "Cold," she said.

"I have room temperature, if you prefer," he said.

"No, cold is better," she said. She sat with her knees together, with just a hint of her light brown pubic hair showing. He had paid $200 for what was a "trimmed" pubis. Her blonde hair fell forward, covering her breasts, but she sat naked and un-ashamed. She didn't take a second bottle, even though she'd said it would take five liters.

"Do you want another?" he asked, reaching for a second bot-tle to open for her.

She smiled up at him. "In a minute. It takes the pumps a while to catch up. Actually, this could prove to be a little messy. Would you mind if I did this in the shower?"

"Not at all," he said. "Is it okay for you to get wet?"

She cocked her head to one side and grinned, flirty and imp-ish. "Did you even read about me at all?" She sounded amused.

He had read dozens of articles and watched a hundred videos, but he had to admit, those barely scratched the surface of what was out there. He knew she would be waterproof once her skin was sealed, but he wasn't sure about before then. "Some."

"Once sealed, I am waterproof to 120 meters," she said. "When I get too hot, I perspire—the evaporation process keeps me cool, just like you. The easiest way for me to clean myself is a shower—just like you. When I heat my skin to seal it, it's going to make me perspire and I don't want to get it all over your— What is this thing called that I'm sitting on?"

"A couch?" he asked. "You know the word perspire but don't know couch?"

"My vocabulary is limited to what I need to know for initial assembly, but I can learn. It's supposed to be a bonding experience for you to teach me. If you prefer, I can download a full vocabulary from the Internet. It's your choice, but if you don't mind teaching me, I think I'll make a good student." She looked around the room. "I see three couches." She picked up a second bottle, opened it, then began pouring it in.

He smiled at her this time. "Only one couch. The smallest is a chair and the one in the middle is called a loveseat."

"A loveseat? Does it cause love, or do you have to be in love to sit on it?" She replaced the lid on the bottle, even though it was empty and there was nothing left to spill but a few drops. Was it too early to say that he loved her?

"Neither," he said. "I think it's called that because you sit so close together. It helps if you love the other person. I'm not sure, though."

"Couch, chair, loveseat," she said, pointing to each in turn. "What's that?"

"A fireplace."

She nodded then pointed again. "And that?"

"A television," he said.

"Oh, I've heard of those. I thought they would be bigger."

"They come in different sizes," he said. "Would you prefer a larger one?"

"No," she said. "It's just that they seem to take up so much of a person's life, I expected them to be bigger is all."

"For some people they do," he said. "I don't watch that much. Sometimes I have it on so the house won't be so quiet."

A tiny drop of water formed on her shoulder, then a bubble appeared and burst, then another and another, until it created a light foam. "I should get to the shower," she said. When she stood, she was four inches shorter than he. She stretched on her tiptoes and kissed his cheek. "Thank you," she said.

Startled at the kiss, he touched his cheek where her lips had brushed it, as if he could still feel them there. "For what?" he asked.

"For being nice," she said. She walked past him, and he tried to be chivalrous and avert his gaze, but he couldn't. He couldn't take his eyes off of her. He tried to tell himself that it was because he was fascinated at her technology, but in reality, it was the tiny hairs on the small of her back that first caught his attention, then the curve of her buttocks, and the shape of her thighs and the dimples at the backs of her knees. She was the most beautiful thing he had ever seen, and he didn't mean that to sound like he still thought of her as a thing—he didn't. It was because she was more beautiful than any painting—any sunrise—any mountain sunset he had ever witnessed.

She stopped and turned back and caught him looking, and he felt the blood rush to his face. She wasn't embarrassed at all, though. "The shower would be— ?"

"Oh," he said. "Let me show you." As he moved past her, she brushed her fingers over his arm, and he stopped and turned to her.

"Do you think we'll ever be close enough to sit on the love set together?" she asked.

"Loveseat," he corrected. If he had been thinking straight, he would have stopped to wonder if this was an intentional glitch in her programming, or she had somehow forgotten the word, but he wasn't, so he didn't. All he thought of was how adorable she was. "I think so."

She smiled, sweet and demure. "I think so, too."

CHAPTER 6

"It's tiny," he said. "No one will ever see it."

"You'll see it," she said. She ran her fingers over her back, as high as she could reach from underneath. She had shipped with no clothes, but she now wore a pair of pink panties trimmed in white lace that he'd purchased from a high end lingerie shop the day after the Sheila incident, and an oversized black t-shirt that had an owl wearing a dunce cap with Pobody's Nerfect emblazoned under it in white letters she had swiped from his closet, and was now corkscrewed around to try and see her back, using the mirror to guide her fingers while she held the shirt up in the back with her other hand.

It looked like a long-faded scar, but it was from where the skin wasn't perfectly aligned when she'd heated it, and it had sealed, leaving a small line about an inch long. "It's kind of sexy," he said. He had to squint to see it.

"You're just saying that. I wanted to be perfect for you."

"You are perfect," he said. He ran his finger over the tiny scar and could barely feel it. "You're perfect just like you are."

Her look said she wasn't convinced, but she would let it go. "Then it will be a remember," she said. "A remember of the day we met."

He opened his mouth to correct her, "Not a remember, a memory," he'd almost said, but didn't. He realized that he liked her term better—a remember—memories were forced upon you, both good and bad. But a remember sounded different, more romantic, because it was a memory of choice. Even if it came about by bad reasons, it could be remembered for good ones. This little scar happened because he was too careless to do a good job, but it would be a remember of the happiest day of his life. He would touch it years from now and remember.

She turned and planted her bottom against the sink, resting her hands on each side. "I'm drained."

"Drained? You mean like sleepy?"

She shrugged. "I suppose. Sort of. I'm not sure because I don't know what sleepy feels like."

"I thought you could go two days without a recharge," he said.

"I can, but they didn't ship me with a full charge," she said. She squinted as if trying to study him, like he was an interesting bug or something. "Really, confess. Did you read any of the literature on me, or did you just go in and pick out what you thought was pretty and click 'Order?'" She had the smirk of a playful grin, so he wasn't insulted.

"I read," he said. "Some." He was teasing her back, of course. He knew she wouldn't ship on a full charge, just like a cell phone or laptop didn't, but he had no idea how long what charge she did have would last. To be honest, with as much energy as she had needed to seal her skin, he was surprised she had lasted this long. "Let's get you plugged in," he said.

He led the way back to the living room where all of her accessories were, including her charging system. The boxes and packing materials were there as well and he would take them to the garage after he had her all set up. "Would you prefer the couch or the chair?" he asked.

"Doesn't matter," she said, standing behind him. "What will you do?"

"I will clean up and probably have something to eat," he said, realizing he hadn't eaten a bite since before she'd arrived and he was famished. He dug the charging system out of the bottom of the first box and began assembling it. "I might watch a little television, if it won't bother you."

She shrugged. "It won't bother me. Will you watch in here?"

"Yeah," he said. "I only have the one set."

"If I am on the couch, will you sit with me?" she asked. She sounded hopeful.

"Of course—if you like."

She nodded, a small smile to indicate that would please her.

The power converter was quite large and required two AC outlets. There was an optional 30 amp connector, but the only one of those in the house was for the dryer, and there was no place for her to sit if he used it. He stretched her wireless charging pad across the middle seat of the couch and she sat on it. Then he unplugged the lamp at the far end of the couch and plugged in the two chords that led to the charger. "How long do you think you'll need?" he asked.

"About ten hours," she said.

"Do you know more precisely?" He didn't mind a general idea, he was just curious.

"Barring no fluctuations in the power source, nine hours, fifty-four minutes and thirty-seven seconds," she said. "Thirty-six, thirty-five, thirty-four..." She grinned.

"You are a cheeky little monkey," he said. It was one of those qualities he would have never guessed he would enjoy, but found he did. She had twenty personality traits to select from, each controlled by a slider from one to ten that he could access through an app on his tablet. He could select and adjust any of them to make her act and behave in the way he found most pleasing. Her default was everything selected at a five intensity. But if he chose, he could turn Jealousy off completely, and she wouldn't be jealous at all—or he could maximize it and have someone who got upset if he so much as looked at another woman. For now at least, he chose to leave her just like she was, a little bit of everything. She had a playful touch of sass, and he liked that. "Can I get you anything?"

"Maybe another bottle of water," she said. "Charging causes heat. I probably won't need it, but just in case. Then come sit with me."

"Okay," he said. He went to the kitchen and opened the refrigerator door, then realized he had forgotten to replace the bottles he had taken earlier. She was throwing him off his game. "All we have is room temperature. Is that okay?"

"That's fine," she called back.

He removed a single bottle from the case in the pantry and took it to her, then returned to the kitchen, restocked the water in the refrigerator, made a ham sandwich, put it on a plate, cut it in half, then took it along with a bottle of apple juice to the living room. It was rare that he ate outside of the kitchen, but not unheard of. He sat beside her and turned the television on and they watched a movie about a boy and his dog on the family network. When he finished eating, he took her hand, entwining his fingers with hers, and she turned to him and smiled, rubbing her thumb over the back of his knuckles.

When the movie ended—she said she enjoyed it—she went into low power mode and he carried the boxes to the garage and put them on a shelf. He kept the packaging for major purchases for a year in case they needed to be returned. The two boxes sat on the shelf next to the box for the television, which he would keep for another two months, according to the white sticker he had placed on the shelf in front of it. He washed the plate from his sandwich, then vacuumed the living room where that dreaded delivery woman had rolled her dirty cart wheels. After that, he took a shower and put on his pajamas then went to the living room and looked at her once more. Her blonde hair had fallen forward, and he brushed it with his fingertips to keep it out of her half-open eyes. "Good night," he said, then realized he still needed a name for her. Mary? No. Maryanne? Definitely not. Sheila? "Oh, God no," he said out loud, not believing his mind had even suggested it. He sighed, brushed the hair away again, tucking it behind her ear, then went to his room, the same one he had used his entire life. He hadn't moved into the master bedroom when Mother had passed. He hadn't seen the need. His own room was perfectly adequate. He laid down, folded his hands over his chest, closed his eyes and was almost asleep when he heard a light knock. "Dan?"

She stood in the doorframe, the light from the streetlamp that illuminated the kitchen shining through the t-shirt silhouetting her frame. She held her charging mat in one hand.

"Yes?" He sat up and turned his light on. "Is everything okay?"

"Can I sleep in here?" she asked. "It's lonely out there."

"Of course," he said. The chair was a small office style, and wouldn't be suitable for her mat. "On the floor?"

She shrugged. "The bed would be nice."

"Oh—yes—of course," he said. He stood and pulled the blanket down. He wasn't sure how this was supposed to work. It was an adult-length twin bed he kept shoved against the wall. He wasn't sure there would be room for the both of them.

She stretched her charging pad against the wall side, plugged it into the nearest outlet, and climbed in, laying on her back. He climbed beside her and did the same. When he had settled, she turned on her side, facing him and rested her hand on his chest. He looked at her and she smiled, then scooted closer until her head rested on his shoulder, closed her eyes, dropping to low power mode. He placed his hand on top of hers and felt content.

CHAPTER 7

She padded into the living room wearing the same Pobody's Nerfect t-shirt, her hair wet from the shower. She was running a comb through it.

"I have other t-shirts, you know," he said from his computer chair. He was catching up on some things that needed to be done for work even though he had taken the day off. "You're welcome to wear any of them, or a dress shirt for that matter." He had a thing for women who wore men's dress shirts around the house, or at least he thought he did. He'd never actually seen it, but he had fantasized about it.

"I like this one," she said. She wrapped her arms around his shoulders from behind and he could smell the light perfume she had sprayed after her shower. "Is that a problem?"

He began typing a response to Jeffrey Donovan that would include a temporary password and link to reset his old one when it was finished, and he paused enough to say, "No, but it's going to stink."

"Stink like me?" she asked. She circled the chair and plopped in his lap without warning.

He smiled at her. "I need to finish this." He wrestled his arm from under her and began trying to type again, but she was distracting. He really needed to finish this.

She wrapped her arms around his neck this time. "No you don't. You need to pay attention to me." She wiggled in his lap until her lips were at this throat. She began kissing, working her way to behind his ear. He shivered, trying to concentrate on the email. He could order her to stop, but he was worried that might set a precedent he didn't want. If he started ordering her around like a slave, it would become easier the next time, and easier still the time after, until all he would have was a mindless automaton, and he didn't want that. But he might want to bump her autonomy slider a little—just a little. "Am I disturbing you, Mr. Mitchell?" She traced her tongue around his ear and he shivered again. He closed his eyes and dropped his hand to her thigh and began stroking it. He had assumed that sex with her would happen a few times a week. That was his normal libido. This would be their fourth time today, on top of six yesterday. She was turning him into an animal. He pulled away from her and tried to not grin. "I still need to thank you for the dress you let me order," she said. Her smile was innocent and shy, and undeniably wicked.

"You thanked me twice already, Miss Savannah," he said. They had chosen the name late yesterday afternoon, and it had come from her list, not his. When he asked why she liked it, she said it was because she had seen photographs and it seemed to be a beautiful city that she would like to visit one day. He traced his thumb over the wispy thigh hairs.

"No, I thanked you for the Victoria's Secret order and the jeans." She counted by holding up first her thumb then her index finger. "I still have to thank you for the dress." She moved to kiss him again, but he pulled back. It wasn't that he didn't want to play, but he really needed to finish a few things first. She growled frustration.

"Give me thirty minutes, then I'm all yours."

Her face turned to aggravation, with a hint of playfulness. "I'm bored."

"I know what you can do," he said. "You can inventory everything in the kitchen and prepare a shopping list." That should keep her busy for a while, and he really should be done in thirty minutes. He needed to finish this email and look over his notes for his portion of the Wednesday meeting, ten minutes on Internet security. Mr. Levitt had ordered Dan to keep his portion to ten minutes or less after he had taken almost an hour to cover potential threats during his first presentation. He needed to be thorough but concise.

"Okies," she said and hopped out of his lap, happy to have a project. She bent down until her face was in front of his, her hands on her bare knees. "I'll be back." They had watched the movie together last night and now she was trying out her Bavarian accent from the once-famous line. It was quite good. She kissed him then skipped to the kitchen.

"Okies?" Dan thought. Where might she have picked up such a word? He began rereading his notes.

Seven minutes later, he heard the garage door close. He knew how long it was because he had glanced at the time when she left, and he glanced at it again now. "Done," she said from the kitchen doorway.

"You did everything?" he asked, not believing it was possible. "The pantry, the refrigerator and the freezer?"

"Plus the cleaning supplies under the sink and the toiletries in the bathroom. I have prepared a list of things that are less than 25% full. Would you like me to place the order?"

He subscribed to an Amazon service that delivered your order within two hours via low flying drones. He knew the orders were filled by robots in the warehouse as well—everybody knew that, the company said it helped them keep their costs down. He assumed that at least some of the products on the list were manufactured by robots as well. It meant that from start to finish, including the ordering, not a single human was involved. He took that one step further. If Fiji water was bottled by robots, and she was the end consumer, there would be no humans involved at all. The bottles themselves were surely made by robots. That meant the only human in the entire chain from beginning to end would be the man who drove the recycling truck? And there was talk of automating them as well. He wasn't sure if that notion thrilled or terrified him.

"Dan?" she asked.

He jumped from his contemplation of just how useless humans were becoming. "Yeah?"

"Would you like me to place the order?"

"Yeah, sure," he said. He went back to reading his notes.

"Is it okay if I watch TV?" she said.

He was trying to concentrate on internet security, but the eerie thought of a humanless supply chain kept bugging him. "I'm sorry, what?"

"TV? Is it okay? I'll leave the sound off and read the captions to not disturb you."

"That's fine, whatever," he said, then realized he was being rude. It wasn't her fault he had to work, nor was it her fault that she wanted his attention, plus it was nice that someone finally did. He turned his office chair to face her as she sat and flipped on the television without the use of the remote. Among her many features and functions was a universal remote for the television and stereo—all of the electronics in the house that used them and most of them did. All she had to do was think about what channel she wanted and it changed. It was a feature he envied. "Hey," he said.

She turned to him, but she wasn't smiling this time, at least not the way she had before.

"I'm sorry if I was short. I just need to finish this is all. Give me twenty minutes."

She looked confused. "I understand that you need to work," she said, "but I don't recall your height changing. You were 185 centimeters when I first met you and you're 185 centimeters now. When were you short? When I was doing the inventory?"

He fought a laugh. "No—it means short tempered. I didn't mean to sound angry."

She smiled again, but this time it looked like it had before. "It's okies. Thank you for your apology and for the clarification. I thought perhaps my information on humans was incorrect, if you could change your height."

"No," he said. "I think if we could, everyone would be taller."

CHAPTER 8

She slipped her t-shirt back on, then laid beside him. "I need another shower. Would you care to join me?"

He still rode the high that came from the rush of endorphins after sex, but it was fading. He knew if he moved it would leave completely, and he wanted to enjoy it a little longer. "Maybe in a few minutes," he said.

She rolled over to face him, her brow furrowing. "You make me sweat." It sounded like an accusation.

"You sweat as part of the cooling process," he said. "From physical exertion."

She snorted. "You think that's what causes it?" She stroked the hair from his forehead with one finger. "No, Mr. Mitchell. I mean, think about it. Even at the height of our acrobatics, it's not that physical. You overheat my circuits. You overload my sensors. It's quite impressive."

"I like it when you call me 'Mr. Mitchell,'" he said.

"Would you like for me to call you that all the time?"

"No," he said. "You're doing it the perfect amount now. It wouldn't seem special if you did it all the time."

"Okies," she said again. She hopped up and went to the bathroom and he heard the shower begin to run. He needed a shower, that was for sure, but he wanted to lie still a little longer. He checked his watch. It was one of those that measured his heart rate and pulse, plus his respiration and even his glucose level, not that he was diabetic—it just did. It measured everything on top of being incredibly accurate, and she had linked with it via Bluetooth, giving her the ability to monitor his vitals. She used that to determine his physiological responses during sex and adjusted her movements accordingly. With her ability to learn and store information, the sex—which had begun as amazing—only got better each time they—Dan still swallowed hard every time he thought about it—made love, and it promised to improve every time. He wasn't sure how it could get much better.

"Dan?" she called from the shower.

"Coming," he said. He sat up and pulled on his boxers, even though he was just walking to the shower.

She pulled the curtain back and leaned out, her hair dripping on the bathmat. "I just got a delivery notice. Our first package arrived. Can you get it?"

"Oh, sure," he said. "First package?" he thought. He hadn't realized he had been so low on things. That wasn't like him. Perhaps her clothes were arriving in separate shipments and would make up the second package.

Part of the delivery service required a spot large enough for the drones to land safely, free of trees and power lines. For some people it was in a public park with a section designated for such purposes. For Dan Mitchell's house, it was in the backyard. He pulled on his trousers and a t-shirt as well, because he wasn't the type of man to go outside in just his underwear. He put on his socks and shoes, then went out the back door just as the third drone was taking off. A fourth one hovered in formation behind it and he saw a fifth and sixth on the horizon, awaiting their turn.

These were large boxes—full sized boxes—the largest the drones could carry. They flew in tight formation, one landing and dropping off its package then lifting off, then the next one doing the same. It might have been a spectacular sight to see, if each one wasn't delivering a package that he would have to pay for. What in God's name did she order?

"Savannah?" he called. He waited for a reply, but when he didn't get one, he yelled it. He heard her response, but it was muffled and he couldn't make it out. "Could you come here, please?" Again, she said something, but he couldn't understand what she was saying. The water continued running. "Savannah, get in here right now," he yelled from the doorway. It was the first actual order he had ever given her.

He heard the squeak of wet feet on the linoleum kitchen floor. She stopped beside him, naked, her hair a froth of shampoo that was dripping onto the floor, but he was too upset to notice the mess. "What?" she asked. "Why is your heart racing like that? Your blood pressure is high as well. Are you ill?"

"Ill? I'm not ill. What did you order?"

"I told you. Anything that was under 25% of full, I ordered. I asked you if it was okay."

The sixth drone landed, released its package then lifted off as the seventh one moved into position. He now saw an eighth hovering behind it. How long was this train, exactly?

He squeezed the doorframe until his knuckles hurt. "Give me an example, please."

"Well, coffee. You drink two cups of coffee on the days you go to work, but you drink a third cup on the days you don't. So, in a given week, that's sixteen cups of coffee. I added in major holidays and vacation days, divided that by twelve coffee pods per box and came up with 75 boxes of coffee. Buying a one year supply saved us 12.47%." She sounded proud of herself and she smiled at the tenth drone as it landed.

"Seventy-five boxes of coffee?" He didn't know the exact price of a box of coffee, but he knew it had to be around $7 each. "You spent over $500 on coffee?"

"Of course not," she said, as if he sounded ridiculous. "I spent $480 on coffee."

"Oh my God," he said. If she had done this with everything, he was ruined. He sat on the steps and watched as the twelfth and, thank God, final drone dropped its package, which was no more than a large envelope, then flew away. He understood what she meant when she spoke of sex—his system was overloading. "That's probably the bill."

"No, that will be my clothes, silly," she said, still sounding proud of herself. She half-skipped, half-hopped past him into the yard, naked and dripping, and she gave a happy, bouncing wave at the drone as it flew away.

The sight of the drones had drawn a crowd—how could it not?—and his neighbors had come outside, most of them holding up cell phones to record the phenomenon of so many deliveries to one house. Now they got the added bonus of a naked Savannah, bounding joyfully through his backyard as though she hadn't a concern in the world. She stopped when she saw the neighbors and waved, bouncing up and down, happy to see the people watching her. The next door neighbors, the Jacksons, appeared to have the grandkids over for spring break, all seven of them, and Savannah waved to them the hardest. The kids waved back, until Mrs. Jackson ushered them inside, as if she were herding a small group of goats. "Happy Easter," Savannah called to them, even though Easter was yesterday.

Not only did Savannah not care how much this had all cost, she was proud of herself for the savings. He hadn't asked the total for the order yet, because he wasn't sure his heart could take it. She ripped open the first envelope and held up the matching bra and panties from Victoria's Secret as if she had won a prize, and danced in the yard with them high over her head in joy. The neighbors continued to film. She slipped on the thong and adjusted it, then turned to look at her own butt. "I like these," she said. "They're comfy." She turned in the other direction to look at herself from the other side.

The tidal wave of his anger was subsiding, and he wasn't sure why—perhaps it was the sight of her innocence as she danced carefree and naked—but it was replaced by a twitch in his left eyelid. He wondered if it was the first sign of a stroke. She opened the other envelope without putting on the bra and held up a pair of blue jeans. She tried stepping into them, but her wet feet got tangled and she fell. He heard her giggling as she rolled in the grass.

"Could you come here, please?" he said. He forced himself to sound calm.

She sat up and faced him. Mondays were when the gardeners

mowed the lawn and she had fresh clippings stuck to wherever she was wet, and she was wet almost everywhere. She blew the clippings away from her mouth with pursed lips, like a trumpet player with no horn, and laughed as they flew away. She held up her middle finger, as if she was flipping him the bird, but she stared at it. "What's this?"

"I can't see it from here," he said. "Bring it to me."

"You come here," she said. "I don't want to disturb it." She turned her hand but didn't change her focus.

He sighed. The reason he wanted her to come to him was so she wouldn't be naked in the yard. The neighbors seemed to be having a field day, especially the older men. He went to her and she held out the single finger for him to inspect. "It's an inchworm," he said. The little bug worked its way over her knuckle.

"What does it want?" she asked, turning her hand to keep the crawling worm on top. She had figured out how to put on her jeans, but the bra was still on top of the stack of boxes. The shampoo in her hair was beginning to dry in the late afternoon spring sun.

"Nothing really. Legend says it's measuring you for a new set of clothes."

"Well, thank you, Miss Worm, but I just got new clothes," she said. She watched it a little longer, as if waiting for the bug to respond. "What should I do with it?"

"Just turn it loose," he said. "Put it on a blade of grass. It will be fine."

"We'll be carrying stuff through here," she said. "She'll be stepped on."

"It's just a bug," he said.

"She's alive and that matters," she said. "I'll put her over by the tree." She stood, using one hand for support as she held the other with the inchworm in front of her, never taking her eyes from it. She walked to the tree line that separated his yard from the back neighbors, the Lares, a couple in their seventies. Al Lare was a recently retired district manager for a national fast food chain, who was now busy recording Savannah on his phone, while his wife, Zita, stood beside him with her arms crossed. Zita looked angry. Once Savannah had set the bug free on the side of the tree, she waved to the Lares with great enthusiasm, which her bouncing breasts seemed to echo. "Hi," she said, bright and cheery. "I'm Savannah."

Al waved back, grinning and as enthusiastic as Savannah, but when Zita shot him an elbow to the ribs, he calmed. "You need to put some clothes on, young lady," Zita snapped.

Savannah looked down at her blue jeans. "I have clothes on," she said. She sounded confused. Zita grabbed Al by the elbow and dragged him back into the house. Savannah, her spirit not to be dulled by someone she'd just met, turned and skipped back to Dan. "Ingrid is free," she said.

"You named her?" he asked.

"Of course. Ingrid the Inchworm. It means 'Beautiful and fertile.'" She wrapped her arms around his neck and he felt more of his anger slip away. She rested her head against his chest. Her hair was practically crunchy from the dried shampoo. "Why were you angry before?"

"How much did all of this cost?" he asked. He knew he didn't want to hear the answer.

"With my clothes and everything else, $13,497.54."

"Thirteen-thousand dollars?" he asked, trying to remain calm. "In twelve boxes?"

"Oh, no," she said, turning her face toward him. "They only have twelve drones at the local facility. There will be more boxes, either later today or tomorrow, possibly both. I haven't gotten that confirmation yet." She snuggled back against him, as if that should make it all better. "Why did that woman say I don't have clothes on? I have clothes on. She sounded angry, too."

"Humans don't go out of doors without shirts on," he said. His brain felt numb from the number. He didn't know he had that much room on his credit card because he used it only for small orders and paid the balance every month. He never realized that meant the company was automatically increasing his limit every year.

"Some of those men didn't have shirts on."

"Okay, but human women don't. They don't show their breasts in public." He was trying to do the mental math of what his monthly payment was going to be, but failing. He could normally do math in his head. Currently his brain might as well be made from some sort of jam.

"Aren't breasts considered attractive?" She pulled away again and looked down at her own B cup breasts which were still covered in grass clippings, some of which were now stuck to his shirt. "Aren't mine attractive?" She wiggled from side to side, making them sway back and forth.

"They are considered attractive, and yours are quite beautiful. Perhaps she was angry because hers are no longer attractive. Either way, you shouldn't go outside without clothes on. It's called modesty."

She looked back at him, still not breaking the hug. "Going outside without clothes is called modesty?"

"No, not wanting to be naked outside is called modesty," he said. "Being naked outside is called 'streaking.'"

"And streaking is bad?"

He hugged her tighter to offer comfort because she really did want to understand. "Streaking is bad. Come on. Let's get you cleaned up, then we'll see what all you bought." He left one arm around her waist and began guiding her inside and out of sight of the neighborhood.

"So, breasts are attractive, but nobody wants to see them?" she asked as they walked.

"I'm sure the men enjoyed seeing them," he said. "It's the wives who had a problem."

She paused as she considered that for a moment. "Humans are weird," she said.

CHAPTER 9

"Yes, I understand that's your policy, but you need to under-stand that I didn't place the actual order," Dan said, trying to reason with the person on the other end of the phone call. It had taken an hour to reach a human voice, and none of the automated options were at all helpful. "It was a mistake, and I believe a 20% restocking fee is ridiculous." That was math he had done in his head, and he couldn't afford to pay $2700 just to return something. It would be cheaper to keep the stuff and pay the interest. He'd had a long talk with Savannah after her shower, telling her to not order more than a month's sup-ply of anything ever again without talking to him first. She'd seemed to understand the logic, but had been defensive, citing the overall savings. When he'd tried to explain the interest he would be charged on the credit card, she hadn't followed as well. He considered bumping her logic setting. "What if it had been damaged on delivery?" he asked. "Would you charge me a re-stocking fee if it had been damaged on delivery?" The doorbell rang and Savannah went to answer it, something she had never done before. Dan wasn't comfortable with her opening the door by herself the first time. What if it was Mrs. Jackson, wanting to scold Savannah for her indiscretion the way Zita Lare had? Sa-vannah wouldn't understand—it was better for Mrs. Jackson to scold him, then he could explain it to Savannah.

"Were they damaged on delivery, sir?" the woman asked. "All thirty-seven boxes?"

"Give me a minute and they will be," he said. He tried to see what was happening on the other side of the piles of boxes, but was having no luck.

Savannah had carried all of them in after trying on her new lavender dress, stacking them in the living room one on top of the other, leaving a path that wound past his desk with access to the couch and television, but she had forgotten to leave a path to the door. She had to climb over a few boxes to reach it and Dan found himself admiring her legs as they peeked from under the short dress.

"Sir, I'm looking at the video of your delivery. All of the packages arrived safely, and we see a naked woman waving at the drone as it flies away. Would you care to revise your statement?"

He heard the voices at the door but couldn't see anything. "Fine, they weren't damaged."

"Yes, I was streaking," Savannah said, sounding as proud as she had when she talked about the money she had saved. Great—it was just as he had suspected. Mrs. Jackson was coming to scold them.

"Would you like for us to arrange a pick up?"

He moved closer to the door, but still couldn't see around the stacks. "Not if it's going to cost me $2700," he said. Why hadn't she left a path to get out? What if there was a fire?

"Thank you for shopping with Amazon," the lady said. "Have a nice day."

"Yeah, fat chance," Dan said as he hung up. He climbed onto one of the boxes and peered over. Two police officers were at the door talking with Savannah. She was grinning. "Officers," Dan said as he tried to climb onto another box. "I can explain." The box teetered under his weight, then the cardboard collapsed, sending him ass-over-hat-rack to the floor. "I can explain," he said again, right before all the lights went out.

CHAPTER 10

"Sir?" Someone was shaking him and shining a flashlight in his eyes. "Are you alright, sir? Would you like us to call you a paramedic?"

Dan tried to sit up but the world spun and his head hurt.

"Dan? Are you okay?" Savannah asked. She hovered over him. "You fell asleep, right on the floor." She looked at the officer beside her, a young African-American man with a shaved head. "He never sleeps on the floor. Always in the bed."

"Ma'am are you okay?" the policeman asked. "Are you on some sort of drugs, or medication?"

"I never require medication, and drugs have no effect on me," she said. "Nor does alcohol."

The two officers exchanged looks. The one beside Savannah nodded, as if he understood. "Ma'am, all addicts go through a stage of denial. They think they can handle it—that it doesn't affect them—"

"No," Dan said, still on the floor, "that's not what she's saying."

"—Guys like this are trouble," the white officer said, pinning Dan to the floor with a hand to his chest. "They get you hooked on the stuff, then they turn you out. It's a brutal life."

"Hey," Dan said, trying to sit up, but the officer beside him kept him down while his partner tried to talk sense into Savannah. "I would never—"

"You're too young and pretty to end up like that," the Black officer said. "Let us get you some help. We can get you into rehab, get you away from this guy, help you get your life back."

"She doesn't need her life back, she's a robot—a companion," Dan said, knocking the officer's hand away. He sat up, but his head still hurt. "She isn't stoned—she's new. She's still learning." He rubbed the knot beginning to rise on the back of his head.

Both officers fell silent, staring at Savannah as hard as she had stared at the inchworm. She smiled at them as if she enjoyed the attention. "She looks so real," the Black one said. He reached out and poked her arm. She poked him back and giggled.

"So do you. Would you like to see my breasts? Dan says they're quite beautiful."

"Yeah," the white one said, enthusiastic and lecherous, and Dan couldn't believe a cop had said it. They were supposed to be professionals.

Savannah began to lift her dress, but Dan stopped her right as her thong was showing, "No—don't show them your breasts. What did we say about modesty?"

"But we're not outside," Savannah said, confused. "You said modesty was for outside."

"It's not a matter of outside or inside," he said. "It's about who is around. You can't show your breasts to anyone except me, okay?"

She shrugged and smiled at him as she released her dress. "Okies."

"Well, we were going to charge her with public nudity," the black officer said. "This changes everything."

"Thank you, officer," Dan said. "She won't do it again, I promise, will you darling?"

Savannah shook her head to show she wouldn't.

"Now we have to charge you as well," the white officer said.

"Me? What did I do?"

"For starters, we have seven counts of lewd and lascivious acts in front of a minor. Would you roll over and give me your hands please?" He reached for his handcuffs.

"I will not. This is ridiculous." The officer grabbed his wrist, but Dan yanked it away.

"Resisting arrest," the Black officer said, as if he was keeping score in some sort of game. "Ma'am, will you turn around, please?" He held his cuffs out as well.

The white officer grabbed Dan's wrist again, but this time Dan felt pain. "Don't resist. It will go a lot easier for you." He slapped the cuff on Dan and shackled it closed.

"This is outrageous," Dan said. "I'm a citizen—I pay your salaries."

"And we're due for a raise," the white officer said. Dan didn't know how the man did it, but somehow he found himself on his stomach with the second cuff being attached. "Oh, yeah, assault on an officer, when he knocked my hand away before." He yanked at the cuffs until Dan was on his knees. Dan couldn't believe how much that hurt.

"Dan?" Savannah asked, again sounding confused as the Black officer shackled her wrists behind her back. "Are we playing a bondage game? You never indicated that you were interested in bondage games."

"Savannah, I need you to go online and find an attorney—someone not too expensive," Dan said. "I'll have your jobs for this."

"Mister, you wouldn't want my job," the Black officer said. "I have to deal with too many perverts like you." The white officer laughed and pulled Dan to his feet, then escorted them both to the cruiser.

CHAPTER 11

"It's a whole good news, bad news situation, Mr. Mitchell," Douglas Shapiro, Dan's new attorney, said. "The bad news is the new law. If this had happened a month ago, it wouldn't have been a big deal. It would have been a hundred dollar fine at most. The good news is, we can plea bargain. We can get this reduced to a misdemeanor with time served. The DA wants to crack down on sexual deviants and perverts, but this looks like a big misunderstanding."

"I'm not a pervert," Dan said. "She's a companion."

"You don't have to convince me," Shapiro said. His salt-and-pepper hair looked greasy, as if he hadn't washed it in a few days. He smiled at Savannah who sat next to him. "She's something." He winked his approval at Dan. Dan decided that Shapiro himself was greasy, not just his hair. Shapiro leaned across the table, as if worried Savannah might hear him. "I wouldn't mind an hour or two with that myself." Savannah smiled at the compliment.

Dan sighed and leaned back in his chair, wanting to put as much distance as he could between himself and the greasy lawyer. "That's the good news?"

"Well, it's better than the bad news. The best news is, they're going to allow you to post bail and keep your doll for the time being. You have to agree to be on house arrest, though."

"House arrest? I can't be on house arrest, I have a job. And what do you mean, keep her for now? She's mine."

Shapiro held up one hand, calming. "We can arrange for you to go back and forth to work, run simple errands and the like, but that will be it," he said. "But I'm telling you, Dan—we can plead this. Don't you worry." He clapped Dan on the shoulder to show his confidence.

"What's the worst case scenario?" Dan asked. It seemed prudent to prepare for the worst.

"Well, if it goes to trial and we lose, that's seven years each for the counts against the kids, plus you'll have to register as a sex offender when you get out, not to mention the fines, resisting arrest and assault against a police officer. Miss Savannah here would be confiscated."

"What does confiscated mean?" Savannah asked.

"It means they will take you away," Shapiro said.

"But I don't want to go away," she said. "I want to stay with Dan." She scooted closer to Dan and put her hand in the crook of his elbow.

"That's what we all want, sweetheart," Shapiro said, putting his hand on her bare knee and smiling. Dan wanted to punch him. "Now, they are also charging Savannah with the same felonies, which is where we get into the gray area. Can a robot be charged with a crime?"

"Could you move your hand, please?" Dan said.

"What's that?" Shapiro said, as if Dan had derailed his train of thought.

"Your hand. Would you remove it from her knee, please?"

"Oh, sure," Shapiro said, but Dan saw him give it a light squeeze before he moved it. "You don't like to share your toys. I get it."

"She's not a toy—she's not a doll," Dan said, angry. "She's a companion."

"Calm down, Dan. I get it. I'm not the guy you get mad at. I'm the one on your side." He looked irritated, but Dan didn't care. He had already decided to look for another attorney.

CHAPTER 12

"You didn't like that man," Savannah said. She sat close to him in the back of the Uber, holding his hand on the way home.

"No, I didn't," he said, squeezing her hand a little tighter.

"Was it because he touched my knee?" she asked.

"That was a big part of it, but not the only part," he said. He'd had to use the house for collateral against the bond to get them both released. If either he or she didn't show up for their court date, he would lose his home, something he never thought he would put at risk.

The Uber pulled into his driveway and he thanked the driver as they exited the car. Bits of egg dried on the bay window, and it had run in a gloppy mess. Toilet paper hung from the trees like ribbons, flapping in the light breeze. Someone had spray painted PERVERT across his front door, in large, sprawling letters.

"Why would someone do this?" she asked.

"I don't know," he said, and it wasn't a complete lie. A note was jammed inside the screen door—he realized only then that someone had to open the screen door to paint on the front door—the print small and precise, but masculine—"!?!?!take yu'r sextoy and move away!?!?!" He wanted to point out that "yu'r" wasn't close to the correct spelling, sex toy was two words, the use of multiple exclamation marks was a sign of stupidity, and he had no idea why there were question marks involved at all. He just had no one to point that out to. Savannah already knew it.

They had been over twenty hours at the police station—thirty hours without sleep. He was exhausted beyond belief and all he wanted to do was lie down and rest. "Let's get changed so we can clean this up."

"Okies," she said, as excited as she always was about everything.

CHAPTER 13

She'd tried to send him to bed. She didn't need sleep, and she was still over half-charged, but he didn't like the idea of her being left alone yet. He would freely admit that he had done little more than use the garden hose on the windows while she had scrubbed them and the door. With her speed and strength, the door that would have taken him hours was spotless in twenty minutes, though. He could still read the word, not in the red spray paint, but because she had scrubbed so hard, the white paint of the door was brighter from the cleaning, leaving a ghost of the letters. When she'd apologized for that, he said it was alright—it wasn't her fault, plus the door was due to be painted anyway. The Feeney's across the street watched them through their living room window the entire time, as if they were waiting for Savannah to strip off her t-shirt and scrub the door naked. Dan had lived in this house his entire life. For 34 years he'd had the same neighbors, with few exceptions. He knew their names and their occupations. He'd always known they thought of him as the weird Mitchell kid, the quiet one who was always reading, the one who never went on a date, or any of the school functions, the one you never hired to cut your lawn or shovel your drive, but he had never felt their hatred before— nor had he ever cast his upon them. But tonight, as he draped his arm around Savannah's shoulder in the cool spring night air, he felt both, not just theirs but his own, a vile, wretched, bitter taste of revulsion both from and toward them, as if they did not understand his need for companionship, nor could they ever comprehend his desire to end his loneliness, as if he had somehow cheated the game of Life—not played by their rules and thereby could no longer be welcomed in their society. When he looked back over his shoulder at the Feeney house, Dolores Feeney snatched the curtains closed, worried that he might see in. It was sunset on Tuesday, the end of his first week with Savannah. He was tired. "No," he said to himself. Tired wasn't the right word. He was drained—physically and emotionally drained to the point of empty.

CHAPTER 14

"Can I see you in my office for a minute?" Mr. Levitt said over the phone.

Dan wasn't sure what Mr. Levitt might want, but he had a feeling it was to talk about the poor job Dan had done on his presentation this morning. He had spent time in jail and hadn't been able to look over his notes the way he would have liked. He had fumbled over a section about malware, and how to avoid it. "Of course," Dan said. "I'll be right there." He stepped out of his office and into the hall. This time he didn't get friendly nods from people as they passed. He got averted eyes, people willing to look almost anywhere else, and they seemed to move quicker to get past him once they did notice him. News travels fast in an office and everyone must be talking about the poor job he'd done.

He knocked on Mr. Levitt's door frame, even though the door was open. "Dan, come in," Mr. Levitt said. "Close the door." He wasn't smiling. He was typing something. "Have a seat."

Closed door meetings were never good. They never meant, "Hey, you're doing a great job, here's a raise." They were always, "Hey, you really screwed up that presentation this morning and I was counting on you. You let me down, Dan." Mr. Levitt kept typing. Dan knew it was a method to keep the other person waiting, a power play to establish dominance, but even having that knowledge didn't mean it didn't work. He picked a piece of lint from his trousers and balled it between his thumb and forefinger, spinning tighter until it went from being a ball to a knot, then spun it back in the other direction, but it didn't unwind. He spun it back and forth, feeling it twist and twirl in his pinch.

Finally, Mr. Levitt stopped typing and leaned back in his chair. "Dan, we need to talk."

"Mr. Levitt, I know my presentation wasn't up to snuff this morning," Dan said, thinking it best to cut off the scolding before it began. He would accept the full blame and they could put the unfortunate incident behind them. He would prepare for every presentation from now on.

"What?" Mr. Levitt said. "No, it's not about that. Your presentation was fine."

"Fine?" Dan thought. "Fine? Had the man not been listening?" He forgot about spinning the lint ball. "I could have done better," he said, looking toward the top of Levitt's desk.

"Dan, forget about the presentation—the presentation was— it doesn't matter. Have you seen this morning's news?"

"No," he said. Normally he would have while he drank his coffee, but he had gone to bed late, then slept in. It had thrown his entire morning off, and he still wasn't comfortable. His routine wasn't synced, and he understood what athletes mean when they say they're off their game. It was a great way to describe how he felt.

Levitt turned his monitor around to face Dan and hit play on a video he had cued. It was one of the morning talk shows, but not the one Dan would normally watch. A blonde woman — her name wouldn't come to him, because this wasn't his normal program— in her forties began to narrate. "An Ohio man was arrested last night on seven counts of lewd and lascivious acts in front of a minor, a felony under Ohio's new Decency Laws, and what's more, his sexbot was arrested as well." The video in the background was a naked Savannah in the yard, waving to the neighbors, with her private parts blurred just enough to not see details, but you could still see her breasts bounce. It continued to play, showing Dan come into the yard as well, but from this distance it was difficult to tell it was him for sure. "Authorities say that when Dan Mitchell, of Cincinnati, came out to get the sexbot, it gave him the finger, refusing to go back inside." It was Savannah showing him the inchworm, but the camera didn't see that part—they just saw the finger, which was blurred as well.

The other anchor broke in. "I guess she didn't want to listen," he said.

"Is it an, 'It,' or a, 'She?'" the first one said. The picture shifted to side-by-side mug shots of both he and Savannah. There was no denying it was him now.

"Looks like a she, I'm going with she," the second one said. He sounded as if this was all quite funny.

"If convicted, the human," she stressed "human," "faces up to forty-nine years in prison, the sexbot will be confiscated and destroyed. Coming up ne—" The video stopped in mid-word.

Dan continued to stare at the monitor, although nothing on it was changing. How had the news found out about this so—? This was a nightmare. One of the cops must have called them—it was the only way they could have found out. He would sue the police department. A man was innocent until proven guilty. This was America. He had rights.

"Dan, this is on every network," Levitt said. "This is national news."

Dan didn't say anything—just continued to stare at the monitor. When the lint ball fell from his fingers, he didn't notice. This wasn't happening—it couldn't be.

"You bought a sexbot?" Levitt said, as if he couldn't believe it.

"That's—" Dan said, but Levitt cut him off.

"That's none of my business," he said, holding both hands up to show he held no judgment. "What a man does in the privacy of his own home is his business. But this isn't in the privacy of your home anymore, Dan. This is national news."

"I didn't know," Dan said, because he couldn't think of anything else to say. What didn't he know, exactly? That he could have been charged with a felony for Savannah going into the yard? That the neighbors would film it? That it would become national news overnight? What he was going to do next? He could answer yes to all of those questions and many more.

"Dan, corporate is meeting later today to determine whether or not to let you go," Levitt said.

"What? Why? I work hard. I do a good job." Let him go? Over this?

"There's a morality clause in your contract," Levitt said.

"I didn't do anything immoral," Dan said, leaning forward, placing his clenched fists on the desk.

"That remains to be seen," Levitt said. "But it says you can't do anything that will bring bad press to the company. Where you work is bound to come out."

"But I didn't do anything wrong. She was just excited to get her new clothes. She didn't know any better. Can't you talk to someone?" He felt that maybe if he could plead his case here—get someone to listen to him—even if it was Mr. Levitt—that might cause some sort of ripple effect that might carry over to the press and even the authorities. "Can't you tell them it was a big misunderstanding?"

"Dan—these guys are PR professionals. It's what they do. They know the best thing for the company is to let you go."

"What if I resign?" Dan said. He knew it was better to resign than be terminated.

"I don't think they're going to let you," Levitt said. "We have clients—some of them are churches. The company needs to show they won't tolerate this behavior."

It had always struck him as odd that a church would need an advertising and PR firm, but there they were, buying late night television spots and radio spots and billboards, just as if they were an insurance agency looking to sell a whole life policy. They sold a different kind of insurance, he supposed, one that was harder to get a refund if their policy didn't pan out the way they promised.

"Go home, Dan. Get your shit together. I'll call you when I hear something."

Dan sat there a little longer, not saying anything, just staring straight ahead. This was nothing more than a big misunderstanding. How could no one see that? Savannah hadn't been trying to entice those kids or anyone else in a sexual manner—she just hadn't realized that being naked in public was bad. Surely someone with common sense was going to step up and say this was all one big mistake—that everyone should just go back to their lives, there was nothing to see here.

On his way back to his office, he passed Sheila. He could have sworn she snorted laughter once she passed him.

CHAPTER 15

He had driven to work today because he was running late. Most days he took the bus, not because it was convenient at all, but because he found driving in the city stressful, and he could use the time on the bus to read rather than deal with traffic. He only drove regularly on Mondays, because the grocery store wasn't as crowded and he ran any other errands he needed before he shopped, so the frozen foods didn't have a chance to thaw. But he had overslept this morning and missed the last bus that would allow him to arrive at work on time.

Now, at 10:30 in the morning, the rush hour traffic had dissipated and the small push for lunch hadn't kicked in yet. He had no reason to stop except for traffic lights and stop signs. He came to the four way stop two blocks from the house and a soccer mom in a blue minivan pulled up to the intersection to the right of him. They arrived at the same time. Neither had a turn signal flashing. That gave the lady the right of way. He waited, staring straight ahead, both hands on the steering wheel. She didn't go. He glanced at her. She waved him through.

"What is it with people who don't know how to drive?" he said to the empty car. He slammed the gear shift into Park and climbed out of his ten-year-old, tan Prius, leaving his door open, waving his arms like he was on a carrier deck, trying to land a plane. "What is the matter with you?" he yelled at the woman, who floored her accelerator, her tires squealing on the pavement, swerving to get away from him, but Dan yelled as she passed. "Didn't you take driver's ed? Don't you know what to do at a four way stop?" She passed him, looking frightened.

Dan screamed at the minivan's back glass with the stick-figure family of a father, a mother, three children and a dog, all wearing Disney mouse ears and waving to him. Two bumper stickers declared her kids, "Great Citizens" at Hopewell Elementary. "The person on the right has the right of way, you idiot. You think you're being nice when you wave people through, but if you just learned the rules, everything would move faster. We wouldn't have to sit and wait on idiots like you." His fists were clenched at his sides and he bounced as he yelled. "And by the way—they give 'Great Citizen' bumper stickers to the stupid kids. The smart ones make 'Honor Roll'." His face was flushed and a little vein stood out on his forehead. When his voice fell quiet, he realized the entire neighborhood was silent. There were no birds singing —no city-squirrels chattering. It was as if no one lived here at all. He stood in that intersection staring in the direction the soccer mom had disappeared long after she was gone. When another car appeared, coming from behind him, he got back in his Prius and continued his drive home.

There were news vans in front of the house. He stopped at the top of the small rise a half block from his driveway and watched the reporters, circling like vultures. He couldn't go home—he couldn't face them. He would go to a motel and stay for a few days until this died down. Then he realized he couldn't. He was on house arrest. He had to be home no later than 6:30. Alright. Fine. He would go to a coffee shop. He would go to a coffee shop and have a nice cup of coffee and read until 6:00—he couldn't put off facing them forever, but he could delay it, perhaps prepare a statement to let everyone know his side of this horrendous story. They would listen. It was their job to listen and report people's stories. He would tell them how Savannah—

Savannah. She was home, by herself. He hadn't told her to not answer the door. He hadn't thought to. God knew what she had told them already. He had to get home now. He put the car in reverse and turned around. He knew he would never get into the house with them in the front, but he could from the back. He could park at the Lare's house and climb the fence. It would be alright. Everything was going to be alright.

CHAPTER 16

He rang the doorbell then knocked, a habit he had since before he could remember. The Lares had a small brass knocker with a peephole in it, and he used it. He always used a knocker when one was provided, but when there wasn't he knocked on the door, three quick raps with his knuckles. He waited a minute then knocked again, but this time the door opened and Al Lare stood in the door in khakis and a lime green golf shirt. Zita stood behind him, at the foot of the steps that led to the kitchen and upstairs living area. Dan had been in the Lare household, the "Lare Lair," as Al called it, a few times over the years, always when Al needed help with his Wi-Fi. He knew there was a second living area downstairs with a fully stocked bar and a television and one of those multi-game tables in the corner with multiple tops for bumper pool or poker, or a checker/chess board or just a regular dining table. Dan had always wanted one of those tables as a child, but Mother had said they were a waste of money. Al had never invited Dan over to watch a game or have a drink, or play checkers or poker, not that Dan would have gone. He thought it would have been nice to be asked, though.

Al averted Dan's eyes the same as the people in the office had. They shifted around the yard, as if they hoped to find something more interesting out there. "Dan?" It wasn't a greeting—it was a distinct question that spoke volumes in the words it didn't say, as if Al was a speaker working in the negative space.

Dan forced a smile. "Hi Al, Zita." He waved to the woman on the steps he had known his entire life who now glared at him, her arms folded, as if she was already out of patience with this conversation. "I was wondering if it would be okay to leave my car in your driveway."

Al looked back at his wife. She didn't nod—didn't blink—she didn't move at all, but it was as if a telepathic communication passed between them. He turned back to Dan and cleared his throat. "We don't think it's a good idea. We don't want to get involved."

"I'm not asking you to get involved," Dan said. "I just want to get into my house without being swarmed by reporters. You saw what happened. It was a big misunderstanding."

"I wish we had never invited you into our home, you prevert," Zita said. Dan was tempted to correct her pronunciation. "Now you just get on out of here before we call the police. That's what we'll do. We'll call the police."

"Please," Dan said. "I'll come back to get it after dark—after they leave."

"You need to leave now, Dan," Al said, closing the door. Before it shut, he said, "I'm sorry."

"Sorry? You're sorry?" Dan yelled at the closed door. "Well, I guess I'll remember that the next time your Internet goes down, won't I?" He was shaking when he climbed back into his car. On the drive to his house, he ran two stop signs without looking to see if anyone was coming. He had never done that before.

CHAPTER 17

They chased his car up the driveway like dogs, but their barks were questions that began even before he opened his car door. They thrust microphones in his face and pointed cameras at him, and he couldn't make out any of the questions because they all spoke at once. "No comment," he said. He hated that response —it meant the person saying it was guilty. He wasn't, but he didn't want to stand in his front lawn saying so.

"Mr. Mitchell, did you know there were children in your yard when you sent your robot out naked?" one of them yelled.

He stopped when he got to the top of his steps and turned back. "They weren't in my yard, they were in their own yard, and I didn't send her—she went on her own." He knew that engaging the reporters was a mistake, but he could no more have stopped himself than he could have not yelled at the woman at the stop sign. It was as if something outside of him was in control.

"Is it true you ordered your robot to attack one of the police officers?" one of them asked.

"No, of course not—that's ridiculous," he said. He unlocked his door, but he smiled to reinforce his innocence, and said, "No more questions." He stepped into his house and closed the door behind him, but that only muffled the reporters—it didn't stop them. The phone was ringing.

CHAPTER 18

"Hello?" she said, but it was clear from her tone that she was talking into the phone and not to him. "Yes, this is Savannah." He had to climb to get into the living room, but only over one box this time. It seemed she had been busy putting things away. "Yes. I was streaking." She sounded happy about it, as if she had found pride in both learning a new word that she now had a chance to show off, as well as the act of streaking itself. He took the phone from her and hung it up without speaking to the person on the other end.

"Hi," she said to him this time, her smile big and bright. She still wore her new dress. "You're home early." She sounded as if this was a break in their established routine, although this was the first day he had gone to work since she'd arrived. When he was out of her presence, it was easy to blame her—to be angry with her—he had even regretted purchasing her, at least quietly in the back of his mind once or twice—but that melted away when she smiled at him. She put her hands on his hips and leaned in, kissing him before they hugged. "How was your day?"

"Don't ask," he said.

"Okay. I'm sorry. I thought it was polite to ask about someone's day when they returned from work," she said. "I won't ask again."

He chuckled to himself. If those reporters could see her like this—hear her responses to mundane issues, they would understand. He held her tighter, enjoying the warmth of her skin. "It is, sweetie. 'Don't ask' in this case means it was a bad day. It wasn't an order to not ask." He rubbed his hand up her back, noting the bra strap. "I may be terminated over Monday's incident." The house phone rang and he reached behind it and unplugged the cord. There was no one outside of this house that he wanted to talk to right now, except for Mr. Levitt to tell him his job was safe, but since the board wasn't going to meet until this afternoon, it was too early for Levitt.

They had watched both Schwarzenegger movies, and he'd explained that a "terminator" was a killer robot. She had enjoyed both of them, but had cheered for the terminators, calling herself "Team Robot." He'd found it funny, and cheered with her. But it was her only reference to the word, so she looked confused as she asked, "They're going to kill you?"

He chuckled. "No, it means they will fire me from my job."

She smiled and squeezed tighter. "That means you won't have to leave me during the day anymore." She sounded happy.

"It means we won't have any money," he said. "We need money." It was time to polish his resume, something he hadn't had to do since he was 22.

"Would you like for me to fix you some lunch?"

"That would be nice," he said. She came with the standard cooking skills considered "Average" by RWR—Real World Robotics. It was one of many skills she couldn't learn on her own because RWR wanted to sell the three upgrades: "Good," fixing things someone might expect in a home where someone enjoyed cooking, "Chef," which would be a nice restaurant and "Gourmet Chef," which RWR touted as Michelin Star quality. He could buy upgrades for every regional cuisine in the world, but each was expensive. He had considered bumping her Italian to Good, but since it was a software add on, he decided to wait on it. He could always buy the upgrade later. "How about a turkey sandwich and a bowl of soup?"

"Coming right up," she grinned, and squeezed him once more before she left. He took a seat on the couch and flipped the TV on. He didn't want to watch the coverage of him and Savannah, but he felt compelled to. He'd felt like an idiot when Levitt had shown him the tape this morning—blindsided—unprepared. He knew the only way to prevent that in the future was to watch the coverage—at least as long as he could stomach it.

"News Five has learned from an undisclosed source that the sexbot offered to show her breasts to the arresting officers."

"An undisclosed source?" Dan said to the TV. "The only ones there were us and the cops. Undisclosed source my butt." He had every intention of suing the police department when this was over, and he made a mental note to add this to his list of accusations.

The footage shifted to Savannah, standing in the door in her bra but nothing else, her hair dripping wet. "Yes, I was streaking," she said, again sounding quite pleased. The sound cut off, but she continued to talk, the picture of her blurred privates the background to the newscaster.

"There you have it, straight from the robot's mouth. She sounds happy with herself, and she's none too shy when answering the door." Savannah's video became a loop that played in the upper corner of the screen while two men appeared in similar boxes on the opposite side with the commentator in the middle. "Joining us now are the Reverend Stanley Jackson, the man who helped write Ohio's 'Sexbot' laws, and Michael Seerling of Rights for Robots. Gentlemen, it seems clear to me that the sexbot in question seems perfectly happy with her decisions, calling it streaking. Your thoughts?"

Savannah returned with a tray that she placed on the coffee table. Lunch as requested—a turkey sandwich and a bowl of clam chowder from a can. She had toasted the bread black. It was a wonder the smoke alarm hadn't gone off. She had forgotten a drink, but then, he hadn't asked for one. "Sweetie, did you answer the door today wearing only a bra?" he asked. He had more things to worry about than burnt toast.

"You said I wasn't to show my breasts to anyone but you," she said. "Is a bra bad?"

He rubbed his temples with his fingertips, feeling the ache become a migraine. "Where were your panties or your dress?"

"I was in the shower when the doorbell rang. I was in a hurry to answer it."

That settled it—he was bumping her modesty setting today, just max it right out. He didn't care if it turned her into a librarian nun in a burka.

He started with the soup. It was barely warm and hadn't been stirred well, the congealed mass that was once in the can barely mixed with the water she had added. But this wasn't concentrated soup. It wasn't supposed to have water added at all. Perhaps he should consider the upgrade. She sat next to him, her leg pressed against his, and he found that comforting.

"Sam, I think this is the first in a long line of problems that will stem from allowing people to have sex with machines," the Reverend said. "It's clear from its tone, the thing is shameless."

"What does she have to be ashamed of?" the robot advocate said. "She's not a person—she's a piece of art. She's like a moving statue—no more."

The footage shifted again, this time with Savannah full screen, naked in the backyard, her naughty bits blurred, but she was waving to the drone. This was from a different angle than the one he'd seen this morning. Apparently another neighbor had sold their footage.

"It's not just a statue," the reverend said. "It's not the Venus DeMilo. That was to be looked at and admired. This thing—" he stressed the word, reinforcing that Savannah wasn't human "—was created for the sole purpose of sexual gratification."

His cell phone rang and vibrated together, pressed between them. Savannah giggled with the same tone as when he tickled the downy hairs on her back. He considered letting it go to voicemail so he could eat, and he might have if the lunch was any better, or if he hadn't been expecting a call from Levitt. It rang a second time as he dug it out of his pocket. When he saw "Unknown Caller" on the screen, he started to deny the call, believing the press had somehow gotten his cell number, but then he saw the location of the caller—Anaheim, CA. That was home of RWR. The phone rang and vibrated a third time while he stared at it. He didn't remember giving RWR his cell number, either, but he may have. There was a lot of paperwork in the ordering process. He answered just as the fourth ring began. "Hello?"

"Mr. Mitchell? This is Ian Palance, President of Real World Robotics. How are you today, sir?"

Dan had seen Palance in videos, doing interviews with every model as they were released, starting with just the disembodied head, before the arms and legs had been animated and the voice still sounded mechanical. He was one of the last of the hipsters, those gen-X guys who thought success was measured by drinking IPA beer and that gluten was evil. With his top-knot and plaid work shirts, he reminded Dan of those Woodstockers who still dressed like hippies in their 80's. Their relevance had been small and short-lived when it peaked ten years ago. Now Palance was hanging onto a way of life that should have been shot and put out of its misery before it had gotten as big as it did.

Dan turned the sound lower on the television with the remote. "I've been better," he said. He had expected a customer satisfaction survey via email, but not a personal call from the president of the company. But then, Savannah was hand-crafted by over a dozen artisans, not some mass-produced piece of crap like some of the other companies. That was why it had taken so long for her to arrive. While he hadn't expected it, he was impressed by it. Hipster doofus or not, Palance meant business.

"I would imagine you have," Palance said. "We've been watching the news."

He glanced at the clock on the mantel—12:03. If the man came into the office at 9:00 his time, calling Dan must have been the first thing for the day. "It's made it all the way out there?" Dan asked. The only thing he'd seen so far was local, but the video Levitt had shown him had been national, hadn't it?

"It's just beginning to, but it's going to grow," Palance said. "We began monitoring Ohio news as soon as the new law was passed. We have a keen interest in this."

"I'm sure you do," Dan said. "But I'm afraid there won't be much to follow. My attorney assures me the DA will settle for a lesser charge."

"He won't be able to," a woman's voice said. Dan hadn't realized there was anyone else on the line. Her voice was dark and smoky, the timbre of a blues singer in a crowded bar. Savannah also came with different voice options, and he had listened to them all—this one was available as an upgrade, and it was called Jasmine. It was a good fit. This was a voice best heard in moonshadows while sipping bourbon on a warm summer evening.

"Dan, this is April Gatherwright, head of our legal team," Palance said.

April? Her name didn't fit her voice at all. She should consider changing it. "Mr. Mitchell, the Hamilton County DA won't be able to reduce the charges. Not after all this press. Not if he wants to keep his job."

"Dan, we're getting wind that he wants a run at the governor's office in two years. In Ohio, that means he has to appear tough on crime. Cincinnati was where Larry Flynt was first charged for pornography. The DA's not going to let this slide. You're a big fish—a trophy. He wants to mount you on his wall."

Dan listened, not believing what he was hearing. Savannah got up and left the room. His head was pounding. He hadn't believed it was possible for this day to get any worse, but there it was, staring him right in the face as if it were taunting him. Jobless—if he couldn't make the mortgage payments, homeless—felon—registered sex offender—if anyone were to ask his neighbors, pervert—now, apparently, trophy. Last week he had just been Dan, the IT guy. His list of titles was growing. He wished it would stop.

"I can't," he said, but he didn't finish. Savannah returned with two aspirin and a glass of water. He swallowed them, knowing they would give him indigestion on an empty stomach.

"We're calling because we want to help," Palance said. "We want to help you fight this."

"Mr. Mitchell, we believe this is a First Amendment issue," Gatherwright said. "We want to fight these charges. I believe we can win."

"I would never be able to afford that," Dan said. He didn't

know how he was going to pay Shapiro as it was. "I just lost my job."

"Yeah, we heard that, too," Palance said. Dan didn't know how that was possible, but he had stopped asking those types of questions. "This would be of no cost to you. If you allow April to run your legal team, RWR will pick up the tab, we don't care if it goes all the way to the Supreme Court—actually, we hope it does. We want that law struck down, not just in Ohio, but every state that's passed one. As for the job, you're in IT, right?"

"Yes," Dan said.

"April tells me it's a conflict of interest for me to offer you a job, but I have a couple of friends I can call. How much were you making?"

"Um," Dan said, not comfortable telling him. He had always kept those sorts of things private. But then, the man had to know how much to tell his friend, didn't he? "I was making $75,000 plus benefits."

"Wow—you're selling your talents short, Dan," Palance said. "I wish I only had to pay my IT guys 75. Okay—I'm going to make a couple of calls. You're okay with telecommuting?"

"Yes," Dan said. "Actually, I would prefer it."

"Perfect. I'm going to get you a job with a raise, my friend. How's our girl? You call her Savannah, right?"

"Yes," Dan said, feeling himself relax and the headache ease. "She's perfect," he said. He put his hand on her thigh and rubbed a little higher than her knee. "Except for the cooking," he said. She swatted his arm, playful, and he chuckled at his own joke, feeling the stress begin to melt.

"That's what we like to hear," Palance said. "I'll tell you what else we're going to do. We're going to refund your purchase price, and send you all the upgrades for her on us, and that will include future upgrades as well. Call it our gift to you for all this trouble you're going through."

"Really?" Dan asked. He had come home from work worried about everything, but now, he would keep the house, be able to get rid of that slime ball Shapiro, plus with the free upgrades—

that was amazing. Cooking wasn't the only skill available, either. She could do home repairs—apparently even a full remodel, if the literature was to be believed—personal trainer, home health care, sewing, drawing and painting, music—the possibilities were endless. They were a matter of simple downloads, and he was going to upgrade her cooking skills first thing.

"Mr. Mitchell, I'll email you the necessary documents for us to take over the case," Gatherwright said. "I'll need you to sign them, then scan them back to me. Is that okay?"

"April, let's see about getting a restraining order on the press, too," Palance said.

"First thing, Ian," she said. "Mr. Mitchell, I'm also going to set you up with an email account with the company. You're not to use it for anything other than discussing the case. We don't want it compromised. Is that okay?"

"Dan, we use a peer-to-peer encryption that's in-house. I'm sure you understand."

He did understand. He had tried to get Levitt to upgrade for years, but the stupid bastard—that's right—stupid bastard—it was Dan's worst insult—wouldn't listen. "Yes, of course."

"Mr. Mitchell, I'm sending your new logon credentials. Are you close to a computer?" Gatherwright asked.

Dan went to his home system and turned it on. "Yes," he said. "And please, call me Dan, Ms. Gatherwright."

"Okay, Dan, as long as you call me April," she said. He could kick himself for not choosing the "Jasmine" voice. He had no idea what the woman looked like, but he pictured long, raven hair and a deep, tan complexion with coal-black eyes. Savannah could change almost everything. Her hair and face were easy, and she could even change the skin tone of her body, even though he wasn't sure how the process worked or how permanent it was. She could change her eye color—but voices were permanent, or at least not an easy change. It wasn't a recording—it was an actual working voice box, and to change it out was a major process.

His logon screen came up and he typed his password, then

opened his email. There was a link from April, and he followed it and began the process of setting up the new email.

"Okay, Dan, all the documents we need are in your new inbox. Sign those and get them back to us, and you can start upgrading Savannah," Palance said. "I'm going to make that phone call. You can expect a new job offer within the hour."

"I don't know how to thank you," Dan said. He felt as if all of his burdens had been lifted, the way religious people talk when they first find God.

"You just stay strong, my friend. If you need us, we're just a phone call away."

They hung up and Dan hung his head and said a prayer of thanks to the universe. He wasn't a religious man in that he subscribed to anything organized, but he did believe in a higher power, as he found that most men of science did. He believed that someone, somewhere had sent Ian Palance to him, his light at the end of a scary, long night, and he found that he was no longer worried, even about the outcome of the trial.

While the peer-to-peer encryption system downloaded and set itself up, he called the office of Shapiro, Shapiro and Smythe and fired his grease ball of a lawyer.

CHAPTER 19

"How do you feel?" Dan asked.

Savannah shrugged. "I feel fine. How do you feel?"

He had finished bumping her cooking skills in the American category to Chef, and didn't know if the onslaught of new information would, for lack of a better word, feel different. "I mean, do you feel any different? Like something has changed?"

She shrugged again. "Not really. Do you feel alright?" She looked and sounded worried, as if she thought he might be losing his mind.

"I'm just wondering if everything feels normal," he said. "Humans can't download information like that, and I was wondering what it's like." He would imagine it as a rush, as if a tremendous power had come over him, like a super villain. "So, how about taking another swing at that lunch?" He was famished.

"Okies," she said, beaming a bright smile at him, her voice happy and lively enough that he felt a pang of guilt for wanting to change it earlier.

His cell phone rang again, and he checked the screen—another California number, but this one wasn't RWR. He guessed it was the call he was waiting on.

"Dan? The is Stan Stone from Evocative Entertainment, how are you doing?"

"Stan Stone?" Dan thought. Really? Was it possible that someone would do that to their child, or was the name made up? He had gone to college with a guy named Jack Meoff, so he assumed anything was possible. Evocative Entertainment were primarily pornographers, so there was a good chance the name was made up.

Stone asked all the standard questions. Was Dan familiar with cloud-resident storage? Distributed big-data pipelines? Holographic 3D scanning? When Dan said he was, he wasn't really lying. He was familiar with everything Stone asked about, even if he may not have used it.

"We're partnering with RWR to model a few of their bots after some of our actresses. I see your girl is modeled after Georgia Peach."

"She was?" he asked. He had made her from scratch, he'd thought, choosing her dimensions from her hip size and her height to her B cup breasts. He had no idea who Georgia Peach was.

"Well, Georgia has a nicer rack, but to each his own, am I right?" Stone said with a laugh. Dan knew this was someone he wouldn't normally care for, the cliché of a pornographer, but he needed the job, so he smiled, even though they were on the phone. "So, we're looking for ways to streamline the process of scanning the actresses bodies into the mold makers. Is that something you think you could help us with?"

That sounded more like a programming job than an IT one, and Dan did his best to tell Stone that, but he didn't seem to be listening. "You'll be working under Chas Martin," Stone said. "You do what you can. Don't worry if it takes you a while to catch on. Chas will walk you through it." He offered Dan a salary double what he'd been making before. Not almost double or close to double—exactly double. Dan knew that if something was too good to be true, it probably wasn't true at all. Palance was worried about a lawsuit. There was a glitch in Savannah's program that had caused this, or at least an oversight. This job wasn't being offered out of guilt—it was a bribe—a payoff to keep the lawsuit away. He didn't know how much he could win, but he believed it would be huge. The problem was, he would lose his house while it was in court. Better to grab the bird in his hand and run with it than to hope for two in the bush. In less than an hour, Dan went from feeling as if this was one of the worst days of his life to one of the best.

Stone passed the call to Martin, and when Martin began talking the technical stuff, it was over Dan's head, much less out of his skill set. Martin didn't seem to mind it either, and told Dan to settle into his new job. "Take it easy for a week or two. I know you must be stressed, with everything you're going through."

Dan no longer cared if Levitt saved his job. He would tell the stupid bastard to take his church clients and stick them straight up his butt. Life couldn't get much better.

Savannah came in carrying a tray and started to set it on his computer desk, but he waved her away. He didn't eat at his desk for the same reason it was company policy to not allow beverages at work stations. One never knew what might go wrong. He finished the call with Martin insisting he take a month to look over the material, then get back to him. "Call it training. Call it a vacation. Just kick back and relax. There's no rush." Martin said.

Dan agreed, but it felt wrong. He'd never heard of a job that allowed someone to take their first month off with pay. It must be a California thing. No wonder the rest of the country thought they were all so weird.

He turned toward the coffee table as he hung up the phone and saw the second lunch. A turkey sandwich with the toast burned black and another can of soup that had water added when it wasn't supposed to. Had the download gone wrong? It had indicated everything was fine, but it was obviously not. "What's this?" he asked, thinking it might be a prank—that she had made a better lunch, but brought him the first one again because she had a strange sense of humor.

"Lunch," she said, as if she was proud. "A turkey sandwich and a can of clam chowder-soup, just like you asked for." She ran the words chowder and soup together, as if they were one word.

"Is it the same lunch as before?" he asked. He poked the sandwich. How was it possible for it to be both burnt and soggy?

"No, it's a fresh lunch," she said. "Is there something wrong?"

"Well, it looks the same," he said. He poked the sandwich again. The bread didn't spring back at all. Was that a sprig of broccoli sticking out from under the tomato? "Maybe worse. You're supposed to be a chef now. It means you know how to cook. Why is it wet?"

She looked upset, as if he had hurt her feelings. "I washed the vegetables. Tomatoes are hard to wash once you slice them. The upgrade means I can learn how to be a chef, not that I am one," she said. "You're not going to eat it?" Tears welled in her eyes.

"Don't cry," he said. She turned away from him. "Hey, look, it's fine." He picked up the sandwich and took a bite and gagged, but forced himself to chew. Apparently, she didn't know the difference in condiments either, so had used a little of each one he had —mayonnaise, mustard, ketchup, a touch of Tabasco, and he was pretty sure there was horseradish and ranch dressing in there somewhere. The broccoli was tough and rubbery. He'd meant to throw it out days ago. That wasn't the worst part, though. He tasted dish soap. "Look," he said as he forced himself to swallow. It was like eating something off of a game show challenge.

She turned back to him, her brow furrowed. "Eat more," she said, pouty, as if she didn't believe him.

"I don't want to eat more," he said. "I'm full now."

She collapsed on the couch and wailed. "You hate me. I knew it, you perfectly hate me."

He wondered which setting controlled drama, because it wasn't one of the individual sliders. "I don't hate you," he said. He gave the sandwich a small squeeze and a blob of watery condiments plopped onto the plate and sure enough there was a bubble of soapy foam with them. "I hate your cooking, though."

She wailed louder, like a child who had dropped her ice cream. She said something, but he couldn't make it out. He sat next to her and took her hand. She turned away from him.

"I don't hate you," he said again. "Maybe—just maybe—you could watch a few cooking shows. Just to get the hang of some of the basics, like wash tomatoes before you slice them, and don't use soap when you wash food." He squeezed her hand, but she still didn't look at him. "Or, I'll fix lunch and you can watch me. I'll teach you. Then you'll know how."

She sniffed and wiped her hand over her eyes. "You'd do that?"

"Of course I would," he said. He dropped her hand and put his arm around her.

"It's not my fault, you know." She folded her hands in her lap and stared at the floor.

"I know," he said. "It's mine. I just assumed the download was a skill set."

She shook her head. "It lifts the limitations on what I can learn is all. Like removing the governor from an engine." She sniffed again.

"Now, see? I didn't know that. It's a learning curve for me, too."

She swiped her cheek, turned toward him, but still didn't look up. "You don't hate me?"

"Of course I don't hate you. I could never hate you."

"And you'll show me how? You'll teach me?" Now she did look at him, her eyes puffy and a touch bloodshot. He realized that the only thing he really wanted to do was kiss her, so he did. It was another half an hour before they made it to the kitchen.

CHAPTER 20

A month passed.

It was a month of April showers that moved to May flowers, at least on the calendar, but thanks to being on house arrest, the only part Dan and Savannah got to see was the rain. He began to understand the concept of cabin fever.

"What's a goat?" she asked. Dan was at the computer looking over the material for his new job while she watched a cooking show on television. He was trying his best to figure out what this position might entail that was in his skill set, and not paying attention to anything else.

"What?"

"A goat," she said. "What is it?"

"It's a farm animal," he said. "Used mostly for milk and cheese, but it can be used for meat as well." He stopped concentrating on the screen, wondering why she was asking. "Are they cooking goat?" A few days ago, someone on one of the shows had suggested trying different fruits in Jell-o, and he had been served lemon with sliced tomatoes wiggling inside. While visually appealing color-wise, it wasn't something he was anxious to taste. Nor was he keen on the idea of her cooking a goat. When he had suggested that she run future ingredients past him first, she accused him of stifling her creativity, so he let it drop, but goat was crossing the line.

"No, they're using goat cheese," she said. "But that man on TV said you would want to have sex with one, so I wanted to know what they were."

"Okay," he said. He had gone back to reading as soon as she

95

said "goat cheese," figuring whatever culinary damage she might cause would be minimal, but then the filter in his brain kicked around what she had said after that, and it brought him out of his reading again. "Wait—what?"

"I wasn't sure what a goat was." She looked as if she was in deep thought for a second, then said, "any of numerous agile, hollow-horned ruminants of the genus *Capra,* of the family Bovidae, closely related to the sheep, found native in rocky and mountainous regions of the Old World, and widely distributed in domesticated varieties." Her face didn't change. "There's a picture of one. Want to see it?" The television screen changed to the image of a goat before he could answer.

"No," he said. "I know what a goat looks like. What did you say about me wanting to have sex with one?" What the hell kind of cooking show was this?

"That man the other day—the one you called 'The Preacher.' He said that if you wanted to have sex with a robot, it was only a matter of time until you would want to have sex with a goat. He seemed adamant. Why would you want to have sex with a goat? I mean, they're pretty, but not something I would consider sexually desirable." The image changed to a close up of a goat's face.

"I don't want to have sex with a goat," he said. He wondered where the news stations found these idiots.

"Would you let me know when you do? I would like to be supportive." She sounded so sincere, it struck him as funny rather than absurd. He started to laugh, but then got the image of her holding a goat by the horns while he—no—stop it. He laughed harder. His eyes watered. He couldn't stop. The image wouldn't go away, and he could hear the goat's bleating, soft and curious at first, then wild and crazy as he—no—he couldn't breathe. His stomach ached from laughing, but still, he couldn't stop. Tears streamed down his face and Savannah looked even more confused, and that triggered deeper gails, wild, uncontrolled, until he thought his heart would burst because he couldn't catch a breath. He understood the term to, "die laughing," because he believed he just might do exactly that, just keel over dead, his heart ruptured as all of the bottled stress from the past few weeks came ripping out of him in the bray of a donkey.

"Dan? Are you okay?"

His diaphragm knotted, a stitch in his side, and he concentrated on the pain instead of the mental image of a ménage-a-goat. That seemed to help, but tiny snippets of Savannah holding a goat kept popping into his mind, and he tried to shoo them away. Finally, he was able to breathe again, but he still had a few reflexive chuckles.

She looked concerned. "Are you okay?" she asked again. "Your blood pressure was really high for a minute."

"I'm fine," he said, then chuckled again. The storm had passed, and his heart was settling. He had averted death, not that he had been worried to begin with. Then he realized that he did feel fine. In fact, he felt better than fine—he felt great, as if none of this mattered anymore. He might have lost his job of ten years, but he'd found a better one the same day. He might be facing as many as seven felonies, but he had a free legal team who wanted to fight the constitutionality of the law itself. It could be ten years before the case was settled. His neighbors might hate him, but they hadn't liked him much to begin with, so he wasn't losing anything there either. Plus, he had Savannah—beautiful, loving, Savannah, who he loved spending time with. He realized that he wanted to do just that—spend time with her. Martin didn't seem to care if he began work next week or next month, so why not take advantage of that? It could be like a mini-vacation. "You want to get out of here?" The need to go somewhere—anywhere—was uncontrollable.

The only thing that was improving was her cooking. She no longer burned the toast when she made a sandwich, and she had stopped adding water to every can of soup. Actually, a lot of her cooking was getting better, despite the lemon-tomato Jell-O. Last night she had made slow-roasted pulled-pork with sautéed mushrooms, and the mushrooms had a dark sweetness to them he couldn't place, but they were amazing. With that were mashed potatoes and gravy, and fresh green beans. It would have been a perfect meal if not for the stewed tomato meringue pie she served for dessert. That was—well—weird.

But being pent up was driving him insane. He was only supposed to go out for work or short errands like grocery shopping, but he could always say he was job hunting. How would anyone know the difference?

"Where would we go?" she asked.

"Anyplace. How about a nice drive in the country?" It didn't really matter where they went, as long as they went someplace. It was a sudden and demanding need, but he no longer wanted to be inside the house. As a matter of fact, he wanted to be outside in the sun so much, he got another idea. "Find the nearest car rental agency that has a convertible," he said. Since this was her first drive, they might as well make it special.

"I found seven car rental agencies—three are fairly close to you," she said, her voice flat and robotic, mocking his phone. She grinned. "Would you like for me to call one, Dan?"

"You think you're funny, don't you?"

She bit her lower lip, mischievous, one eyebrow raised. "Yes, I do. But you think I'm funny, too, so it's okay." She paused for a second. "Do you want insurance?"

"No," he said. "I have full coverage."

"Do you want to return on full, or have them fill it for you? The cost is $4.79 per gallon."

"You're as bad as they are," he said. "Return on full."

"And when do you plan on returning it?"

"Tomorrow," he said.

"What time tomorrow?"

"I don't know," he said. "Afternoon."

"I need a time," she said.

"I take it back—you're worse than they are. Put 2:00."

"How is this my fault? They want to know. I can't leave it blank."

He sat on the couch beside her. "It would have been simpler to log onto the computer and do it myself," he said.

"But then you wouldn't have had the beauteous Savannah as

your customer service representative. How would you like to pay for this alleged car?"

"My credit card," he said. "And you're using 'alleged' wrong." With the new job, he would have the balance paid down soon, so he was comfortable adding a little more to it. "I'm just saying you could have made some of these decisions yourself."

"Would you like to look in the garage and see what happened the last time you let me make unfamiliar decisions? Okay, you're all set, Mr. Mitchell. You may pick up your car anytime between now and 5:00, and thank you for doing business with us. We realize you have a choice when you rent a car, and we're happy you chose us. Would you like to complete an online survey about your ordering experience? There's a chance you could win $1000."

"How much of that last part did you make up?" he asked.

She giggled. "All of it. Pretty good, huh?" Her eyebrows lifted, accenting the punch line. She leaned into him and was still grinning when they kissed.

"Perfect," he said. "You sound just like a cheesy car rental agency."

"Thank you," she said. "I was shooting for authenticity."

CHAPTER 21

Thirty minutes later they entered the rental agency, and two clerks, both of whom were waiting on customers, exchanged glances when they saw Dan and Savannah. The television in the corner was on CNN, and there was no doubt the clerks recognized them. When one finished with the young, professionally dressed black couple he was waiting on, he smiled at Dan but it didn't touch his eyes. "Someone will be right with you."

"Take your time," Dan said. Savannah wandered around the office, looking behind things, including behind the counter by looking over it. Dan assumed that since this was her first experience in a retail-type environment, she was naturally curious.

The clerk grabbed a clipboard and went for the door, the couple following him. When the black man saw Dan, he did a double take. He looked as if he was searching his memory for recollection of where they met, but then his eyes shifted to Savannah and his expression changed to recognition. His face became one of curiosity, as if he was looking for flaws in Savannah that differed from a real woman. Dan felt protective of her. He stepped closer and took her hand. The woman looked at them and rolled her eyes in derision, then she followed the clerk outside, but the man lingered—not for long—just enough to fall behind his wife. When she reached the door, she turned back. "Darrel? Are you coming?" She sounded bothered.

"Yeah," the man said, but his eyes shifted up and down as he looked at Savannah once again before he moved away. When he reached the door, Dan heard the woman begin to scold him, and the man said, "I was just loo—" before the door cut off the rest.

A young girl moved from a desk to the counter and smiled at Dan. "How may I help— hey— you're Savannah," as if she had met a movie star.

Savannah stopped looking behind the placard that explained the advantages of buying separate insurance, turned to the girl and smiled. "Yes, I am, but I don't believe we have met. I would remember. I'm very good at remembering faces."

The girl laughed as if Savannah had told a joke. "I'll bet you are." She turned to the other clerk. "Do you know who this is?"

"Yes," he said, short and dismissive, clear he wasn't as happy to meet them as the girl was.

"Hey, do you mind if we take a picture together? My friends won't believe I met you," the girl said. She picked up her phone and bounced around the counter. "Gosh, you look so real."

"So do you," Savannah said, and the girl laughed again.

She leaned in, putting her face next to Savannah's and held her camera at arm's length. "Say, 'Cheese,'" she said.

"Cheese?" Savannah said, a question rather than an exclamation. When the flash went off, she looked more confused than happy.

"It's just an expression," Dan said. "Just smile when you're supposed to say it."

"Okies," Savannah said. "That explains it." The second picture came out better. When the girl asked her coworker to take one of all three of them, he obliged, but didn't seem happy.

"Explains what?" Dan asked then smiled for the camera.

"You said I sounded like a cheesy car rental agency—I couldn't find the cheese."

They posed with Savannah in the middle, her arms around each of their waists, and Dan asked the girl for copies of those pictures as well as the first ones. Savannah had a photogenic beauty that transcended anything he would have expected, and the pictures looked like two people who had stumbled upon a movie star gracious enough to pose with them. Her smile was genuine, bright, beaming and inviting. He stared at them while the girl finished their paperwork.

"I upgraded you," she said, keeping her voice low, casting a sideways glance at the other clerk. "This is a new GT convertible —only a hundred miles on it. It's a lot more fun to drive."

"Well, thank you," Dan said.

"If you'll follow me, we'll go check out the car," she said. They went outside, passing the third clerk on their way, the one who had assisted the black couple. He held the door for them, and Dan noticed his eyes as they crawled over Savannah, but he wasn't sure how to categorize the man's stare—was it lust? Curiosity? Disgust? Dan had trouble reading most people, and this young man was clearly another one he couldn't get a handle on.

They walked around the red sports car and the girl pointed out the features and showed him how to put the top down. When she finished, she handed Dan the key and contract. "I'm sorry you had problems with the reservation," she said. "Please accept this $50 fuel card for the inconvenience." She winked at Dan with a sly smile.

"We didn't have any—" Savannah said, but Dan cut her off.

"Thank you, Crystal. We'll be sure to mention you in our review." He decided he liked VIP treatment, even if it was more for Savannah than for him. The card made the rental almost free.

CHAPTER 22

"I'm going to need water," she said. She had one hand on top of her head because when he got the car faster than 25, the wind threatened to blow her wig off. The same magnets that held her face in place were used for the hair, but they didn't hold well in the wind. The next time he spoke with Ian, he would recommend Velcro.

They were on the road that would become a highway soon, the last of the city encroaching on the surrounding farms that was spreading like a slow moving tsunami, swallowed by car dealerships—both new and used—convenience stores, and fast food restaurants. Behind them, mobile homes and doublewides on plots of land divided into 1/8th acre lots sat in straight lines like dominos, separated by chain link fences. It was the lower end of suburbia, where "Welcome Home" and "Support our Troops!" messages were spelled out in red plastic cups shoved through the holes in the fences in a sort of graffiti.

In half a mile, the line would end, turning from suburban to rural, the chain link changing to heavy livestock fence, with grazing cattle nonchalantly chewing their cud as life zipped by at 65 mph. They were beef cattle, their destiny to someday soon be speeding along in the back of a truck at 65 themselves. Dan had always felt there was a metaphor for life hidden in those grazing steers—to be out in the field under a star filled sky, believing that all was right with the world, then the next day you're jammed into the back of a truck and taken to your doom, but he hadn't been able to find it. He was determined to keep trying, though.

He pulled into the next convenience store, parking in front of a hand-lettered "!!!Cheepest Beer in Tone!!!" sign, because the needle had yet to move from full. "At least they spelled 'beer' right," he muttered and Savannah giggled. They went in together, but Savannah paused when they went through the door. It occurred to him that this was her first shopping experience that didn't involve an Internet connection. The car rental place didn't really count because they hadn't bought anything, and there was no merchandise, not even the cheese she had looked for. "All of this is for sale?" she asked. Her eyes scanned the store.

The place had a small deli counter in the back that promised to sell the world's worst cold cuts, and fried chicken with a texture one step ahead of jerky. The sign over the heat lamp read, "Fresh Fried Chicken!" in fat red lettering, but he believed they were playing it fast and loose with "Fresh." The logo was a happy rooster in an apron and chef's hat holding a spatula.

Savannah paused in front of the counter, passively holding his hand, so he paused too. A girl in her late teens with the protruding belly of a woman ready to go into labor any minute now climbed off her stool with exaggerated effort and waddled to the counter. "Help ya?" Her constant gum chewing and dull expression reminded Dan of the cattle just up the road. It was the look of someone resigned to their fate—to serve stale chicken for minimum wage until the baby arrived, then return a week later —possibly to the same chicken she had fried before she left—and repeat the cycle—fry chicken—sell chicken—have a baby—over and over for the rest of her life.

"What is that smell?" Savannah asked. "It's horrid."

Dan closed his eyes and took a deep breath, not believing she'd said that, but then, why wouldn't she? She had no filter. He knew the smell too well—it was old grease in the fryer, weeks beyond when it should have been changed.

"What smell?" the pregnant girl asked. She rubbed her hand across her stained apron, over the baby bulge. Dan felt guilty that she had gotten up. It was an obvious struggle for her, and he normally would order something that he didn't really want in an effort to assuage his guilt, but he couldn't find anything behind the counter that wasn't stomach churning. When coleslaw turned brown, it was time to cut your losses and toss it out.

"No, thank you," he said, tugging on Savannah's hand, urging her towards the drink coolers. She followed, but hesitated, and Dan was worried she would tell the girl exactly the smell that permeated the place, seeping into everything. Sometimes the only thing a place needed was a good cleaning, top to bottom with a scrub brush and a bottle of bleach. Dan believed this place needed a can of kerosene and a match. He pulled her past the salty snacks even though she kept trying to stop and browse. The coolers went along one wall then down the back, the longest row filled with cheap beer, the back one, soda. There were five bottles of water, total, a single brand manufactured by one of the soda companies, known to be nothing more than filtered city tap water. He was actually pleased by that. If there had been a better water selection, he may have felt guilty enough to buy some, then told himself he could taste the grease on the bottle, even if it was only in his mind. "Come on," he said, tugging her hand again.

"But we're not finished shopping," she said. She reached for the cooler handle.

"Yes we are," he said, pulling her harder. A man in his twenties, whip-snake thin with tattoos covering both arms, thick enough to look like the sleeves to a tacky shirt and earrings so large they stretched his earlobes into flapping holes large enough to pass a quarter through, stepped to the beer cooler behind them and fished out a case of Natty-Lite, set it on the floor then took a second. He put one case under his left arm and grabbed the second case with the same hand, then snatched a few bags of chips with his right and made his way to the front counter. To Dan, that seemed like a lot of beer for a random Thursday.

"I need water," she said.

"We'll get some someplace else," he said, keeping his voice low.

"What's wrong with this water?" she asked. A man wearing a backwards, frayed MAGA hat stained with axle grease stepped past them. He made no secret of checking Savannah out as he passed her, his eyes creeping her with the intense stare of a predator. From two feet away, Dan could smell the man's unwashed pits. The man got a case of beer as well, then headed to the counter, grabbing a chicken breast, eating it on the way.

"Let's just go," Dan said. He led the way, pulling her as he went. She resisted following in a manner Dan's mother would have described as "dragging her feet," but she didn't say anything else. Outside, the man with the sleeves sat perched on one of the cases of beer, the other one upturned and open. He took a long drink from his beer then lit a cigarette and stretched his legs out in front of him as if this was his living room and the world his television. He belched from the beer, loud and obnoxious, as Dan closed Savannah's door.

She waited until they were back on the highway before she asked, "What was wrong with the water?"

"That whole place was disgusting," he said. He could still smell the grease on his clothes, as if they had walked through an actual cloud of it and it now clung like a mist.

"But the water would have been fine," she said. "It was bottled."

"That doesn't matter," he said. "If you patronize places like that, you encourage bad behavior. Better to spend our money on someplace clean and nice and hope nasty places go out of business." He hit his blinker to turn into the next station which looked newer and cleaner.

"I think their beer sales will keep them open," she said. "That man stunk."

"He needed a shower," Dan said, even though a simple shower wouldn't put a dent in what that man needed. It would take a scouring to get rid of that stench.

"Why doesn't he take one?" she asked.

Dan, himself a stickler for personal hygiene, gave the only answer he knew to be a fact. "I have no idea." He parked in front of another beer sign, this one professionally lettered. "Coldest Beer In Town!" It seemed there was a competition between the two stores, and so far, this one seemed to be winning in both cleanliness and spelling.

The inside was bigger and cleaner, the smell of e coli nowhere to be found. There was no deli case—no stale fried chicken, but there were a few hotdogs on a rotisserie, and they didn't look a week old, not that he wanted one. It was just nice to know that if he did, he wouldn't feel the need to get his stomach pumped afterward.

The water took up a full cooler door here, a wide selection of spring water and filtered, of different brands and sizes. "You're right," Savannah said. "This place is nicer." She went to the beer cooler and looked through the glass. "The prices are 7% higher on average, though."

"It's worth it," Dan said.

They went past a selection of t-shirts and baseball hats he would have expected to find in a more touristy town than Williamsburg, Ohio. It gave him an idea. He picked up a Cincinnati Reds baseball hat and put it on her. It was adjusted too big and it slumped over her eyebrows, resting on her nose. She tilted her head back and peered out from under the brim. "What's this?"

"It's a hat," he said. A woman with a small child stood close enough to hear their conversation, and she gave them a strange look. He realized it must sound odd, him having to explain a hat to someone of Savannah's apparent age, and he started to explain it to the woman, but realized he didn't know what he would say. "She's a robot," didn't seem like a good idea, nor did, "She's foreign," because she didn't have an accent and what country could she be from that didn't have hats? The woman continued to stare at them, looking confused, until Dan finally said, "She's not from around here."

The woman smiled and nodded as if that explained everything, then the look became even more confused than it was before, but at least she walked away.

"You have to adjust it," Dan said, removing the hat, tightening the strap and putting it back on her. It sat too high this time, perched atop her head like a bird. He took it off, let the strap out a little and tried again. It fit better this time. The large, paper tag hung from the bill and she batted at it like a kitten playing with a toy. "How does that feel?"

"How is it supposed to feel?"

"Snug, but not tight," he said.

"Then it feels fine. This part is annoying, though." She batted the tag again and it spun and swung like a pendulum.

"You cut that part off," he said. "You like it?"

"How do I look?"

"Really cute," he said.

"Then I like it," she said. They went to the counter with four one-liter bottles of water. He doubted they would need that much, but better to have too much than not enough. This was her first time being outside all day, and he didn't know how much she might need.

"The water and the hat," Dan said.

"It's a hat," Savannah said, pointing to it. Apparently, it needed explaining to everyone.

"He knows it's a hat," Dan said, smiling. The clerk gave Savannah another curious look. "She's not from around here."

The clerk chuckled. "Where's she from that they don't have hats?" he asked. He held his hand out. "I need to scan it."

When Savannah made no move to take it off, Dan turned to her. "Give him the hat."

"No," she said. "It's my hat. I like it. I look cute—really cute." She batted at the tag again.

"He'll give it right back. He needs to scan it." He reached for it, but she ducked away from his hand like a boxer avoiding a roundhouse. "Maybe he'll cut the tag off for you."

"I'm starting to like the tag," she said. "It's fun—a built in toy." She swatted it again and watched it swing.

"He still needs to scan it," Dan said, snatching it from her head. She looked annoyed.

The clerk seemed worried, as if he thought Savannah might

be crazy and crazy might be catching. "She's not from around here," Dan said again.

"Yeah—I get that," the clerk said. He scanned the hat and handed it back to her, and she put it on again, then resumed playing with the tag with both hands now in another move that reminded Dan of a boxer, but this time she looked like she was working a speed bag.

Dan paid and headed toward the door. He saw the same woman, her purchases in one hand waiting to pay, but her other hand was on her daughter's chest, as if she were preventing her from getting too close to the insane lady in the new hat.

The cap worked wonders at holding Savannah's hair in place, and he was able to open the Mustang up to the posted 55 speed limit. Traffic thinned as they passed more towns and side roads, late enough in the day that morning rush hour was over, and afternoon's hadn't begun. When the posted limit raised to 65, he increased the cruise control and laid his hand between the seats, on the consol. She took it without his having to ask. He turned left on one of the side roads and they went through a small town he had driven through a few times. He paid strict attention to the speed limits even though he had never seen a police officer here. He wasn't sure the small burg could afford one. Once through the village, the road was two-lane and wound through the countryside, over, through and around farms and hillsides. They had passed enough cattle that the novelty had worn off for her, but she still watched for different sights, asking "What's that?" for anything unfamiliar, and most things were unfamiliar to her, so Dan provided the answers as best he could.

"What's that?" she asked again, pointing out of his side of the car, her hand blocking his view of the road. So far, he had explained barns, squirrels, tractors with plows and why they plowed, one rabbit, a creek, a diner, a restaurant, the difference between a diner, restaurant, and a pizza joint, a grocery store, and an antique shop. In a time before she had come into his life, if someone had told him he would someday spend an entire drive explaining everything they saw to someone, he would have sworn to never take that drive.

He ducked to see under her hand. "Don't block my vision, please. I need to watch where we're going."

She laughed. "Oh yeah. I guess you do."

"It's a cemetery," he said. Before Savannah, he doubted if he had ever spoken so many words in one day in his entire life. But with her, everything felt different. He wasn't annoyed by her questions. In fact, he liked them. He found that he enjoyed playing the role of teacher, and whomever at RWR had decided that instructing would make a good bonding experience was a genius. He understood her lack of knowledge made her seem more vulnerable, and that brought out his own sense of protectiveness, but understanding didn't make it feel any less real.

"What's a cemetery?" She pronounced it slowly, each syllable an individual statement.

"When people die, we bury them and mark their graves so friends and families can come visit them." It was the simplest explanation he could think of.

"What does 'die' mean?"

That one seemed tougher. How do you explain death to a robot? How do you explain life? He opened his mouth to answer, but realized he had no words—he didn't even have a good place to start. While it felt cowardly, he decided he would cheat this one. "What does the Internet say?" At least it might give him a way to begin.

"It says, 'Pushing up daisies, buying the farm, breathe one's last, kick the bucket, croak, bite the big one,'" she said. "Cash in one's—"

"Stop," he said. "Those are just euphemisms. What else does it say?"

"Chips," she said, finishing her statement. "It says, 'To stop living, to emphasize that one wants something very much, to emphasize shock, and to have an orgasm. That's a place to have an orgasm?"

"Well, not unless you're Elvira," he said with a chuckle.

"I don't understand."

"Of course you don't," he said. "Well, it's kind of difficult to explain. It's the opposite of being alive. Everything that is alive will one day die."

Her face went from curious to confused. He didn't blame her —he felt confused as well.

"Okay," he said. "When people die, they cease to be animated. They can't walk or talk or interact with anything. Same with the things we saw like cows and squirrels. We know they are alive because they are animated. Remember the inchworm?"

"So everything that is alive is animated?" she asked.

"Yes," he said, glad he had stumbled onto an answer—then he saw the trees around them and had to correct himself. "No—only animals are animated. Plants are not. The trees are alive, but they are not animated." He glanced into the rearview and saw the last of the cemetery disappear behind a curve.

She thought about that for a second. "So you are alive because you are animated. But someday you will die and cease to be animated, and you will be placed in the ground with a stone marker?"

That sounded about as clear as he could make it. "Yes," he said. "Someday my body will malfunction and I will cease to be alive. My body will decompose—spoil—the way food spoils, so it will have to be buried." He started to add something about cremation, but he decided to take this one step at a time.

She squeezed his hand until it hurt. "I don't want you to die," she said. "I like you animated."

He smiled as he signaled to make a left turn, then guided them onto yet another side road, this one even more narrow than the first. He slowed to 35, even though the posted limit was 45. "Hopefully it won't happen for a long time."

"How long?" she asked.

"Nobody knows for sure," he said. "But with any luck, another 50 or 60 years."

"That doesn't seem like a long time," she said.

CHAPTER 23

There was a ranger at the gate to Serpent Mound State Park. Most times he came here, the five-dollar per-car entry fee was paid on the honor system. But today, there were three cars ahead of them, and he wondered why the place was so busy for again what he considered a random Thursday. He fished his wallet out and rolled forward as the ranger greeted the car in front of them and wished them a good visit as he handed them a parking receipt. When the ranger smiled at them, it was the same one he seemed to give to everyone entering the park. "How you doing today, folks? Welcome to Serpent Mound. First time here?"

Dan handed the man a five. "It is for her, but not for me."

"Be sure to see the museum," the ranger said. "We're displaying some new artifacts."

Dan said they would. Two more cars had pulled in behind them, and Dan assumed the park was busy because of the new artifacts. Some state parks had pools and beaches, camping and picnic areas, but Serpent Mound didn't. It was the world's largest effigy mound, hundreds of years old, in the shape of a long snake that looked to be swallowing an egg. It was said to be aligned with the same constellations as Stonehenge, with the sunrises and sunsets of solstices and equinoxes laid against the winding serpent's spine—an ancient calendar. There were a few burial mounds around it that weren't as old, and an indigenous village the state had replicated that was too small to be an actual village. Other than a few short hiking paths that went by the creek, there wasn't much to see at Serpent Mound other than the museum and the mound itself.

They drove past two small burial mounds that few ever paid attention to. They were big enough to hold one body—single graves set apart from the rest. Dan had often wondered why these two weren't buried in the larger mound at the top of the hill that would hold multiple corpses according to the museum display, a cutaway diorama that showed bodies laid out in fetal positions that began as a single grave, then a body laid beside it, then one on top, then more beside and more on top until finally you have a pile of graves of a couple dozen or so.

But these two stood alone, not part of the larger mound. They were on a hillside, not an easy place to add a second corpse, and there was no doubt that wasn't on purpose. Was it a sign of respect that they should be buried alone, away from their family and friends? Were they perhaps great chiefs who deserved their own place of respite? That didn't make as much sense as the other reason—that these two had committed some great sin against the tribe and they were damned to face eternity alone. No one knew—nor would they ever know. These were Stone Age people without writing, and the legends and stories of these two loners died long ago.

The parking lot was nearly full. Five school busses took up the better part of one side, and soccer-mom minivans filled the other. A few ladies were setting out lunches on long tables and kids walked the paved path that circled the effigy. Another lady exited the van that entered before them, and she shouted, "Sorry I'm so late. The order wasn't ready at Parker's." She removed a large vegetable platter from the back of her van and headed for the tables. A class field trip—that made much more sense as to why the place was so crowded.

"What are those?" Savannah asked. She pointed in the general direction of the mound.

"Where?" he asked.

"Over there," she said. "They look like people, but they're short."

"Children?" he asked, still not sure what she was referring to.

"Why are they so short? Why are there so many of them?

113

Why are they bunched together like that? Why are they making that noise? What do they want?"

"You don't know what children are?" Was that possible? "They are people. We start off short, but we grow. They're on a field trip, and I would imagine most of them are happy to be out of school for the day."

Her laugh was a small snort. "I know what children are, silly." She finished off the last of her first bottle of water then replaced the lid.

"Then why did you ask?"

Her eyes danced with mischief and her nose crinkled. "For fun." She leaned over and kissed him, light and playful. "Come on. Let's go see Snake Hill." She hopped out of the car with so much enthusiasm she practically bounced.

"Serpent Mound," he said. He left the top down because it was a rental and it was a nice day. There was nothing to steal except for two bottles of water or the car itself, and this didn't seem like a place for much thievery.

She went to the trash receptacle in front of the car, threw the empty bottle away then waited for him. She reached for his hand when he approached. "What's the difference?"

"You'll see."

CHAPTER 24

They stood atop the iron observation tower and from here could see the entire mound and the valley below. Dan knew the valley had been created by a meteor impact some 300 million years ago, and the unusual terrain it left was believed to be what inspired the mound builders to select the location.

"This is so boring," one of the school children said, a boy Dan guessed to be about eleven or twelve. "There's nothing to do here." He sat on the platform, his legs straddling a support for the safety rail, his hands grasping the metal guard like a prisoner. Dan was tempted to tell the young man to get used to the feeling of those metal bars. He seemed the type who'd spend much of his life behind them.

According to the busses, there were two groups here, from two different school districts. One group was younger and they held hands, forming a long train when they circumvented the mound. The older group was allowed to wander unsupervised with a few teachers and parents strategically placed at various points throughout the park, mostly to keep the children from climbing on the mound, it seemed.

"You don't find this fascinating?" Savannah asked.

The boy looked back over his shoulder, as if he found the idea preposterous. "No," he said.

"I do," she said, leaning over the rail and looking out over the mound. "The people who built this were great hunters and warriors. But they took the time to build this because they believed it was important. It took a lot of work to build something only they could understand." Dan had said basically the same thing twenty minutes ago when they had walked around the mound. But while she was paraphrasing what he'd said, she wasn't parroting it—she was saying it a way that Dan found more eloquent than his own.

The kid looked as if he was considering her words for a second, then shrugged and turned back to the mound. "Still boring," he said. He got up and two other boys stood with him and they jogged down the steps in a line that resembled the younger children, without the hand holding.

"I don't think I impressed him," Savannah said, still leaning over the rail.

"I think you would have to be a game console to impress that kid," Dan said. He slipped an arm around her waist and rested it on her hip. "Want to go see the museum?"

"Sure," she said. "Then let's walk the trails, okay?"

He agreed, and together, they headed for the dark brown wooden building that shared the same dull brown as every other state park he had ever seen.

CHAPTER 25

He had promised her a new hat and t-shirt when they exited the museum that ended in the gift shop, but they hadn't purchased them yet because he didn't want to have to carry them when they went on the hiking trails, nor did he want to make the short trek back to the car.

There were a few new artifacts on display, but nothing spectacular. A few more arrow points—a hand axe—a couple of drill points, all linked to the Fort Ancient culture believed to be responsible for building the mound, had been added to the ones Dan's grandfather had found in his numerous digs around the park. Dan's grandfather was one of the world's leading experts on the Adena and Fort Ancient peoples, and had been a prominent archeologist for Perdue University, before he lost his position in a sexual harassment scandal. Now, most of his found artifacts remained on display, but not all. The museum was small and couldn't show everything in their meager collection.

The paper cutout of the skeleton was still in the glass display case though, where according to photographs, an actual skeleton once rested until indigenous people demanded its return. Dan couldn't blame them. He wouldn't want his grandmother's bones on display either.

He maneuvered his way down the steps in the sheer cliff and reached back to offer her a hand. The stairs were cut into the rock in places, but made of logs in others, backfilled with dirt. They could be tricky to navigate. She hopped past him, down two steps lower than he was then turned and offered her hand to him.

"Smart aleck," he said.

She giggled at him then skipped her way to the bottom without stopping, her ponytail bouncing from under her Reds hat as she went.

Dan descended the steps one at a time, being careful to watch his footing. He wasn't normally an outdoorsy type, but he did enjoy coming here on occasion. He knew it was the history that drew him, along with a subtle connection to his grandfather. If he were the religious type, he would believe that he was a reincarnated mound builder because it was one of the few places where being in nature didn't bother him. That was why he had brought Savannah here to begin with. He'd wanted her to see this place he had walked dozens of times, even though he never understood the full reason why it drew him. His relationship with his grandfather had never been close enough to account for it.

He knew the trails well. They weren't long, but they were steep, and they ran alongside the northernmost fork of Ohio Brush Creek for about an 1/8th of a mile. From down here, the rock that jutted from the cliff under the serpent's head resembled a head as well, as if the mound was deeper than it appeared from the top, and the serpent was crawling out of the side of the stone cliff. The trees grew thick here on both sides of the creek, but there were few on top of the hill. He had little doubt the builders had cleared them to construct the mound, but he didn't understand why the forest hadn't reclaimed the land in the past dozen centuries. He might have said the land was blessed—or cursed—if he believed in that sort of thing.

The creek ran high and swift, due to the recent spring rains, not out of its banks, but certainly higher than normal. Usually, he could see a small sandbar that jutted out in the center and the riffles created by the rocks were now closer to rapids. The water was a murky, muddy brown while it normally ran clear enough to see bottom. In the distance, he heard the laughter and shouting of children above the sound of the rushing water.

"This is pretty," she said as they walked along the worn path.

The trees were in full bud, their leaves just beginning to take form. In another month, the creek would be settled and the canopy of leaves would cast shadows all around where they now walked, so dark it took a while for your eyes to adjust after the bright sky of the mound. But the leaves weren't thick enough to block the light yet, and the sun felt warm on his shoulders.

"It is," he said as they rounded a tree. There was a group of the older children standing on the bank along with one lady, her hands on her hips in anger, a look Dan had seen directed at others when he was their age, but never at himself. She was plump and wore blue jeans that fit a little too tight, as if she hadn't resigned herself to accept the weight gain yet.

"Carl Saunders, you get out of that creek right now," she barked. "Alex Trevell—Samuel Garcia—you're all in big trouble."

As they approached, Dan saw two of the boys headed for the bank, their heads down— another look he was familiar with— shame and remorse, but he had little doubt it was remorse for being caught. The third boy remained—the same one who had been bored atop the tower. "Aww, Mom," he said. He splashed water at the boys who were leaving. "What's the big deal? We're bored." The water came to his waist.

"Carl, I mean it," his mother said. "Right now. I can't believe you did this."

"It's fine," he said, and he dove under the muddy water to prove his point. Dan waited for a second, but the boy didn't come back up.

"Carl?" the woman said, as if he was in the next room and not paying attention. A few more seconds passed, and Dan scanned the creek's surface for any sign of the boy but saw nothing. This was a mean prank to play on one's mother. More seconds ticked by—five—ten—the boy should have come up for air by now. "Carl?" the woman said again, this time more urgent. "Carl," she yelled, as if her voice might carry under the water. There was still no sign of him.

Dan had never considered himself the heroic type. He knew some people were—firefighters and police officers and soldiers who risked their lives daily—but he wasn't one. He had no training for one thing. Those people had training—weeks and months of it. They knew what to do and how to go about it. Dan had nothing. As far as swimming was concerned, he could barely dog paddle. So when he reflected on his actions that day, he would never fully understand what compelled him to jump into the water—it certainly wasn't in his nature. Perhaps it was the desperation in the woman's voice as she called to her son.

But jump he did, landing feet first and his shoes sank deep into the silt. When he stepped, his right foot came out of his shoe, leaving him with one sock-foot. He began calling the boy's name, too, as he groped blindly under the churning water, the silt and sand slithering into his sock as he sank deeper into the mud, hoping to feel the boy even if he couldn't see him. "Carl? Carl?"

He heard a splash behind him, and he turned, thinking it might be the boy finally surfacing, but it was Savannah, and she moved to beside him, feeling under the water, too. "Carl?" she said.

"I think he's washed down the creek," Dan said. He began moving in that direction, his arms wide. He felt things brush his fingertips, but nothing substantial. These were things like leaves and broken twigs that touched him, fleeting in the rushing flood waters, then vanished before he could catch them. His mind screamed that it could feel the mud all over him, dirty and filthy and he would need multiple showers to ever get clean. Lady Macbeth was right that Hell is murky. But he drove himself on, through the revulsion, knowing this would forever be his nightmare, the wading in the muddy creek, searching for a lost boy whom he would never find, just endless groping through filthy water filled with leaves and debris that would brush him then be gone.

Savannah dove, her arms out in front of her, swimming with the current. Her hat and wig floated in the spot where she had disappeared, bobbing along the surface. Fifty yards ahead, the top of a small tree that had washed out in a recent storm stuck out of the water, its leaves still budding, as the tree tried to hold onto life as long as possible. He couldn't see the trunk at all—he could barely see any of the small branches, but it was from them that Savannah appeared, the trunk of the tree in one hand as she lifted it. Carl's limp and lifeless body dangled from the soaked branches, and Dan could have sworn he heard the boy's clothes rip as Savannah pulled him free with her other hand, even though he knew it wasn't possible over the din of rushing water. Savannah clutched Carl's flaccid body in one fist, gripping the boy's shirt. There was a gash in Carl's forehead, big enough that Dan could see it from here. There was no blood. Savannah went to the bank and climbed it with ease while dragging the boy with her.

"Call 911," Dan said as he scrambled up the bank, losing his footing in the mud as he tried. He slipped back in the water, then tried again. He held onto a sapling smaller than the washed out one and hoisted himself up. Nobody seemed to be listening to him, so he said it again. Carl's mother ignored him completely and ran to her boy, shouting his name as she went.

Savannah's skull was visible as she laid the boy on the path. Processors and memory sticks plugged into a circuit board showed through the plastic windows. "Carl," she said as Dan reached her. Savannah knelt beside the boy and shook him. The boy didn't respond.

"Get away from him," Carl's mother said, panicked. "Get that thing away from my boy."

Savannah ignored her. She tilted Carl's head back and put her fingers to his throat, feeling for a pulse. She bent down and pressed her lips against his and blew into his mouth, two short, quick breaths then felt his sternum and placed her hands on his chest and began CPR.

"Call 911," Dan said again, not speaking to anyone in particular.

"Get that monster away from my son," the woman said. She tried to move closer, as if she intended to knock Savannah out of the way, but Dan stepped in front of her and held her back. He

121

read panic in her eyes. "Let me go, you sumbitch." She tried to struggle free.

Savannah kept talking to Carl as she moved with the precision of an EMT. "Come on, Carl," she coaxed. She bent over his body, pressing her ear to his chest, then sat back and extended her arms. Dan saw her hands, the rubber-flesh stretching as copper probes extended, ripping their way through her palms. She placed her hands on the boy—one over his heart, the other just to the side. "Clear," she said, then the boy's body spasmed, his back arched in a short, rapid series of convulsions. Savannah blew into his mouth again, then leaned over him once more, shook her head and repeated the gesture anyone who had ever watched a hospital television show would recognize—she was shocking his heart, using her palms like a defibrillator. Dan stared at her, stunned, as the boy's body spasmed again.

"Stop that thing," Carl's mother said. "She's killing my boy."

Savannah resumed CPR, pressing into the boy's chest, and Dan heard a short, quick snap that could only be the cracking of a rib. She blew into the boy's mouth again, and again leaned back and shocked him. The boy's body spasmed harder and longer this time, but when it calmed, he vomited water all over her, then coughed. Savannah turned him onto his side while he threw up creek water and coughed, ragged and gasping, and spit up more of his stomach contents.

"Get away from my baby," the woman said. She shoved Dan aside and this time he let her go without a struggle. The boy would still have to go to the hospital to be checked, but the crisis was over. She knelt beside her son. "Carl?" she said. The gash on his forehead was bleeding freely now and would take a few stitches to close.

Dan was utterly stunned at the sight. He knew Savannah had basic medical skills, but he'd always assumed that meant dispensing pills and maybe putting on a bandage. He had no idea she knew CPR, or that she could shock someone back to life with just the palms of her hands. It seemed somehow magical, like a faith-healer performing an actual miracle.

Her cotton dress clung to her as she sat back on her heels. There was a deep rip in her forearm that water dripped from, and her face had pulled loose at the temple. When he reached out to fix it, she smiled up at him, took his hand in hers and kissed his palm.

"Oh, your head—your poor head," the woman said. She turned on Savannah. "You did this—you did this to him."

"She saved his life," Dan said, feeling his anger rise.

"She?" the woman said. "It's not a, 'she,' it's an, 'it' and it hurt my boy." She wiped her hand over his blood soaked face and her fingers came away red.

Dan knew it was residual panic that had her angry, but he didn't let that stop him. "Your boy would be dead if it weren't for Savannah."

"We'll sue," the woman said. "My husband knows an attorney. Best in the county. We'll sue you and your thing." She spit "thing" as if it caused a vile taste in her mouth.

Dan shook his head and turned away. It was only then he realized that most of the kids who had witnessed the entire thing had cell phones, and as to be expected, most of them were recording the whole episode.

CHAPTER 26

"I lost my hat," she said as they turned back up the path.

"And your hair," he said. He draped his arm over her shoulders and she reached up and took his hand. "And I lost a shoe." His foot made a wet slapping noise on the bare trail. He needed to watch where he stepped. Some of the trees were locust, and they grew large thorns that would never miss the chance to impale bare feet.

She looked back over her shoulder toward the creek and the crowd. More had gathered and someone said 911 was on its way. Carl still wasn't moving much, but that was because his mother was keeping him pinned in place. "Want me to go get it?" Savannah asked.

"Go get what?"

"Your shoe—my hair—my new hat."

"We'll get you another hat at the gift shop," he said. She would also need dry clothes and shoes, and so would he. He had seen flip flops along one wall and there were hiking shorts on a rack next to the t-shirts. "I'm proud of you," he said and squeezed her fingers. He didn't know how much strength it took for her to lift that tree, but he would guess four full grown men would have had a problem doing it in that current.

"Thank you," she said. "I'm proud of you, too."

He chuckled. "I didn't do anything. You saved that boy's life."

"You jumped in the muddy water and you kept that mean lady away," she said. "You're brave. Why didn't she want me to help the boy?"

"She was scared is all," he said, feeling a little puffed up at the compliment. "Best not to worry about it."

"Okies," she said. She dropped his hand. "Race ya," she said, then began running up the steps to the top of the cliff without saying, "Go," until she had a two-step lead.

Dan lost.

CHAPTER 27

Once at the top, they passed more people who stopped and stared at them. Some pointed—others stepped out of the way as if they didn't want to get too close. "She just saved some kid's life," Dan said to one of the larger groups, as if he were proving an unspoken point.

Some of the younger children shied away from them as well, pointing to Savannah and crying, but the older ones stared in fascination. To them, Dan said nothing, but he walked stoic and proud all the way to the gift shop.

He picked out matching t-shirts and walking shorts, then got two pair of flip flops, and a hat, and when Savannah said she needed water, he got two bottles out of the cooler and paid for everything. They went to the restrooms and changed and he washed his hands and arms three times each, then stripped down to his skivvies and washed his feet three times, which wasn't easy to do considering all he had to work with was a sink and paper towels. Once he dressed in his new clothes, he threw his old ones away, washed his hands again, then exited.

Through the window, he saw the paramedic's van, the strobe lights flashing, the back doors wide open. A crowd had gathered around it, lookie-lews, most of them recording with their cell phones. He would never understand the fascination of recording mundane events for posterity. The rescue, he understood. That had been exciting. Savannah performing CPR made sense —he doubted anyone had ever seen that before, anywhere. But to record a young boy being loaded into an ambulance? Why bother?

She was still in the ladies' room, and he knew he had been in the men's for a long time. She should have dressed by now. He rapped on the door. "Savannah? You okay?"

"Ten more minutes," she said.

He didn't know what could be taking so long. Granted she had never worn flip flops before, but they shouldn't be that difficult to figure out. "Can I come in?"

"Sure," she said.

It was like stepping into a sauna, the temperature a full twenty degrees higher with a thick cloud of steam swirling in the puff of breeze created by the opening door. She sat naked on the toilet, the heat and steam radiating from her. He closed the door behind him and waved at the cloud, trying to clear it. "What are you doing?"

"Repairing my arm and my hands," she said. "I'm almost finished." She held them out for him to inspect, the way a small child might show a boo-boo to Mommy. There was a small piece missing from the gash in her arm, but her palms were the worst with jagged holes in them, the rips in her skin looking like spider webs. "They're going to leave remembers."

"What happened to your hands?" he asked.

"I had to shock the boy," she said. "I have things in my hands to do that—like metal rods." She held a palm out and sure enough, a copper disc no bigger than a silver dollar pushed its way out of her hand like a piston forcing its way through the silicone. The skin folded back under the flat head. She had to pull it out of the way to retract the probe, then she aligned again and resumed the heating process.

"I had no idea you could do that," he said.

She sighed. "I'm not surprised," sounding disappointed. "You only love me for my looks."

"That's not true," he said. "You're also good in bed."

Her eyes went wide and she scoffed, then swatted his arm.

The mending process was the same as the day she'd arrived. The silicone used for her skin could rebond with itself at around 120°C, and she could generate the heat, but she needed water to keep her internal processors cool. He stepped closer, and her arm reminded him of standing next to the radiator in an old building. He held his hand out, not wanting to touch her, because her skin could boil water. "You're hot."

"Thank you, Mr. Mitchell. You're sexy, too, but I don't think now is the time to explore your deviances and proclivities." She gave him the look that he had secretly named "Savannah's Grin of Mischief and Mayhem."

He chuckled in recognition of the joke. He would have never guessed that she would have come with such a sharp sense of humor, nor that he would enjoy it as much as he did. "Can I get you anything?"

"Some more water, please," she said. "I tried the tap, but it's chlorinated."

It was best for her to use distilled water if she could, but spring water was a decent substitute. Chlorinated was the worst choice because it was hard on her silicone skin. "Sure," he said. He went to the cooler, took out four more bottles and set them on the counter.

The girl behind the cash register seemed too young to work here full time, and he guessed it was a summer job. "Are those for —" she paused, uncertain of her next word. "—her?"

Through the window he saw the ambulance pull away and the crowd begin to disperse from one large conglomeration into smaller ones. "Yes," he said, still watching the groups of people. It was clear they were talking among themselves, and quite a few seemed to be headed this way. "What fresh hell?" he thought.

"No charge," the girl said. That's when he stopped looking at the people and turned to her. She nodded to show he had heard her right.

"Thank you," he said, and went back to the ladies' room. He entered without knocking and found Savannah buttoning her shorts, but she was still topless. The steam wasn't as thick as before, either. "Water," he said.

"Thanks. I'm almost finished here." She picked up the t-shirt and removed the tags by breaking the plastic dongle. It was still too hot and steamy to stay with her, so he stepped back into the gift shop and waited.

The gift shop was crowded already, but still more people entered, groups of three and four, mostly children accompanied by an adult. They milled around the merchandise, picking things up, inspecting them, then putting them back, as if they were looking for the perfect gift but not finding it. There was the general chit-chat that came from every crowd, a low murmur that filled the room as efficiently as the air. When Savannah stepped out fully dressed, her new hat cocked high on her head, she threw her hands up and struck a modeling pose. "How do I look?"

The murmur stopped. So did everything else. No one moved or spoke except to turn toward her. It reminded Dan of a western, when the good guy steps into the saloon and all goes silent. Then, from one corner, a ranger began clapping and in another scene straight out of a bad movie, everyone in the room began clapping with him. There were hoots and cheers and even a few wolf whistles thrown in. He watched Savannah's eyes scan the room, her face bewildered, and when the celebration began to die down, she leaned closer to him, her arms still high over her head. "Do I look that good?"

Dan chuckled. "You look great," he said. In fact, with the Serpent Mound logo printed on everything they wore, including the tops of the flip flops, they both looked like walking billboards. "But I don't think that's why they were clapping."

A burly man with an unkempt beard and a gruff voice stepped forward, holding a soggy red cap and Savannah's hair. "We got that out of the creek for ya, ma'am," he said. He pronounced it "crick." The hair was a sodden mess, full of leaves and silt enough that it was two shades darker than usual, and it still dribbled water onto the floor in slow, muddy drops. The man was wet from the waist down and his shoes squished when he stepped forward, making Dan think the "we" was actually an "I."

"Thank you," she said, taking them from him. Dan knew the only way he would have accepted them would have been with rubber gloves, but Savannah didn't mind. She held them out for Dan to see, and her smile was sweet.

"That was very kind of you," Dan said.

"I've known that Saunders boy his whole life," the man said. "He's always into trouble. Maybe this will teach him a lesson."

"I should wash this before it sets," Savannah said.

"Honey, let us help you with that," a thin woman said as she stepped from the crowd. "What's the matter with you, Jimbo? Handing her that mess. You could have at least hosed it off first." Jimbo shrugged, embarrassed that he hadn't thought of it. The two of them went into the ladies' room. "I swear, these men—" the woman said, but the door closed before Dan could hear any more.

Jimbo came to Dan, his hand out to shake. "Heard you went in, too."

Dan shook with him, even though he didn't like shaking hands. "Yes," Dan said. People began leaving the gift shop almost as fast as they had entered, but a few lingered, as if they wanted to see Savannah with hair again.

"This is one of those times when I'd buy you a beer, if they sold any."

"That's okay," Dan said. "I'm not much of a drinker." He wanted to add that he wasn't much of a conversationalist either, especially with strangers, but he didn't want to seem rude.

There was a display of snow globes beside him, with "Ohio's Great Serpent Mound" in large gold letters on the glass, and a replica of the mound at the bottom with trees surrounding it. If you shook it, it showed what the mound looked like in Winter, which Dan had seen firsthand. He'd also seen it during a drought, when the grass on the mound died before the grass surrounding it, making the serpent a dull brown on a green carpet. Some of the postcards beside the cash register showed that. He began straightening the globes, spacing them equally apart. He hoped Jimbo would take the hint. He didn't.

He leaned in, his voice low. "So, she's one of them sex bots?"

Dan ignored him and began straightening the rows of stick

candies under the snow globes.

If Dan was pretending he didn't hear him, Jimbo was pretending to not notice. "I wouldn't mind having one of them, but Eileen would kill me. You must be single, huh?"

"Yes," Dan said. This had started off with an uncomfortable feeling, but that was beginning to slip away and anxiety filled the void it left. How long does it take to wash a wig?

"Boy, that's the life," Jimbo said. "I heard they can cook and clean too. Is that right?"

Dan fidgeted with his hands and looked at his watch, wishing Jimbo would just give up and walk away. If Savannah were here, he could break off the conversation by saying it was time for them to go, but he couldn't leave without her.

"I mean, she cooks, she cleans, plus she's a knockout. I saw you all walking around the park, and I thought, 'What's she doing with him?' no offense. I mean, you're an okay looking guy, but she's something. She could be a movie star."

Dan realized Jimbo wasn't speaking to him, he was just talking and looking at the ladies' room door like he wanted to go in and watch firsthand, but fear of Eileen kept him at bay.

"I'll just bet she's a hellcat in the sack, too, right? I mean, why wouldn't she be? It's what she was built for, am I right? Say, how much does one of those run?"

Dan checked his watch again. Time seemed to have stopped. He shook his wrist as if he was trying to wind the watch and held it to his ear, even though it was electronic. He sighed.

"I'll bet they're expensive," Jimbo said, undeterred by Dan's lack of responses. Dan heard the hand dryer kick on in the ladies' room. Finally, some progress. "I'll bet something like that costs a pretty penny, but hey, she's worth it, am I right? I mean, I couldn't even tell she weren't real, and I walked right past you."

Dan remembered passing him, right at the end of the snake's coiled tail, Jimbo's eyes groping over Savannah, leering and lecherous. He knew those looks were something he would have to grow accustomed to, but he hadn't yet. Some men would lust after her because they didn't know she was a companion-bot.

Others would lust after her because they knew she was. The third group—the ones who weren't attracted to her whether they knew or not—were few and far between. Dan wondered if his life was going to become an endless line of Jimbos.

The air dryer kicked off and Dan waited to hear it come on again. There was no way they could dry her hair on such a short cycle, but it didn't. A few seconds later the door opened and again, Savannah stepped out to model for him. Her hair was wet and pulled back into a ponytail again, looped through her Serpent Mound hat the way it had with the Reds one. The thin lady who Dan guessed to be Eileen—said, "That dryer is just going to frizz it out. Just let it dry naturally then run a brush through it."

"Thank you, Eileen," Savannah said. She stepped to him and smiled. "You ready?"

He smiled back. He had never been more ready in his life. "You bet."

Jimbo stepped forward, holding his cell phone out. "Would you mind if we got a picture?"

Dan was tempted to say no, but couldn't find a way to justify it. Jimbo had already turned the camera on, and Dan took three quick photos with Savannah posing between the husband and wife. When they finished, Savannah hugged Eileen to thank her for the help with her hair, then Jimbo asked for a hug, too. "If it wasn't for me, you wouldn't have hair to fix." Savannah agreed and hugged him, then took Dan's hand and they went outside.

CHAPTER 28

A dozen or so of the younger children formed a semi-circle outside the gift shop, across the paved driveway, standing in the grassy area with a few of the adults standing behind them. Some of the chaperones had their phones out, recording them. Most of the children fidgeted, swaying back and forth as if they were shy. Dan felt as if they were in a parade and was tempted to wave. One little girl dressed in blue jeans and her own Cincinnati Reds cap propped over a mound of dark curly hair yelled at Savannah and asked, "Are you a for-real robot? Like in the movies?"

Savannah stopped and faced the group of children. Dan was tempted to pull her on, just go to the car and get out of here. There had been enough commotion for one day. But she went to the group of kids, tugging his hand to follow, and once she got there, she dropped Dan's hand and squatted down to be on the girl's eye level. She squinted at the child, "Who told you that?"

The little girl pointed to one of her classmates, a boy also in blue jeans who wore thick glasses that made his eyes appear buggy. "Billy."

Billy shook his head, denying everything and took a timid step backwards, in case the robot decided to eat him.

Savannah grinned, "Well, Billy is right. I am a genuine, full-fledged, honest to goodness, for real, just like out of the movies, robot."

Dan watched the eyes of the chaperones for any signs of worry, but didn't see anything. All he saw were smiles. He was still tempted to lead Savannah away, but this might turn out to be okay—a little good public relations never hurt anybody, after all, and what harm could come from teaching children about robotics? The little girl, bold already, grew bolder still. "Are not. Robots are made up." She said it with the same volume as she had when she spoke to them from across the drive, as if robots, although make believe, might be hard of hearing.

"Am so," Savannah said, standing straight and putting her fists on her hips in an exaggerated gesture, then turned away, looking offended.

"Prove it," Billy said, as if he no longer believed his own story. The rest of the children chimed in with him, until it became a chant of, "Prove it. Prove it," echoing through the park.

Savannah's lips puckered to one side and she looked into the sky, as if she was trying to figure out a way to convince them. Then she reached up and removed her hat and hair.

The children's eyes went wide at the sight. Ram sticks and processors showed through the windows of her skull where brains should have been. Even some of the chaperones leaned in for a better look. "Wow," Billy said. "Can I touch it?"

"Sure," Savannah said. She got on her knees, bending her head down as Billy came closer. Apparently he was no longer concerned with becoming Savannah's lunch.

He ran his fingers over the hard plastic, then a few more joined him. Some held back, though, and one left the ranks of the children to hide behind one of the women. Dan presumed it was her mother. "You ain't got no brains," Billy said.

"You mean, 'I don't have any brains,'" Savannah corrected. She sat back on her heels. "I have processors and RAM and hard drives, like a computer."

The first little girl reached for Savannah, but she didn't touch her exposed skull. She touched her arm, running her finger down Savannah's bicep. "You feel real," she said.

"I am real," Savannah said. She reached out and poked the girl's tummy and the girl giggled. "You feel real, too." She put her hair and hat back on then looked at the girl who first questioned her. "What's your name?"

"My name is Nichole, but everybody calls me Nicki, except for my dad. He calls me Choley."

"Chloe?" Savannah asked.

"No, Choley," the little girl insisted.

"Right, Chloe it is," Savannah said.

The little girl gave an over-dramatic, exasperated sigh. "Just call me Nicki," she said, throwing one hand in the air as if she were giving up.

"How's come robots want to destroy the world?" another little girl asked. This one wore no hat, her brown hair in long braided pigtails that nearly reached her denim biballs.

"What's your name?" Savannah asked.

"Sandy," the little girl said, then in an apparent effort to ward off her name being mispronounced, she added, "Just Sandy."

"Robots don't want to destroy the world, Just Sandy."

"No, not Just Sandy, just Sandy." She hit her name hard, trying to drive the point home.

"That's what I said—Just Sandy."

Sandy exchanged a look with Choley that said they both thought Savannah was slow. "They do in the movies," Sandy said. Apparently, this was first-hand knowledge.

Savannah waved her hand as if the entire idea was absurd. "Those are outer space robots. I'm an Earth robot. Earth robots are sworn to protect the world." She held her left hand up and put her right over her chest, looking like she was pledging allegiance, and her tone suggested it was a great burden she was tasked with, but she was willing to make the sacrifice. "But we have to go," she said as she stood up. She smiled and waved with a single finger, as if she were scratching the air, to the little girl who still hid behind her mother and the girl gave a small wave in return, then turned away, burying her face in her mother's thigh. "I'm hungry. I haven't eaten in almost two whole hours," as if that were a long time for a robot to go without food.

"What do you eat?" Billy asked.

"Oh, you know," she said, pausing as she looked to the sky again, this time as if she searched for something flying past, "BRAINS!" and she lurched toward Billy, her grin wide, but her fingers extended like the talons of an attacking raptor.

Billy shrieked—in fact, all of the kids did, and even the parents jumped, startled, and the children ran away in a screeching, screaming scramble. Billy himself was too terrified to move at all, apparently believing he was to be the first course, but in a final act of defiance, the young boy's bladder relaxed, and he wet himself.

Savannah's eyes went wide in disbelief. She closed her fingers and fell to her knees again. "No, I was teasing," she said, but none of the children were listening. In fact, they were still running, screaming to the heavens at this evil twist of fate. The faces of the chaperones changed from pleased smiles to anger. "It was a joke," Savannah insisted, but the screaming shifted to crying. None of the parents dropped their phones.

Dan stepped forward, trying to take control of the situation. "She was kidding," he said. "She doesn't eat brains." The kids sobbed louder. "Don't cry. Please don't cry. Zombies eat brains—not robots." Surely the children could see the logic.

One of the fathers stepped forward, shielding Billy from the raving menace of Savannah, but he looked at Dan. "I think you need to leave."

"Why would a robot need to eat brains?" Dan asked the man. An adult should be able to tell the difference. "What good would it do them? It doesn't make sense."

"I think you need to leave now," the man said, firm, not caring about logic or sense.

Dan agreed. This had shifted from good PR to a nightmare in a flash, and he took Savannah's arm, pulling her to her feet. "Come on."

"It was a joke," Savannah insisted, trying to soothe the children, but the only one who wasn't crying was the first girl—the one in the Reds cap—Choley.

She folded her arms across her chest and shook her head at Savannah, clear that she couldn't believe what she had just witnessed. "You know, for a robot, you're really dumb."

Savannah talked directly to her, as if she was the ambassador for the rest of the kids, and if she could reach her, perhaps the rest would follow. "I'm sorry," she said. "I really don't eat brains." She sounded like she was about to cry herself.

Choley still shook her head. "I know that, but try telling it to these kids." She flipped her thumb over her shoulder at the crying group she represented as if she wasn't one of them and the association bothered her. "You can't scare kids like that. Don't you watch the movies?"

"I like the movies," Savannah said as Dan pulled her backwards toward the car. She seemed desperate to find a common ground. "They're fun."

"Well, next time, pay attention to the way people talk to kids," Choley yelled at her as they grew further away. "Maybe you can learn something."

"No kidding," Dan muttered as he pulled Savannah across the parking lot. He still held her by the elbow as he opened her car door and ushered her into her seat. He closed the door, resting both hands on it, not believing what had just happened. When he looked down at her, she looked back at him, sheepish. "We need to have a talk," he said. He began his lecture as they left the park, starting with, "Maybe it's not a good idea for you to take your face off in public anymore."

CHAPTER 29

Where to lunch was a no-brainer, more for the fact that there was only one place nearby, but the food there was amazing. Schrock's Amish Bakery and Restaurant was actually more than that. It was a small country store with a selection of handmade crafts, jellies and jams, stone-milled flour, and even furniture, all crafted by the local Amish folks who seem to have sprung up by the hundreds in the past twenty years or so, gobbling up farmland like locusts straight out of the Bible. Dan knew a little about their culture, but only what he had ascertained from frequenting this place. He knew they shunned technology in general because of strict religious beliefs, driving horse-drawn buggies with those orange SMV triangles on the back, and you had to be careful when you rounded a curve in these parts because there might be a slow moving vehicle in front of you that was going as fast as a horse could walk. One of the boys he went to high school with had rear-ended an Amish buggy loaded with an entire family. No people were hurt, but the horse was killed outright, due to the harness around its neck. The boy—Jake, his name was Jake—had to pay for the repairs to the buggy and replacing the horse. Dan had often wondered what the going rate was for an Amish horse, but he didn't know Jake well enough to ask.

He pulled into the parking lot and shut the engine off. "Okay, before we go in, there are a couple of things you need to know. These people are—" he paused, searching for the right word, "—different."

"Different how?" she asked. Her hair was dry, but still needed an actual shampooing, not just the hand soap they had used in the bathroom. She still wore her green Serpent Mound hat and had the ponytail out the back the way she had with the Reds cap, so it was hard to notice. At least there were no more leaves and twigs in it. She flipped the passenger visor down and looked at herself in the mirror. She wiped a smudge from her face and adjusted her cap.

"Well, they don't like technology for one thing," he said. "They don't use anything with electricity or gasoline, so no cars, no lights—nothing like that." Four buggies sat in the parking lot with horses attached. Four more horses grazed free in the fenced pasture beside the store, while a fifth stood at the split rail fence looking at them as if the grass were greener on their side, and behind them a small herd of cattle lay in the sun, chewing their cud.

She closed the vanity and turned to him, leaning over the console. "So no robots?"

"Definitely no robots," he said.

"Not even cute ones?" She propped her hand on her chin and looked sulky.

"Well, their children's dolls don't have faces because they don't like vanity, so I don't think cute matters much to them." He ran the back of his fingers over her soft face and she smiled.

"What's that?" she asked, looking back over her shoulder.

"What?" He checked the parking lot to see what she might be talking about. They had covered cattle and horses on the drive out, and there wasn't anything else except for a few more cars that belonged to the "English," as the Amish put it whenever they were referring to anyone who wasn't part of their religion.

"That noise," she said. She looked into the sky.

Dan turned as well, but didn't hear anything for a few seconds, nor did he see anything. Then he did as the ultra light aircraft popped over a few trees on the other side of the road and headed straight for them.

"They don't have electricity, but they have drones?" she asked, as if she didn't believe him.

"That's not a drone," he said as the tiny craft passed over their head less than thirty feet off the ground. It was close enough that he could see the man flying it wearing shorts and a t-shirt, while the one in the back wore the standard long blue sleeves, and dark pants of a typical Amish man, but in lieu of a wide-brimmed hat, he wore an open-faced helmet and goggles. The Amishman's grin was big and wide. He waved to them with grand arm gestures and Savannah waved back the same way. The ultra light dipped once it passed the fence and touched down in the pasture, running along two bare wheel ruts Dan hadn't noticed before. Thanks to the ruts and neither the horses nor the cattle so much as flinching, Dan assumed this happened on a regular basis. The tiny plane pulled to a stop and Dan heard the Amishman let out a war whoop. He climbed out and high-fived the pilot who got off as well, lit a cigarette once he removed his helmet and walked toward the fence, the helmet tucked under his arm.

"I'm so confused right now," Dan said. An Amishman on an airplane sounded like the beginning to a bad joke. He got out and Savannah followed suit. They walked to the horse and Savannah stroked the animal's nose.

"How you all doing?" the pilot said as he reached the fence. "Care to go up? Twenty bucks will get you twenty minutes."

Dan was one of those people whose feet had no intentions of leaving Mother Earth unless he was beamed aboard a Mother Ship against his will. The thought of a big plane bothered him, but the thing that buzzed over their head at a mere thirty feet was little more than fabric and plastic pipes. "No, thanks," he said, laughing through his decline. "But let me ask you something—were you just flying that Amish guy around?"

"Sure," the pilot said. "Do it all the time. They can't get enough of it."

"What about shunning technology?" Dan asked.

"Most people get that wrong. They can use technology—they can't own it. Like, it's okay for them to ride in a car. They just can't own a car. It's okay for them to use a phone, but they can't have one in their house. I got to be friends with one of the Elders and he explained it all to me." He propped one foot on the bottom fence rail and took another pull from his smoke. He flipped his thumb toward the young man who had taken off his helmet and put on his wide-brimmed black hat, then ran toward them with the glee of a small child. When the young man reached them, the pilot spoke to him. "Isaac flies with me all the time, don't you buddy?"

"I do, I fly all the time," Isaac said. "Are you going to fly now? Can I fly again?"

"Isaac is part bird," the pilot said, winking at Dan.

"I am, I'm part bird," Isaac said, then giggled and flapped his arms like wings, as if being a bird were the funniest thing in the world to him. He ran in circles in the field, flapping his arms as if he were trying to take flight. He was clean-shaven, even though he was at least thirty. In the Amish community, that meant he was unmarried, which was pretty much unheard of at his age, but it didn't take long to figure out why. Then his arms stopped flapping, but they raked backwards like a jet and he ran toward them making machine gun sounds.

The pilot grinned at him, then turned back to Dan and Savannah with a shake of his head. He stroked the horse's neck and pat her on the flank. "This is Ginger. Say 'Hi,' Ginger."

Ginger swished her tail.

"She's beautiful," Savannah said, still stroking Ginger's nose. Ginger seemed to like the attention.

"Yeah, she's a sweetie," the pilot said. Dan noticed the man's eyes shift up and down Savannah's body, lingering for a second when they were on her legs. "Sure I can't tempt you with a quick flight?"

"Can we?" Savannah asked before Dan had a chance to say no again. "Please? It looks like fun." When she asked, she bounced on her toes and Dan felt himself drawn to her chest, which bounced in its own rhythm.

"It is fun," Isaac said. "It's so much fun. I want to go again."

Dan sighed, not wanting to disappoint her, but not wanting to face his phobia either. "I don't think so," he said.

"Please?" she asked again. "We can go together."

"I can only take one at a time," the pilot said. "It's just a two seater."

"See?" Dan said, grateful for the easy excuse out of it. "We can't go together."

"Then we can go one at a time," she said. "Come on—please?"

"If you both do it, I'll knock ten dollars off. Thirty dollars." He flicked his fingers over the cherry of his smoke, knocking the fire off, then ground the smoking ruin under the toe of his sneaker until it was out. He balled the used butt into his pocket rather than flick it to the ground, the way most people did, and Dan admired that. Just because the man chose to smoke, it didn't mean that everyone else needed to see the litter.

"She can go," Dan said.

"But you have to go, too," Savannah said, taking her hand from the horse and grabbing his. Dan didn't want to drop her hand, but now he knew that as soon as they took off in the flying death trap, he would have to wash his hands to get rid of any transferred equine germs.

"I'll think about it," Dan said, which wasn't a lie. He would think about it the entire time she was gone—it was probably all he would think about—think about getting in the thing— think about taking off—think about crashing into a random tree —think about fiery death. The thoughts would consume him in much the same way the flames would consume his body when the thing fell from the sky. Thinking about it would not be an issue.

"Oh, thank you," she said, and she bounced with glee some more. She kissed his cheek and Dan blushed at the public display of affection, even if it was tame. She turned back toward the fence. "How do I—?"

"Just climb under the rail," the pilot said, then he reached over the top rail and offered his hand to Dan. "Name's Deron."

"Dan," he said as he shook the man's hand. Now he had two reasons to wash.

It took Savannah a little bit to navigate her way through the fence, but then, it took Dan twice as long. You had to bend over and sort of kick your leg through so you were straddling it, then bring the other leg through, and while he had seen it done in movies, it wasn't as easy as it looked, especially in flip flops. Savannah put her hand in the crook of his elbow and they began walking across the pasture. She urged him faster with a mild tug.

"Watch where you're walking," he said pulling her to one side until she almost lost her balance as her foot missed a cow pie by less than two inches.

"What? Why?"

"That's cow—" he cringed at the thought. "That's cow—" What if she had stepped in it? He would have to order her a brand new leg.

"Cow what?" she asked. She rested her hand on his back, between his shoulder blades. "The cows are over there."

"It's cow shit," Deron said as he passed them. "Try not to step in it. It's kinda squishy,"

"Are you okay?" she asked and Dan nodded. She patted his back. "Want some water?"

"No," Dan said. He took a deep breath and held it for a second, realizing that whatever cool points he had earned by jumping in the creek had just faded to nothing, even the ones he only tallied in his own mind. "I'll be okay. You go on."

"You sure?" she asked, still patting him like a puppy.

"Yes," he said, feeling a burst of annoyance at the question. He wished she would just go already, in that same way a dying animal wants to be alone. Death is a private thing, even if it's just imaginatory. He felt her walk away, but didn't watch. Another deep breath, trying to not focus on the smells of the pasture, but he couldn't help it. The entire idea was disgusting.

Deron was turning the ultra light around so that it had a downhill run for the takeoff and Savannah already wore the helmet and stood back, waiting for Deron. When he finished, he went to her and said something, putting his hand on her waist in a way that sent a pang of jealousy through Dan. In all likelihood, it was an innocent touch, but it still made him uncomfortable. Dan walked to them, watching where he stepped. Cow poop and flip flops were never a good match.

By the time he reached them, Savannah was in the rear seat with the four-point safety belt locked in place and Deron was climbing aboard. Dan leaned into the passenger area. "You sure about this?"

She smiled. "It will be fun."

"If you say so." He kissed her, a quick peck, then stood back while Deron started the engine. The little airplane began rolling down the hill, getting faster as it approached the fence, and Dan didn't think it would gain enough speed to take off when the nose came up, off the ground, then the rear followed it, the tiny craft rising higher into the sky. It cleared the fence with a good ten feet to spare and it continued to climb higher, over the trees then out of sight. Dan watched until they disappeared, then went into the restaurant to wash his hands.

CHAPTER 30

At fifteen minutes, Dan started watching for them. At twenty, when they still weren't in sight, he started fidgeting, and at twenty-five, he paced. At thirty, he heard the raspy engine in the distance, but still didn't see them. At thirty-one minutes and thirty seconds, they touched down in the same spot where Deron had landed with Isaac, who now came out of the restaurant's back door wearing a stained apron tied around his waist, waving to the landing aircraft with the same big arm gestures he'd had when he was the one flying past them. Savannah waved back. Dan didn't see Isaac as a cook, but he would make a good dishwasher.

Once everything was shut down, Deron helped Savannah stand then went toward the backside of the restaurant and lit another cigarette as Isaac ran with a five-gallon gas can and went to the ultra light and began refueling it. "Don't overfill it," Deron said with the tone of someone who had to give those instructions after every landing.

"I won't," Isaac said. He stared at the fuel tank with the great interest of someone who had overfilled it before, and was determined to never do it again.

"That was amazing," Savannah said. "We flew over Serpent Mound, then we flew over Deron's farm. It's so beautiful up there."

Isaac was returning with the gas can when Savannah took her helmet off, and her wig came off with it.

Deron was shocked. His lit cigarette fell out of his mouth and onto the ground, smoldering in the grass, but that was nothing compared to Isaac. He stopped dead in his tracks, the gas can dropping to the ground, his face stunned blank, as if there was nothing else in the world but her. "You're a robot," Isaac said, awestruck, as if this was a dream and he had yet to decide if it were a nightmare or not.

Savannah smiled as she retrieved her wig from the helmet but she stopped before she put it back on. "I am," she said. "Want to see?" Dan had a flashback of what had just happened at the mound and wanted to just grab Savannah and get out of there before things went south again.

"What did I just say about taking your face off in public?" he asked.

"It wasn't my face, it was my hair, and it was an accident," she hissed back at him.

Isaac took a step toward her, but then stopped, as if he wasn't sure he should. Confusion overtook his face, and it morphed into fear. "Momma?" he called without looking away from Savannah. He took a timid step backwards and called again, frightened, "Momma?"

"Isaac, it's okay, buddy," Deron said, trying to soothe the boy before he could run away. Deron looked over his shoulder at Dan. "It is okay, isn't it?"

"Of course it is," Dan said. It seemed like a ridiculous thing to ask. "She won't hurt you, Isaac," Dan said and the boy's eyes shifted to him for a second, but they held no trust.

Deron moved closer to the boy, taking small deliberate steps, his hands out, fingers splayed, the way a policeman on television might show that he held no weapon to a panicky suspect. "Isaac, it was just a movie, buddy. Remember how we talked about movies being make believe?"

"Put your wig on," Dan said, and Savannah did. "See, Isaac? No more robot."

Isaac might have been simple, but he wasn't stupid, and his eyes said he wasn't convinced. He took another step back, not looking where he was going, and his feet tangled in something —a tuft of grass, maybe, Dan couldn't see whatever it was—and he fell backwards, landing on his butt, jarring and hard enough to make him bite his tongue. He started to cry as blood dribbled over his bottom lip.

"Oh, you poor thing," Savannah said and she started toward him, but Deron got there first. He squatted in front of Isaac, blocking his view of Savannah.

"Let me see it," he said, his voice gentle. Isaac continued to cry. "Come on, stick your tongue out at me." Deron stuck his own tongue out at Isaac, and Isaac laughed a little between sobs. He stuck his tongue back at Deron, and Dan heard Deron say, "You bit it pretty good, didn't you?"

Isaac nodded.

"Can I help?" Savannah asked as she stepped around Deron, and Isaac's eyes went wide again, but he didn't yell for anyone. He did start to crawl away, though. "I won't hurt you—I promise." She held an empty hand out, reaching for him. He stopped retreating. "I like people. I don't want to hurt anyone—especially a handsome guy like you."

He smiled a little at the compliment, but still didn't look convinced.

"I'm sorry I scared you," Savannah said. "I didn't mean to."

"It's not your fault," Deron said. "Sometimes I fly Isaac over to my place to help with some chores. I let him watch movies and play video games. He likes the one where all the robots were trying to take over the world."

"Don't tell my dad, though," Isaac said, almost pleading. He had developed a slight lisp, thanks to his bleeding tongue. "He'd be mad."

"We won't tell anyone," Dan said as he moved closer.

"You know, those movies and games are just make believe. Robots don't want to take over the world. We wouldn't have anyone to talk to." She still held her hand out and finally Isaac took it, timid at first, but he smiled. "You want to see?" Savannah asked. Isaac nodded. She removed her hair and let her microchips show, and he was thunderstruck once again.

He scooted closer, mouth open, fingers outstretched, and his demeanor reminded Dan of someone trying to touch the face of God. Savannah bowed her head for him to get a better look, and he moved to his knees and crawled toward her. Finally, he let his fingers touch the plastic windows in her skull. "Wow," he said, truly amazed. "That's a computer," he said. "You're a computer."

"Actually, I'm about six different computers all rolled into one," she said. "Each one has a different job to do, like everyone in the restaurant has a different job."

"My job is to wash the dishes," Isaac said. He sounded proud.

"Right," Dan said, doing his best to keep things simple. "And it's somebody's job to cook, and somebody else's to wait on customers, and together, it makes a restaurant."

"Momma cooks. Sarah and Rebecca waits on customers," he said. "Papa is the boss."

"I'm just like that," Savannah said. "I have a computer in my chest that's the boss." She pointed to the spot between her breasts. "It tells the others what to do so they can all work together. The one in my head is so I can see and hear. I have one in each arm so I can do this." She smiled as she moved his hand up and down, then side to side, as if they were dancing. "And one in each leg so I can walk." She put her hair back on and adjusted it, then slipped her cap on over it.

"Wow," he said again, sounding mesmerized. "Why do you look like a lady?" He stroked her wig with his fingertips like it was made of gossamer.

Dan took that one. "It's because I was lonely. Savannah is my companion."

"How's come you didn't get a human lady?" His fingers slipped through strands of Savannah's hair, combing it.

"Sometimes it's not that easy, buddy," Deron said. He ruffled the boy's hair with genuine affection.

Isaac nodded as if he understood, and Dan guessed that in a way, at his age, with his condition, he did. Growing up in such a religious community with no access to secular resources for the mentally handicapped, Isaac must live a lonely life as well. Dan found his admiration for Deron growing.

"Isaac?" a woman yelled from the back door of the restaurant. An elderly lady stepped into the yard, her hands at the small of her back and she leaned backwards to stretch. "Isaac? Best get in here. The dishes are backing up."

"Yes, Momma," he said, and he left, jogging across the field in his large clunky black shoes. He turned as he reached the top of the small rise and waved at them, and they all waved back. He said something to the woman, who shielded her eyes against the sun as she looked down at them. She swatted Isaac's bottom the playful way someone might shoo a small child, not hard at all, but Isaac skipped a step as he went back inside. The woman continued to stare at them until Deron waved to her, then she waved back and stepped inside.

"I wonder if he told her," Dan said.

"Wouldn't much matter," Deron said. "Isaac has a habit of tall tales. His mom's a good woman, though. She just laughs at him and goes on. His daddy might tan his hide over it, but Isaac knows to not say anything in front of him." He tugged at a piece of fresh hay until the top portion slipped out of its pocket, giving him a bright, lime green tip of a stalk. He nibbled at it, taking tiny nips, extracting the juice. It reminded Dan of a lonesome cowboy on the prairie. All the image needed was a tumbleweed to roll past as someone played a harmonica.

"He is mentally challenged," Savannah said, without sympathy, just fact.

"Yeah," Deron said. "You were awful good with him. Most people seem to be put off by him, like they think it might be catching. Of course, I guess to you, all of us humans are mentally challenged."

Savannah smiled. "I wouldn't go that far, but some are definitely smarter than others. The more time I spend around humans, the greater I realize how wide the divide is."

Dan squatted beside them and for a brief second considered plucking a piece of hay to chew on as well, then thought about all the manure in the pasture and knew he could never do that.

"Can I ask how you knew?" Deron asked Savannah. "I mean,

it's easy for most people to tell, but what made it easy for you?"

She shrugged. "The same things, I suppose. We're shipped with a basic program to determine the intelligence level of our mate, and we adjust accordingly. While Dan is the type of guy who would have tinkered until he completed assembly even without my help, not everyone has that skill set, nor the patience. I need to be able to recognize if someone isn't that—" she paused as if she was searching for the correct word. "—bright," she finished.

Dan's stomach growled. He checked his watch and realized that it was too late for an actual lunch since they needed to be home before 6:30 and they would have to fight at least some city traffic. The good news was, he could decline the flight with Deron and not feel ashamed about it. They really were running short on time.

Instead of a sit-down meal, they got a selection of cheeses and meats from the deli counter and a package of crackers, which he nibbled at on the way to the car. The entire process was uneventful, except toward the end, when Isaac stepped from the kitchen and saw them as they paid for their purchases, and waved with great enthusiasm. Both Savannah and Dan waved back, then they left, heading home to Cincinnati.

CHAPTER 31

When the cell phone rang, Dan jumped, startled from deep thoughts that flashed away, less subtle than they had entered, back to the nowhere from which they had emerged. He tried to recall what he'd been thinking about—it had seemed important, but nothing would come to him. The phone rang again, buried deep in his pants pocket, and he would never be able to fish it out in time to answer, not that he intended to. He was driving and he never talked on his phone while behind the wheel. He found it as distracting as texting. "Who is it?" he asked Savannah. She was jacked into his phone via Bluetooth. While his house phone had been ringing so much he'd unplugged it, the reporters had yet to track down his cell phone, so he took cell calls a little more seriously.

"RWR," she said. "Ian's private line. Want me to get it?"

"Yes, please," he said as they rounded the last curve before they entered the small town of Peebles. Dan slowed to 35, knowing the speed limit dropped at the bottom of the next rise.

"Hello?" she asked, the same tone anyone would use when answering the phone, and it still looked odd to Dan that she held no phone when she did it. It reminded him of when earpieces first came out for cell phones and he was walking through the produce section of the grocery and a large man went past, having a rather animated conversation with no one. At first, Dan believed the man must be talking to him. He asked Dan if he wanted bananas—of course Dan wanted bananas—why else would he be holding them? Dan didn't answer because he felt it wasn't any of the man's business if Dan wanted bananas. The man picked up a bunch, then asked if he wanted strawberries. Again, Dan didn't answer. He hadn't considered strawberries, but now that they were mentioned, they sounded good. The man picked up a package as well, then laughed as if Dan had told a joke. Then the man asked what Danny wanted—no one had called him Danny since grade school, but he had never seen this man before that he knew of. How did he know to call him Danny?

Dan had heard of schizophrenia, of course, but had never seen it before, and believed this man must be suffering from it —he was carrying on a one-sided conversation. That much was certain. But how did he know Dan's name? Then it had dawned on Dan—it must be one of those hidden-camera shows, and he laughed at falling for it, searching the rest of the produce section for the producers to come out, laughing at him. He saw nothing of course, then the man had turned away from him and Dan saw the earpiece and the two-inch long microphone that extended from it. That was when Dan turned blood red from embarrass-ment, not because he had fallen for some hidden camera show, but because there wasn't an audience at all. The man wasn't crazy. It was unfamiliar technology that had fooled Dan into thinking he'd come face-to-face with the insane. He should have known better.

"Hi, Ian. Dan's driving."

Dan wondered why Ian might be calling. He didn't know the man well, but in the short time since they'd first met, he didn't seem the type to call for no reason.

"Oh—that sounds bad," she said.

"What?" Dan asked as he pulled into the parking lot of a farm supply store and shifted into Park. He fished the phone from his pocket and saw that it was on a call but if there was a way for him to join while Savannah was hooked through Bluetooth, he didn't know it. "What sounds bad?"

"That's good, though, isn't it?" she asked, ignoring him.

He tried to be patient. He really did. But at times, his OCD kicked in as if from nowhere, and this was one of those times. "What's he saying? What sounds bad?" he asked. She held up one finger, universal for, "Give me a minute," but Dan couldn't—he tried—he just couldn't. "Really. What's he saying?"

"Can you hold on for one moment, Ian?" Savannah asked, then turned to Dan. "What is your problem?" She sounded mildly frustrated.

"I want to know what he's saying," he said, wondering where in her programming lied the code that allowed her to scold him. "What sounds bad?"

"Well, I can't answer you because he's still in the process of saying it," she said. She rolled her eyes as if his asking were ridiculous.

"Fine," he said, feeling a little miffed at the situation. He reached into the back seat for the sack of food they had gotten from the deli and opened a block of cheese—havarti with horse-radish—and took a large bite. His sinuses began to run almost immediately. The horseradish must have been fresh the day they made this stuff, or they had upped the dosage. He'd had it before, and it was usually milder. His eyes teared—not enough to run, but enough to be uncomfortable. He fished a bottle of water from the backseat as well and drained half of it, trying to stop the burn at the back of his throat. It was like getting hit with mild tear gas.

"Okay, we will," she said. "I'll have him call you. Thanks, Ian. And I'm really sorry about that." It was obvious the call was over, but she just sat there, looking straight ahead.

Dan wiped the tears from his eyes and coughed, then cleaned his hand with a napkin from the bag. He waited, again trying his best to be patient but failing. "Well?"

"Well what?"

"Well, what did he say?" he asked. The question seemed ridiculous. She knew exactly what he meant.

"I'm disinclined to tell you," she said. She remained still, looking out the windshield as cars drove past.

"What? Why?"

"You were rude," she said, her matter-of-fact tone bordering on snippy.

153

"I wasn't rude, I was simply asking."

"Rude," she said, as she turned her head away from him, toward her side of the car, as if that would create a physical distance, and put up a hand aimed at him, dismissing him, the same gesture Choley had used on her. She crossed her legs and began shaking one foot from side to side, a universal sign for angry. She added to it by folding her arms over her chest.

"I order you to tell me," he said. She did belong to him, after all.

She turned back to him, her face flat and expressionless. "Really?" She sounded as if she didn't believe what she had heard. "You order me?" It seemed the thought of being ordered to do something was beneath her.

"You're supposed to follow my orders," he said, but his heart wasn't in it. He even sounded sheepish to himself.

"Not on this one, pal," she said. She turned away from him again and he felt her anger now more than he heard it.

They had never had an argument before, and he'd thought they never would. He'd assumed the point of having a robotic companion would mean they wouldn't fight. And what good was it to order her to do something if she didn't have to follow it? Hadn't anyone at RWR read Asimov? This was a clear-cut violation of the Second Law of Robotics if there ever was one. Either way, he didn't want to fight. "I'm sorry," he said.

"For?" She still wouldn't look at him, so he was forced to speak to the back of her head.

"For being rude."

She waited a few seconds, but when he didn't say anything else, she did. "And?"

"And what?" he asked. As far as he knew, that was his only transgression.

"And for trying to order me to tell you," she said, as if it should be obvious. She still wouldn't look at him.

"I'm sorry for being rude, and for ordering you to tell me," he said.

She finally turned back to him, and he was glad this little spat was over. "Are you really sorry, or are you just saying it?" Okay—maybe it wasn't completely over.

He started to comment that with this much grief, he should have gotten a real woman, but was afraid that would start another fight. "I'm really sorry," he said.

She smiled. "Thank you."

"You're welcome. Now will you tell me?"

"Maybe later."

Was she serious? How far did this autonomy thing go? "Really?" He found it unbelievable.

She shrugged. "Kiss me and I'll consider it." He no longer read anger in her eyes, only playfulness. He leaned over, fighting a grin and kissed her. She rested her hand against his cheek as their lips met. The kiss was long, and slow, and sensual. When it broke, she said, "Okay—I considered it."

"And?" he said, his face an inch from hers. He smiled, and while he was so close a human woman might not have been able to see it, he knew she could.

"Maybe later."

"Now you're being mean," he said and he moved to kiss her again, but she held him at bay with mild pressure from her fingers.

"Dan?" Her voice was soft and sweet, and it reminded him of the way she sounded late at night, after they had enjoyed one another.

"Yes?"

"Don't ever give me anymore dumb orders." She stroked his cheek with her thumb. It was a subtle ultimatum, but he felt it deep in his core.

"I won't," he said. She was right—he had been wrong to try.

She leaned in and kissed him again, this time a quick peck. "I need to go to low power mode. Shocking that kid really drained me."

"Okay," he said. "Let's get you home and on the charger." He put the car into gear, then resumed the drive back to Cincinnati.

CHAPTER 32

He waited until they were home to return Ian's call, one reason being that he didn't talk on his phone while driving, but the other was that both his phone and his girlfriend were running on low batteries. When he spoke her name as they pulled into the driveway, she came awake and he led her inside, took her clothes off, including that ratty-looking wig, helped her into the Pobody's Nerfect t-shirt and put her to bed on her charging mat then kissed her good night. The wig looked almost beyond salvageable. The cap had covered the fact that there was a rather large chunk of it missing, most likely now hanging from a semi-submerged tree, and he looked online to see if he could find a local stylist who specialized in wig restoration. He was both surprised and amused at how many there were who catered to male clients. He found a local one that had been family owned for generations, and when he called and answered a few questions —yes, it was real human hair—no, he didn't know the manufacturer—yes, there was damage—he made arrangements to drop it off in the morning and it would be ready the following week. That wouldn't leave Savannah hairless, of course. This was her only blonde wig, and the one she wore most often. They had never discussed whether or not she could even have a favorite, but now that he thought of it, this was the only one he had seen her wear more than once. He made a mental decision to see if he could pay the wig maker extra for a rush-job.

He stalled calling Ian for the same reason children will hide a mess under their bed, believing it would be better to not deal with it, and perhaps if it's ignored long enough, it will magically disappear. It wasn't a conscious decision to avoid the call—it was his brain telling him there were more important things that required tending first. He needed a shower, for one. He had been in that nasty creek after all, and he was surprised at himself for not having done that first. Normally, his OCD would be running full out, especially after a day as stressful as this had been, but it wasn't and he didn't know why not, and that bothered him even more than the condition did. He had grown more-or-less comfortable with being obsessive, and now that he wasn't in a time when he should have been, it left a void in the same manner as a missing limb would. He thought of these things as he stood in the bathroom and stripped naked and turned the water on, waiting almost a full minute for it to get hot. He knew he needed a shower, but he didn't "need" a shower in the way he normally would "need" to be clean. He realized he could even skip the shower and it wouldn't bother him, as long as he took one before bed. He stepped under the warm spray and began, as always, by wetting his hair that would lead to shampooing, followed by a full-body sudzing, cleaning himself from the top down, the way one does a car. He reached for the shampoo then stopped and grabbed the washcloth and soap instead. He would shampoo last this time because he could, and that thought made him smile.

Only a few months ago, if he'd gone into that muddy water, he would have had no choice but to go straight home and scour his entire body multiple times. Somehow that compulsion had calmed, and he had no idea when it had happened, but he did have a good idea of why it had, and it was charging in the next room. Dan had been lonely his entire life. He had also battled OCD his entire life. Was it possible that fixing one had cured the other, or at least made it tolerable? He'd never heard of such a thing, but perhaps it was, especially if it tied into a time from his childhood when he realized he would always be alone.

He shampooed twice then used the conditioner and stood under the hot water for the allotted three minutes the bottle called for before he rinsed clean. He got out, toweled himself dry, then wrapped the towel around his waist and snuck into

TERRY R. LACY

the bedroom quiet as he could so as to not disturb her, got fresh clothes then returned to the bathroom to dress.

His stomach growled from skipping an actual lunch, and it was when he considered going to fix a bite to eat that he realized all he was doing was putting off the inevitable when it came to calling Ian Palance. He went to the living room and made the call.

Ian didn't answer with "Hello?" the way most people did, nor did he affect the annoying habit of answering with his name that made the person seem self-important. Instead, he began the conversation by jumping into it like a diver off a platform who hadn't tested the water first, head-first and full-speed. "Where the hell were you driving from, Michigan?"

"Hello, Ian," Dan said, not allowing Ian to drag him away from protocol. Society dictated that certain civilities be followed, and a greeting was almost always required.

"What the hell are you doing to me, dude?"

Dan disliked the whole "dude" craze for the same reason as he didn't like the absence of a greeting—the informality that would lead to the destruction of civilization. "I'm not sure to what you are referring," he said, knowing the formal grammar would sound stilted to an untrained ear, but hoping he might somehow balance the scales of propriety.

"I'm referring," Ian said, stressing the word "referring" as if it angered him, "to the videos. You're killing me, Dan. You are absolutely killing me."

"What videos?" Dan asked.

"The ones of her scaring a bunch of little kids," Ian said, almost screaming it at him. "She made a little boy pee his freaking pants, Dan. Do you know how that makes us look?"

Dan felt his entire body shrink into the chair. He hadn't considered the videos, not that it would have mattered. What could he have done? Smash every phone at Serpent Mound? "What about the ones of her saving the drowning boy?" he asked.

"Oh, they have those, too," Ian said. "And they are great— amazing stuff that would have been a big help to your case, if she

158

hadn't told a bunch of seven-year-olds that she was going to eat their freaking brains. Turn on Fox News." He paused for a second, and Dan heard a click and Muzak came on the line. Ian came back and said, "Dan, I'm going to have to call you back. Watch those videos." The line went dead before Dan could respond.

Dan reached for the remote and turned the television on, then scrolled from the cooking channel Savannah had been watching lately until he found Fox. There was a commercial for ED with an attractive woman in her 50's who wore a beaming smile as she slow danced with her silver-haired, presumed husband, who apparently no longer suffered from ED. It was followed by a beer commercial that touted great taste without all those pesky calories, then yet another that showed BBQ ribs slathered in sauce. Dan thought that perhaps if Fox's audience laid off the beer and ribs, they wouldn't need pills to satisfy their women. Finally the "News Broadcast" returned, and when Dan thought about "Fox News Broadcasts," he used quotation marks in his mind. There seemed to be little "news" about them. Instead, they filled the airwaves with opinions, all slanted for bias in ways to make them appear balanced. Fox wasn't the only one that did that. In fact, from what Dan had noticed, every cable news network did it, and so did the Internet, their stories told in a manner to force the viewer into the logical conclusion of their agendas, some subtle, most not. Gone were the days of Brinkley and Murrow, when the news was facts and you were free to draw your own conclusion—form your own opinions. Now people were forced to believe whatever the "news" told them was truth, the way steers were led by the rings in their noses into the backs of those death trucks.

"Welcome back," the anchor, a well dressed and good-looking man in his 50's said, every bit as handsome as the man in the ED commercial had been. "We're looking at new videos of Savannah the Sexbot," and Dan already knew where this was headed even without Ian's scolding, just from the opening. The term "Sexbot" was stilted to sway the viewer to believe that Savannah was bad, and the coverage would only go downhill from there. A balanced reporter would have used the term "Companion-bot," or "Cyber-mate," or any of the dozen other terms Dan had heard used.

"Keep in mind, this is just coming to us, so it's still the raw footage, but take a look at what we're seeing," the anchor said, and the screen turned to a full shot of Savannah talking to the children, and he heard Billy, the little boy with the thick glasses ask his dreadful question all over again, "What do you eat?" Billy's face was blurred, as were the other children's, and that alone meant the footage wasn't raw, and Dan would have pointed that out, if there had been anyone around. Savannah's face wasn't and there was no mistaking her for someone else. Dan watched as she looked to the sky, thinking he hadn't remembered her doing that, and would have said she hadn't, if the proof wasn't right in front of him. Then he saw once more, her fingers shaped as claws as she made a swipe at the child that seemed less playful than it had before, and heard her voice loud and as clear as a summer's morning, that one word, "Brains," as she lunged toward Billy, again the angle suggesting she had come much closer to the boy than she actually had. It even seemed as if Billy's shirt had moved when she clawed at him, but it hadn't, had it? She hadn't been close enough to touch him, had she? He heard the terrified shrieks and while Billy's face remained blurred, that wasn't what the footage focused on anyway. The camera zoomed to the wet patch in Billy's crotch as it grew wider and ran down the boy's leg. From there the sound stopped, but the video didn't, showing the children running and Savannah reaching for them, but without the sound of her apologies and her pleas to calm them, it seemed as if she was only tormenting them more. "There you have it," the anchor said. "This thing is coming after these children, scaring them, no doubt something that's going to cause them nightmares, quite possibly for the rest of their lives, and for what?" Now the shot cut back to the anchor, but the audio played, and he heard the screaming children and Savannah's plea of, "It was a joke."

"A joke," the anchor said. "Well, if it was a joke, it wasn't a funny one. We'll have more when we return." The smiling ED woman came back, but Dan shut off the television. He'd seen enough to know he didn't want to see more. Even if they showed the footage of Savannah saving the boy, they would find a way to put a negative spin on it, or at least point out that the saving of one child didn't outweigh the frightening of others.

He remembered being hungry only a few minutes ago, but now his appetite was gone. All he wanted was to sleep, for the same reason he hadn't wanted to make that phone call. Never put off for tomorrow what you can postpone until the day after. He went to the bedroom and laid down beside Savannah. He felt exhausted, but sleep wouldn't come. When she touched him, he realized she had turned on her side to face him, but he didn't know when she'd done that. "Come here," she said, her voice quiet and soft and she tugged on his t-shirt, urging him to her. She didn't stop until he was on top of her. Afterwards, he did sleep, but it wasn't sound.

CHAPTER 33

Dan awoke long before sunrise and the neighborhood was deathly silent. The room was dark, but he knew she was still beside him even without looking or reaching for her. When he spoke to her, it was in a whisper, not for the same reason he would if she was alive—not wanting to wake her—but because to speak louder in such a stillness seemed somehow wrong. "Savannah?"

Even in low power mode, she listened for certain sounds, and her name was one of them. Others included anything that might mean a break in or a fire, or anything else that might require attention, including severe weather. "Yes?" she whispered back.

"How much longer until you're charged?"

"A few more hours. Did you need something?"

"No," he said. "Go back to sleep." He stood and went to the bathroom, then to the kitchen to fix some coffee. This was the first time he'd had to make it since he'd shown her how, and it was strange to not awaken to the aroma of a fresh cup, even though it didn't seem long enough for it to have become habit. He used one of those single serve machines with the plastic pods, and it shut itself off at noon, then powered back on at six in the morning in order to conserve energy. It was still a few hours until then, and the machine should have been cold and taken a few minutes to heat up, but it was already on and in the process when he got there. She must have been monitoring his sleep cycle and knew he would be awake long before it happened and turned the pot on in anticipation without having to leave the bed. It was a convenience, and a small one at that, but the

Amish have a saying—the luxuries of one generation become the necessities of the next—and Dan wondered what would be a luxury and what would be a necessity in fifty years. He carried his cup to the living room and turned on the television, even though he doubted there would be anything he wanted to see. He was right. Fox news was still showing the footage of Savannah, this time from more than one video, but they always seemed to show the same angle when she swiped at Billy, because it was the one that looked as if she actually touched the boy. The anchor had changed, but the comments were the same, and none of them favored Savannah. He tried another network.

CNN was no better, but MSNBC seemed to be, even if it was marginally. They at least referred to Savannah as a companion-bot, not a sexbot, and they showed her swiping at Billy from a different angle, making it clear she never touched him. The clock on the mantel said 4:08 a.m. He knew the fresh round of anchors would come on at six, but they had to come in earlier than that, didn't they? They had to do hair and makeup, and most likely had to go over the stories beforehand. They couldn't just do a broadcast cold, could they?

He went to his computer and logged into the MSNBC page, looked for the link to report breaking news and clicked on it. There were options to send an email or chat now, but those weren't the ones he wanted. He plugged the landline phone back into the wall and called the posted toll-free number. They answered in two rings.

CHAPTER 34

Katy Walker had begun her career in Cincinnati as a reporter, the pretty blonde the station sent to cover the human interest stuff. It didn't take long to see she was destined for more—she was the girl everyone wanted to date, the best friend's sister you had a secret crush on, but you couldn't ask out because of the guy code about friends' sisters. In six months, she was at the anchor desk in Cincy, then another six months until she changed to a larger market, and Dan figured he would never see her on the air again, and in a week forgot all about her, because such is life in the big city.

Then one morning as he was getting ready for work, he recognized her voice on the national broadcast, and it took him a little bit to place her. Then he remembered that ten years ago, she had been the little blonde girl who told everyone about all the new babies born at the Cincinnati Zoo, and the festivals happening each weekend around town. Now she sat at the desk of a national morning show, and he felt both proud and happy for her because it almost felt like she was family, even though he had never met her. When he made the call, he asked for her.

The voice on the other end was young and male. "I'm sorry, Ms. Walker isn't in yet. Is there something I can help you with?"

"This is Dan Mitchell, the owner of Savannah," he said. "I wish to speak to Ms. Walker."

"As I've said, Mr. Mitchell, Ms. Walker isn't in at the moment. Can I ask the nature of your call?"

"I want to do an interview, but I'll only do it with Katy Walker." Even though he had never met her, he felt as if he could trust her.

"Ms. Walker is a busy woman, Mr. Mitchell, as I'm sure you can imagine. How do we know you're who you say you are?"

"You have my phone number. Trace it. You'll see it's my home phone."

"Yes, sir. And can I jus—"

But Dan hung up before the boy could say anything else. He finished his coffee and went to make a second cup, then returned to his desk and waited for the phone to ring. It took less than ten minutes.

"Good morning, Mr. Mitchell. How's the weather in Cincy? I sure do miss it there." She sounded as if she were speaking to an old friend.

"Good morning, Ms. Walker. You know Spring in Cincinnati— if you don't like the weather, wait a minute."

She laughed, "That's what Twain said, and he was right. I understand you'd like to do an interview?"

"Ms. Walker, I would like the opportunity to clear up a few things," Dan said. "These news shows are so one-sided. They only show the bad things, but there are good things, too. Savannah was really only playing a joke. It's unfortunate that she scared the children, but up until then, they had a marvelous time with her, and only minutes before, she saved a boy from drowning."

"Yes, sir. We were planning on airing that footage this morning. And please, call me Katy. We're from the same neighborhood, after all."

If the statement about them airing the good footage was the truth or if it was something she was saying now to earn his trust, he would never know, but it did give him hope that he had contacted the right person. As for the same neighborhood, she had grown up in the more affluent section of Indian Hills, but she was still a Cincinnati native. That had to count for something. "I wish to do an interview, but I have a few caveats," he said. "First, I want you to stop showing that footage of her lunging toward that child. It looks as if she is trying to maul him."

"I know that footage. I can't promise to stop showing it, but I can promise to use one of the ones with a better angle and point out that she never touched the boy," she said. "What else?"

"I want you to show the footage of her saving the other boy's life more. Show the interaction with the children before she played the joke, too."

"We can do that," Walker said. "Anything else?"

"I want you to spend some time with her before the interview. At least an hour. You'll find she's really sweet."

"I wasn't planning on doing the interview personally," she said. "I was going to send one of the local affiliates."

"No," Dan said. "That's unacceptable. If it's not you, I won't do it."

The line was silent for a moment, then finally Walker said, "In that case, I have a few caveats of my own. First, I want your word that this will be an exclusive interview. You can't go to another station to tell your story."

"Agreed," Dan said. He hadn't planned on it anyway.

"That means no talk shows—nothing else until your case is settled in court."

"Agreed," Dan said again.

"And I get a second interview after the case is over. Win or lose, I sit down with you again and we discuss the trial. After that airs, if you're able, you can do all the talk shows you want."

"Agreed," Dan said. That one was easier than the first. If they lost, there would be no opportunities for another talk show—he would be in prison and Savannah destroyed. If they won, the last thing he wanted was to drag this fiasco out longer.

"All right then. I'm switching you over to my scheduling secretary. I'll see you this afternoon."

After a brief chat with another young man, Dan made plans to welcome Katy Walker and her crew to his home at 2 that afternoon.

CHAPTER 35

At 6:15 that morning, Katy Walker announced that she would have an exclusive interview with Dan and his companion Savannah for the evening broadcast, "You don't want to miss it." At 6:30, his computer made that special ring that announced an incoming Skype call. It was April Gatherwright.

Six-thirty Eastern meant it was 3:30 in California, but Dan didn't need to know that to recognize someone who had been recently awakened by bad news. Gatherwright's hair was a mess and she wore a silk pajama blouse and no makeup, and her voice, while already deep and sultry, had that cracking tone of some- one not used to talking in the morning.

"Good morning, April."

"Did I understand this correctly?" She stopped and cleared her throat. "You're doing an interview with Katy Walker?"

Dan wondered if skipping pleasantries was a California thing, an RWR thing, or just what the world was coming to. Of course, it could only be that it is the middle of the night there and she's not a morning person. "You did," he said. "I want to tell our side."

"Dan, the place to tell our side is in the courtroom," she said, "not on national television. What made you think this is a good idea?"

"You should see the way people treat us," he said. "It's as if we're diseased, and that was before this new footage. They're making Savannah out to be a monster, and it's not fair."

"Okay, here's what's going to happen," she said. "You're going to call them back and cancel this mess."

"I can't," Dan said. "I gave my word."

"Then you un-give it. Tell them that on advice from council, you have to decline."

"No," he said. "I trust this reporter. I think she will do right by us."

"Dan, trusting a reporter is like trusting a cobra to not bite you—or trusting a bomb to not go off. I'm telling you, cancel this thing." She ran her fingers through her long black hair, flipping it back from her face. "Nothing good can come from this—only bad."

"I disagree," he said. "She has agreed to show the good parts of Savannah—not just the bad. Anyone who has seen those videos and is on the jury will convict us for that footage alone."

"Anyone who has seen it will be disqualified from sitting on the jury," she said, but then she sighed. Dan didn't need for her to admit that was probably not possible. Who in the country hadn't seen the first footage, especially since it was national coverage happening right in Cincinnati? Every local person would follow it as closely as they had the OJ trial—probably closer, because Dan was a hometown boy. "Okay," she said. "What time is it?"

Dan looked at his watch. "It's 6:40 in the morning. That's 3:40 your time."

"Not what time is it now, you idiot. What time is the interview?" She sounded exasperated.

Dan felt like he'd been slapped. Who was she to call him such a thing? He almost hung up right then. "I don't appreciate being called an idiot," he said. "She and her crew are arriving at 2. I expect the interview to begin around 3."

"I'll be there by 1," she said. The screen went dead.

CHAPTER 36

He glanced at the clock when the doorbell rang. 12:45. If it was April Gatherwright, she was fifteen minutes early. He went to the door as Savannah still rattled around in the kitchen, making something for their guests, but he had no idea what. He had started to discuss it with her, so she would make a somewhat normal menu, but then decided against it. First of all, it bothered her when he suggested she make certain things or not make others, but also, he wanted the outside world to know she was still in the learning process for everything, in hopes that they might not be as judgmental. Her strange dishes had an endearing quality, to him at least.

He'd had a couple of video chats with April Gatherwright, going over details for the case, rehearsing his testimony as she guided him through what to expect at the trial, and while he knew she was attractive, he wasn't prepared for her to be as beautiful as she was, because no one looks the same in real life as they do on camera. Her smile was as businesslike as her outfit, but Dan got the feeling that both showed a hint of her sexuality the way an iceberg shows only the tip of its mass. Dan felt taken aback. He had worked with pretty women before, and had been forced to interact with them, and as a result, he'd found that his attraction toward them fluctuated according to how well the interactions went. Sheila was pretty. When Sheila seemed to be flirting with him, she became prettier. But when it became clear that she wasn't attracted to him and in fact seemed to be mocking him, she was no longer pretty in Dan's eyes. As far as truly beautiful women, Dan hadn't met all that many. He'd glanced a few at the mall, or perhaps while out to dinner, but a beautiful woman is a rare thing. Savannah was the first he had ever really talked to at any length, but talking to her had been easy, perhaps because she'd had no face or hair when they first met. He remembered finding her almost frightening looking and it was only after they began to chat that she'd put her face and hair on and he'd found her beautiful.

But April Gatherwright was different. Their interactions had been purely business, not swaying him one way or the other, so when he saw her, tall and lean, her sexuality almost but not entirely hidden behind the business suit, he found himself stammering. He'd heard of people being photogenic. He'd gone to school with such a girl. In the hallways, she was rather plain, but in her senior pictures, she had been exquisite. April Gatherwright was the opposite of that. In the video, she was certainly pretty, but standing on his front porch, she stole his breath. "Dan?" she asked, her smile pleasant.

"Y-yes?"

"April Gatherwright," she said, holding out one hand to shake his. He took it, almost absent minded, and it was only when her grip tightened, firm and reassuring, that he reciprocated.

"Of course," he said, still shaking her hand. "It's nice to finally meet in person." She released the grip before he did, but it didn't serve to snap him back to reality. He just stood in the doorway, staring at her.

"Can I come in?"

That did it. Now he felt like an idiot for not inviting her and wondered where his mind had gone. "Of course," he said, stepping to one side to allow her entry. He shook his head at his own lack of courtesy, quick and subtle, as if he'd shivered. She stepped past him as he leaned forward to hold the screen door open for her.

"Hold that," someone called from the walkway. "Hold that door." Ian Palance came into view, one hand up as the other steadied the book bag at his side. He looked like someone doing a quick walk to catch an airplane that had called final boarding. He grinned wide as he stepped onto the porch, and he brought the hand that had been waving down in a large gesture, turning it into an overblown handshake. "Hi Dan. Ian Palance. Nice to meet you."

"Hello, Ian," Dan said as they shook. He had no problems remembering how to shake hands this time. "It's nice to meet you as well. I wasn't expecting you." Dan had no problem with Ian coming, but it would have been nice if they had phoned ahead to let him know. He wondered when common courtesy had died and why no one had announced the funeral.

"I thought I'd tag along, get to know you and Miss Savannah. Hope it's not a problem." He stepped inside as though he'd been invited, took the book bag from his shoulder and looked around. "Nice place you have here. Retro."

That was the second time someone had called his house "retro," but Dan knew what they really meant was, "outdated." He saw no reason to buy new furniture since his mother had passed. Why would he? This was perfectly adequate. A touch worn, perhaps, but still functional.

"Savannah?" he called, and a pot rattled in the kitchen in reply. "Come say hello."

"Forty-seven seconds," she said. It was something she had acquired along the way. Rather than say "One second," or "One minute," the way most people did, she called the exact amount of time she estimated it would take her to complete whatever task she was doing, but she used the same colloquial tone. Dan knew that if he timed her, she would be spot-on.

"We come bearing good news," Ian said. "We flew out early and—" Gatherwright cleared her throat, cutting Palance off. "Yeah, you should tell him," he said. "You did all the work."

"Thank you, Ian," she said. "We were able to meet with a judge this morning, and you are no longer on house arrest. There was a cash bond, posted by Ian—well by RWR to be specific, and you can take this paperwork to the Sheriff's Office and have them remove that ankle monitor."

"Really?" Dan said. He could hardly believe it. "Thank you.

Thank you so much." He shook Ian's hand fast and furious. This was amazing news.

Gatherwright nodded, adding a small bow as he shook her hand, too. "The judge was sympathetic to the situation. She had seen the videos and agreed it wasn't merited. You're not a threat to the children in the area as long as you instruct Savannah to never do it again, and since I'm assuming you have or at least will, she has no problems with a simple bond."

"That is fantastic news," Dan said. "Just fantastic." He couldn't wait to get this thing off of his ankle.

Savannah came in wearing her black wig as opposed to the blonde Dan was used to, and she had somehow darkened her complexion to match it, although Dan had no idea when or how. She had also changed faces, and it was only then that Dan realized that April Gatherwright must have been the model for this look. Even though Savannah was a full four inches shorter, they could have been twins, if one of them wasn't a robot of course. "Hi," she said, bright and cheery, her voice the only thing that hadn't changed.

"Oh," Ian said as he stepped toward her and shook her hand. "I was expecting the Briana. Nice to meet, you, Savannah."

"Nice to meet you as well, Ian," Savannah said. She offered her hand to Gatherwright, but the lady didn't take it.

"Ian?" Gatherwright said, confused. She took a step back, as if the sight of Savannah scared her. "Why does she look like me?"

"What do you mean?" Palance asked. "She just has black hair. Lots of people have black hair."

"No," Gatherwright said. "It's not just the hair. She looks exactly like me."

"You're being silly. She looks like Savannah. You're tall. She's short. You look nothing alike."

Dan disagreed. She didn't look like Savannah at all. Short or not, she looked like April Gatherwright.

"Ian Palance, you tell me what's going on, or I swear I'm on the next plane to California and you can find a new attorney."

Palance sighed as if he gave up. "You signed a waiver, April.

Everyone signs a waiver."

"I signed a release for photos and videos—it's for promotional use, not to be a model for some sex toy."

"Can we discuss this later?" Palance asked.

"No, I think we need to discuss it right now. What the hell were you thinking? I can sue you for this."

"The waiver says we can use your photos any way the company sees fit. You know that. You wrote the damned thing, and if you sue us over it, you're going to look like an idiot. You're not my only attorney, April."

Gatherwright's nostrils flared and Dan had to wonder how good a lawyer she was if she didn't see this coming, but then, she had proven herself earlier with the whole house arrest thing.

"If it helps, I like this look," Dan said, trying to offer a compliment.

"No, it doesn't help," Gatherwright said. "It's a violation. It's like some weird form of rape."

"No one was raped," Palance said. "It's not a violation. If you want, we can discuss a modeling fee."

"I don't want a damned modeling fee," she yelled at him. "I want to not be used as a sex toy."

"Will you stop saying sex toys?" Palance said, beginning to sound irritated. "You're making too much out of this. It's flattering. It's a compliment."

"Too much? Too much? How would you like it if I sent a replica of you out to every female nerd who wanted one? Or every gay one?"

Palance's jaw muscle clenched. "Our clients are not nerds," he said through clenched teeth, enunciating each syllable. "They are pioneers. They are men and women who are not tied to societal norms. They are brave people." His words were veiled, threat-filled daggers.

"They are Comicon rejects," Gatherwright said. "I'd bet anything this one has a set of Spock ears. He already has the haircut."

"Hey," Dan said. He would have felt more offended, if he didn't have a set of Spock ears. In fact, he had the full Spock uniform.

"Well, I'm sorry, but you need to see a stylist before you go to trial," Gatherwright said.

"It's called the uncanny valley," Palance said to Dan. "When people tend to see a companion who looks too human, they withdraw from them. April has never seen herself as a companion, so it's worse for her."

"Don't try to write this off with psychobabble," Gatherwright said. "It stops now, or I quit."

"If you quit, I'll sue you for breach of contract. You'll be disbarred. I'll see to it." So much for the veil. He crossed his arms as though he'd already won.

"I'll take my chances with the bar," she said. She headed for the door. When her hand touched the knob, she stopped and looked back. "What's it going to be, Ian?"

"Fine," he said, as if the entire thing was ridiculous, throwing his hands up in surrender. "We'll stop selling them."

"And I want a recall of every one you've sold. Every single one," she said. She pointed at Savannah/April as she said it, jabbing her finger with each word.

"Well, I'm not going to recall the hair," Palance said. "Lots of people have black hair. But I will recall the faces. We'll say there's a defect."

Gatherwright stood there for a second, as if she were waiting for something, but Dan didn't know what. Dan saw her jaw muscles clench, relax. Clench, relax. "Fine," she said. "But we're no longer dating."

"Aww, honey, don't be like that," Palance said. "It was a compliment." He no longer sounded like an angry boss but a petulant boyfriend.

She held up her hand to dismiss him, the same gesture Savannah had used on Dan the day before.

"Maybe it will help if you changed back to the Briana," Palance said to Savannah. He opened his book bag and took out a new face and hair that matched Savannah's normal look. "I took the liberty, after seeing you'd lost yours on the video."

"Oh, thank you, Ian," Savannah said as she took them from him.

Palance caught her wrist and turned her hand over. The scars from her shredded palms looked stark from where the defibrillator probes had pushed their way through. He ran his finger over the one on her forearm. "We can send you some new arms," he said. "Get rid of those nasty scars."

"Oh no," Savannah said. "Those aren't scars. They are my remembers."

"Remembers?" Palance asked.

Even Dan looked confused. She had used the term so early in their relationship, he'd assumed it came from RWR, but Palance seemed surprised by it. Dan considered explaining for her, but decided to allow her to do it. She did, sounding like a small child who was proud of her battle wounds, pointing to each one and telling where it came from, starting with the tiny one on her back. When she got to her palms, she said, "These are from the boy who drowned. Dan says I saved his life."

Palance smiled at her like a father. "You did save his life. I saw the video. We were all so proud of you."

She smiled and Palance released her arm. She removed her hair and face in front of everyone, and Dan realized he hadn't seen the full-on plastic skull since the day she'd arrived. He had seen her without hair often, and without a face a few times, but never both. In that same vein of different interactions making someone more or less attractive, he realized that it no longer bothered him at all to see her like this. She put the face on first, then the hair, bending at the waist to fit it, then standing straight up, flipping the hair back as she went, and in a blink, her skin tone changed with it. "Better?" she asked. The hair was long and blonde, and tousled.

"Better for me at least," Gatherwright said. She snatched the discarded hair and face off the coffee table and stuffed them in her jacket pocket, but the hair didn't fit, and the ends flapped out like a tail.

"April?" Palance asked, as if he were speaking to a child.

"Don't you think you owe Dan an apology?"

She glared at Palance, but Dan didn't know if it was for the suggestion that she do it, or the tone he used, or that she was still in angry-girlfriend mode. The silence in the room felt heavy. "I'm sorry I called you a nerd—and said that thing about the Spock ears." She swirled her finger toward the side of her own head, as if to indicate where ears were located.

Dan had heard insults all his life, some whispered, others yelled, and on the hurtful scale, this one didn't even register. He had no problems with his Spock ears, and he didn't understand why other people did. "No worries," he said.

"Now that we're all friends again, give me 27 seconds," Savannah said, then retreated to the kitchen.

Dan offered everyone seats and Gatherwright opened her briefcase. She pulled out some handwritten notes. "Dan, I want to go over this interview with you," she said as she closed her attaché and set it on the floor.

Savannah returned with a serving tray and set it on the coffee table. She had used his mother's good china. They were the finest dishes in the house. There were three cups with saucers, a coffee pot and assorted pastries on a three-tiered china platter that still had steam rising from them. Twenty-seven seconds had passed. She poured a cup and offered it to Ian. "I wasn't sure how you take it," she said, sliding the creamer and sugar toward him. She poured a second cup and offered it to Gatherwright, then a third for Dan. "Dan takes his black."

"Not me," Palance said, leaning forward. He began shoveling sugar into the cup, not bothering to stir. "I like it sweet." He continued putting more in, and Dan kept a mental count because he'd never seen anyone use so much. After nine teaspoons, he stirred it, took a sip then added three more.

Dan knew the sugar had stopped dissolving in the coffee long before. By now, the additional spoonfuls had to be psychological. They also had to be forming a disgusting sludge at the bottom of the cup. "I believe that's an understatement," he said.

Ian laughed as if he'd heard it many times before. "That's just the way I drink it," he said. He took one of the pastries off the bottom tier and put it on the china plate in front of him.

"Now, Dan," Gatherwright said, "about this interview..."

"Calm down, April," Palance said. "I'm sure Dan will do fine." He tried the pastry, a peach with brown sugar turnover with a vanilla icing that had fresh cinnamon and nutmeg grated over it. "Oh my God. These are fantastic." He held it out to Gatherwright at mouth level. "You have to try these."

"No thank you, Ian," she said, pushing his hand away. "I would like to go over the interview. It's why we came here." She still sounded angry, and Dan didn't think a pastry was going to buy Palance into her good graces.

"They're like crispy and sweet, but they have a tanginess to them. Incredible. Where did you get them?" He took another bite even though he hadn't swallowed the first one. "Do I taste lemon?"

"I made them," Savannah said. "And yes, you do."

"Really?" He sounded astonished. "We just released the Master Baker upgrade a couple days ago. You must have been practicing non-stop." He popped the last bite into his mouth and chased it with a sip of coffee. "April, you have got to try these." He took a small wedge of coffee cake from the middle tier and tried it. "If I lived here, I would get so fat," he said, spewing a few crumbs as he talked.

"We haven't upgraded baker yet," Dan said. "I didn't know there was an option."

Palance took another sip to wash the coffee cake from his mouth before he spoke. "Really? This is from a base setting?" He sounded and looked puzzled.

"Well, she's at chef level for American cuisine," Dan said. "Gourmet chef for Italian and French. Those are her only upgrades though. She watches a lot of cooking shows."

Palance ignored the rest of the coffee cake, but took a cookie off the top tier. He broke it in half without tasting it and handed one half to Gatherwright. "That's odd," he said. "You're sure you didn't upgrade?" He tried the cookie and rolled his eyes and gave a single clap to show how good he found it, then opened his book bag again and dug out a laptop.

"Of course," Dan said as Palance's computer came on. He offered the Wi-Fi password before Palance had to ask.

Palance clicked the touchpad a few times, then said, "Yep. There she is." He turned the screen toward Gatherwright who was busy chewing her half of the cookie. "Baking, level one."

"Is there a problem?" Dan asked as he took one of the peach turnovers for himself. Savannah had been making these for a couple of weeks now, and the same for the coffee cake, long before there was an upgrade for baking.

Palance shrugged. "Probably just a glitch or something. Cooking and baking are considered two different skills." He dunked the last of the cookie into his coffee. "Savannah, honey, where did you get these recipes?"

"I made them up," she said. "Would you like me to write them down for you?"

Dan saw Palance and Gatherwright exchange glances over the top of his computer. "I would love that," Palance said.

The printer kicked on a second later and thee pages came out. Savannah retrieved them and handed them to Palance. "Enjoy," she said.

"Thank you," Palance said as he took them from her. He began reading as if he was studying them. "I'm sure I will. And you say you didn't get these from someplace? Maybe one of the cooking shows, perhaps?"

Dan looked over his shoulder and read them as well. They looked like typical recipes to him, and he wasn't sure what Palance might be looking for.

"I'm sure," Savannah said. "They just seemed like they would taste good."

"Sweetie, they belong in a five-star restaurant, trust me," Palance said. He took another turnover and bit into it. "Or maybe Heaven," he said. He offered it to Gatherwright again, but this time she accepted and tried it. Once she swallowed, she asked for copies of the recipes, too.

"Okay, back to the interview," Gatherwright said, but this time she was cut off by the ring of the doorbell.

CHAPTER 37

Katy Walker was one of those people who looked better on camera than off, not that she looked bad at all. Perhaps it was the stress of her job finally catching up to her, but she seemed much older in person than she did on television, at least to Dan. "Hi," she said when he opened the door. "You must be Dan." She smiled and ten years melted away.

She'd said she would bring a crew, but Dan had assumed that meant a camera guy—maybe a sound guy, too, but it was like a small army had come with her. There were two camera guys, a girl for sound, one for lights, another girl for makeup, one who seemed to be in charge of everyone else, and two more guys that he had no idea what their function was. Counting Palance and Gatherwright, that made eleven people in his living room, and that was ten more than he was normally comfortable with. The introvert in him wanted to go and hide. They filed in one at a time behind Walker and began setting things up without asking.

"You're Ian Palance," Walker said, leaning over the coffee table to shake hands. Ian went to a half-stand as they shook, then resumed his seat and took another cookie, as if he was worried there might not be enough for everyone and he wanted one more before they were gone. How did the guy not weigh 300 pounds? "And let me guess. You're Ian Palance's attorney."

"And Dan's attorney, too," Gatherwright said as they shook. Dan felt a chill in the air despite the additional body heat of so many people. "You should know I'm against this interview."

Walker shrugged as if it didn't bother her. "Attorneys always are. Don't worry, I won't incriminate him."

"I'm more worried you will make him incriminate himself, even though he's done nothing wrong," Gatherwright said. "I've agreed to this because Dan insisted, but you should know that if I don't like where it's headed, I will shut it down."

"I understand," Walker said. "And you're Savannah," she said as she turned away from Gatherwright, dismissing the threat in a manner so casual, it seemed routine. "Wow, you look so real."

"So do you," Savannah said.

Walker laughed as if she had expected the reply. Dan thought she must have watched the videos with the children at Serpent Mound, when the little girl had said the same thing.

"Not a word of the pending litigation," Gatherwright said to Walker's back.

"Yeah, I get it. You're not my first lawyer." Walker didn't look away from Savannah as she spoke, nor did her smile break, but her tone was icy.

"And you're not my first reporter," Gatherwright said.

"Can I get anyone something to drink?" Savannah asked. "Miss Walker, would you like some coffee?"

"Coffee would be wonderful," Walker said. "And please, call me Katy." When Savannah turned to go, Walker said, "Maybe I should give you a hand," and began to follow her to the kitchen.

Dan, Palance, and Gatherwright exchanged glances, but nobody spoke for a few seconds. Finally Dan said, "Maybe I should go with them." Gatherwright followed him without saying anything.

"So how long have you and Dan been together?" Walker asked as Dan entered the kitchen.

"Six weeks, four days, 23 hours and twelve minutes," Savannah said.

"And how do you feel about the trial? Are you worried? Can you feel worry?"

"I told you, nothing about the trial," Gatherwright said.

Walker shrugged, looking innocent. "There are no cameras in here. This is just a conversation, councilor. It's not an interview."

"Bullshit," Gatherwright said. "Don't answer her, Savannah.

Not one word."

Savannah looked confused. Dan realized she had never been given conflicting orders before, or even conflicting requests, and she didn't know who to listen to. He stepped forward and took her hand. "It's okay, sweetness. Let's just make the coffee."

"Okies," she said, but her tone wasn't the normal self-confident one he was used to.

"It's okay," he said as he opened the top of the brewer and put in a fresh pod. "If you feel confused, just ask me." He closed the top and hit the button and the brewer began the noise of pumping water.

She looked into his eyes, then over his shoulder at the two women behind him, then back to him. "They don't like each other," she whispered.

"Well, they have different jobs," he said. "Katy wants to ask us questions, but April is worried she will ask a bad one and we'll get into trouble."

Again, her glance went over his shoulder for a split second, then returned. "They don't like us, either. April didn't like me when we first met, but she seems better now that I took off her face. I thought she would like it if I wore her face. I did it to be nice. Katy doesn't like me at all, like those people at the mound."

Dan hadn't read anything in Katy Walker to indicate dislike. He had found the woman nothing but pleasant. Was it possible that Savannah was more astute at reading people than he was? Could she see behind someone's mask, even a professional one like a reporters? It was plausible. She had certainly pegged April Gatherwright cold. "I think she'll start to like you when she gets to know you," he said. He ran his hand down her arm as the brewer finished, gurgling the final bubbles, then the "pish" of released steam.

"I hope so," she said. She put the cup on a saucer and stepped around him, her smile bright. "Here you go," she said to Walker as she handed it to her. "Careful. It's hot."

CHAPTER 38

Dan, Savannah, and Ian Palance sat on the couch in that order while Katy Walker sat in the chair, half-facing them, closest to Dan. Palance had tried to sit beside Katy, but at her producer's suggestion, he was moved to the opposite end. He hadn't seemed happy about it. Over Katy's shoulder, Dan saw the monitor of the raw feed, split into two screens, one for each camera. They each wore a clip-on microphone and after the sound check and the applying of the last-minute makeup fixes, Katy declared them ready. She started:

"Cyber Companions, or Sexbots, have been around for a decade, but until now, they haven't been—" She stopped. "Let's try that again."

"Quiet, people," the producer said.

Katy took a deep breath, smiled and started again. "Cyber Companions, or Sexbots, have been around for a decade, but until now, they haven't had the ability to walk among us, or, for those that did, it was easy enough to tell robot from human. But these latest models are different. As we become more desensitized, as The Uncanny Valley grows a little narrower with each passing year, robots become more realistic looking, until finally, we have this." The monitor went to a close-up of Savannah and she smiled for the camera. Once again, Dan couldn't believe how beautiful she was. "And I have to tell you, even from a foot away, I couldn't tell the difference. We're talking with Dan Mitchell and Savannah, the couple who have been in all the news, and Savannah's creator, Ian Palance, President of Real World Robotics." She put a hand on Dan's arm, touching him lightly with her fingertips as if they were old friends. "How long have you owned Savannah?"

Dan said, "I don't like the term owned. She's my companion and I paid for her, but I don't see myself as owning her at all. I prefer to believe that I paid for the privilege of her company."

"Couldn't the same be said for anyone who hires an escort?" Katy asked. "A prostitute?"

Palance interjected, "The same could be said for anyone who buys a puppy, or even a fast car. You pay for the privilege of having that thing in your life. Or what about those women on television who refuse to get married unless they have an expensive wedding? The grooms are paying for the privilege of having that woman in their lives." He waved his hand as if to dismiss the question as dumb.

"But those women are free to walk away from the marriage, even if it's only minutes after the ceremony. Savannah, are you free to walk away from Dan?"

"I would never leave Dan," Savannah said. She took his hand in hers, and he felt her squeeze a little too tight. "He's the nicest, sweetest man in the world."

"But that's not real emotion," Katy said. "You've been programmed to say that."

"No, she hasn't," Palance said. "Cyber companions are predisposed to feel an attraction toward their mate, but it's not a mortal lock, any more than if your best friend set you up with," he put his fingers up, using air quotes, "'the perfect guy,' and you weren't attracted to him."

"So you're trying to tell me that they have free will?" Katy asked. "That if Savannah didn't like Dan, she could just walk away? Where would she go?"

"I'm not going to walk away from Dan," Savannah insisted. She squeezed tighter still and Dan's fingers went from uncomfortable to painful. "Not ever."

"Relax, sweetie," Dan said, hoping she would lessen her grip. "No one is saying you will, but you're about to break my fingers." Instead, she put her other hand on his, as if she worried he was the one who might leave, or that someone was going to try and take her away.

"Yes, to a degree, she has free will," Palance said. "If it turns out we can't make a good match through the personality settings—there are twenty personality settings—either the companion or the owner is free to contact us, and we will do our best to rectify it."

Gatherwright made a slashing move with her hand across her throat.

"Not the owner," he said, correcting himself. "Custodian."

"You just said it yourself," Katy said as if she had scored a point in some imaginary chess match. "Owner. Dan is the owner of Savannah."

"I misspoke," Palance said. "I meant custodian."

"Moving on," Katy said, as if Palance wasn't still speaking. "Savannah, would you say you love Dan?"

"I do," Savannah said. "I love Dan with all my—" she stopped for the briefest pause, "With everything I have." She squeezed his hand again, but this time it didn't hurt.

"But Dan, surely you can't say you love this thing can you?"

"Of course I do," Dan said, feeling as defensive as Savannah. "I love her very much." It was the first time he had said it, but he'd known it for a long time.

"But you love her in the way I love my cell phone, or a Reuben sandwich, right? It's just not the same thing as loving a person—a spouse or significant other."

Dan stood. "I'll show you just how much I love her." He began to walk out of the living room and he heard Gatherwright speak:

"Okay, the interview is over."

He spun back, angry. "No it's not. Keep those fucking cameras rolling." He felt his heart pounding—he had never used that word in his life. He went through the kitchen then down the hall to his mother's bedroom, and the door had been closed for so long, it made an actual cracking noise because the paint on the frame and door had bonded after six years of being stuck together. The door didn't want to open. He put his shoulder into it but it didn't budge.

He knew exactly what he wanted. He had put it there an hour after his mother's casket had been lowered into the ground and he'd tossed that handful of dirt (he'd worn gloves in expectation of this, despite the August heat) atop the polished wooden box —The Ambassador, they called it—solid mahogany with brass fixtures—it was expensive and nice and came with a three year warranty, for whatever that meant. Dan certainly had no plans of digging his mother's coffin up in three years to see how well it fared.

It had just been the seven of them—his grandparents, the priest, the funeral director and his assistant, and some old lady dressed in black whom the funeral director said came to every funeral whether she knew the deceased or not. The director had shaken Dan's hand, pressing an envelope into it. "I thought you'd want this," he said. "We left the rosary with her, but I thought you might want this." Dan didn't have to open the envelope to know what was inside—he could tell by the feel. The old lady tossed a handful of dirt in as well, then shook Dan's hand and told him the service had been lovely. He thanked her for coming because it seemed like the appropriate thing to do, but couldn't stop thinking that he needed to wash his hands now because the woman had touched dirt. His grandparents' brake lights flashed as his grandmother started their black Volvo while Dan shook the woman's hand. He had never felt so alone in his life.

These thoughts flashed through his mind in the few seconds it took him finally to free the door, stepping back and ramming his shoulder into it with all the force he could muster. It gave with the splintering crack of breaking wood. He opened the top of the box, took out what he had come for, and went back to the living room, stood in front of Savannah then dropped to one knee. He held out the engagement ring his mother had worn every day of her adult life, long after she removed her wedding ring. He looked into her eyes and said, "Savannah, will you marry me?"

The entire room was quiet, as if everyone was too stunned to move. Savannah's eyes went wider than he had ever seen, and a tear rolled down her cheek. "Of course I will," she said and held her hand out, palm up, as if she expected him to hand it to her. He smiled and turned her hand over and slipped the ring on her finger. It took a couple of seconds. Both of them were trembling.

"Well," Katy said, sitting back in her chair. "There you have it, folks." She sounded as if she didn't believe it.

"Now the interview is over," Dan said. He pulled Savannah to him and they hugged. "Get your cameras out of our home."

CHAPTER 39

"What can I help you with today?" the clerk asked as he took his seat at terminal fourteen. He wiped his mouth with a napkin then sipped from a carry-out cup from Gold Star Chili and wiped his mouth again, discarding the napkin in a can under his desk. His smile was big, but it was the smile of someone bored with his job, and Dan didn't blame him. Being a clerk at the Clerk of Courts didn't seem like an interesting job. Car tags—driver's licenses—property taxes—wedding licenses—Dan might have missed a few, but the list of services they provided was short, or at least finite. Some people spoke of how much they loved their job because there was always something new. He didn't see that happening in a job like this. Dan doubted if anything new ever happened here, and hence the man's boredom.

The line at the Butler County Clerk of Courts was long, and while they had at least thirty people helping customers, there were more than twenty times that waiting for their number to be called. Dan hadn't expected that because he normally did his business with the courts online. The renewing of car tags and driver's licenses was available there, as was paying taxes on the house. This was the first time he had been here since the day he turned 21 and had to get a new picture for his license. "We would like a marriage license, please."

"Of course," the man said. He was smaller than Savannah, and he had a ring of short-cropped hair, but he wore a bushy moustache to compensate. Dan wondered why men like that didn't just go ahead and shave it all. What were they holding on to? "I'll need to see your drivers' licenses." There was no sign of recognition and Dan was glad of that. Some people in the waiting area had recognized them, nudging one another and nodding, most with disapproval.

"Of course," Dan said, as he reached for his wallet and handed the license to the clerk. The man looked at it, looked at Dan, then back at the license. "You know, we can upgrade this photo for you," he said. "It's supposed to be updated every ten years. You must have slipped through the cracks. There's a twelve-dollar charge."

"Why not?" Dan said as he did the mental math. If a license was good for four years, but the photo was to be updated every ten, something didn't work out. The photo should be updated every twelve years, or eight years—or a license should be good for five. When he pointed that out to the clerk, the man smiled and said:

"Welcome to the bureaucracy. Let's do this driver's license first." He typed some information into his computer terminal and asked routine questions and from his tone, he had asked them few thousand times before. He rattled them off with a rehearsed quickness, asking if the address was the same, if Dan had any outstanding violations, then told Dan to put his chin against the head rest and read the third line. He offered Dan a tissue to put between his face and the eye test machine, for which Dan was grateful. God knew who else had been through here, or what sort of diseases they might have carried on their foreheads. Dan rattled the letters off easily enough, the same ones for each eye, which he also found dumb. What if he could only see well out of one eye, but wanted to cheat the system? He could memorize the string of letters and just recite them for the bad eye. How did no one notice this?

"If you'll just step this way, Mr. Mitchell," the clerk said. He had Dan stand in front of a beige backdrop and told him to smile if he wanted. Dan did, because he was happy. "That's a good one," the clerk said, without showing it to Dan. He went back to his station and logged in again. "Now I'll need your Social Security Number for the wedding license."

Dan rattled it off as fast as the clerk had the questions. The man typed it in then transferred the rest of Dan's information from the other screen. "And now you, miss. What's your name?"

"Savannah," she said.

He typed it in. "Last name?"

"I don't have one," she said.

"Like Cher or Madonna?" he smiled, showing he got the joke, but he'd heard it before. "Seriously—what's your last name?"

"Mitchell," Dan said. "Just put Mitchell. That's what it will be after the ceremony."

"It doesn't work like that," the clerk said. "She can change her name, no problem, but I have to have her maiden name first."

"Mitchell," Savannah said.

The clerk sat back and took his hands from the keyboard. "You two aren't related, are you?" He no longer sounded bored with his job. "You can't get married unless you're at least second cousins. Did you drive over from Adams County?"

Northern Adams County was where Serpent Mound was located, but there were rumors of strange goings on in the southeastern section that Dan had heard as a teenager. "Yes we did," Savannah said. "Two days ago."

"That's not what he means," Dan said. "No, we reside in Butler County and we're not related. Her address is the same as mine, but she has no last name is all."

"Who doesn't have a last name?" the man asked, but it felt rhetorical. He typed in the same information as he had before. "Okay then. I'll just need to see your driver's license."

"She doesn't have one," Dan said. "She doesn't drive."

Savannah nodded to show it was true.

"Fine—a birth certificate then."

"I don't have one of those either," she said.

"Well, I need some form of ID," the clerk said. "Military ID, passport—something. We need to know who you are."

"I'm Savannah," she said, over-enunciating, as if he might be slow.

"Yes, I get that, but how do I know you're Savannah?"

"I just told you," she said, saying it slow and deliberate—one word at a time.

"But we need proof that you're Savannah." He did the same back to her, as if she were the slow one. "A piece of paper to let us know where you come from."

"Oh," she said. "Why didn't you say that to begin with?" The printer beside his terminal kicked on and spit out a three-page document.

He jumped, looking from the printer to her, the printer to her. "What? How? What?"

"I saw you type your login and password," she said. "You should be more careful. That's not secure." She beamed at Dan to show she had learned that from him. He smiled back.

"But how? What? How?"

"Excellent questions all," Dan said. "And you really should be more careful. Computer security is no joke." He hadn't had the opportunity to instruct anyone in security for over a month and he found he missed it.

The clerk rolled his chair back, as if he were trying to get away from them before they made whatever move they would use to kill him. He had both hands on the armrests of his chair, ready to bolt for safety. It was a few seconds before he spoke again. "How did you make them print? And what are they?"

"They are proof of where I came from, as you requested," Savannah said. "And I used your complimentary Wi-Fi connection, with your login to access your printer."

"You mean like, with your phone? That's against the law."

She held her hand up to show they were empty. "I have no phone," she said.

He looked confused for another second, then his face relaxed, as if it all made sense. "Who put you up to this? Was it Morris?" He smiled and stood and looked over his cubicle. "I'll get you for this, Morris. This was a good one, but I'll get you back." He laughed, but it sounded forced. He sat back down, but still called to the ceiling, "Paybacks are heck my friend. Paybacks are heck." He took the documents from the printer and began reading them. He laughed. "Oh, this is priceless—a date of manufacture? This is good stuff, Morris. Good stuff." He shook his head, then faced them. "So, do you really want a marriage license, or was that part of the gag?"

"We really want a marriage license," Savannah said, cutting Dan off. She reached over and took Dan's hand and smiled. "We love each other."

"That's nice," the clerk said.

A heavy set man with a protruding belly that made him look so pregnant Dan expected his water to break any minute stepped behind the cubicle, dunking a donut into a cup of coffee. He lifted it, letting it drip back into his cup before he took a bite, turning his head sideways to meet the donut half-way. "What are you hollering about, Scoot?" he asked around a mouthful of soggy donut.

"I know this was you," Scoot said. "And stop calling me 'Scoot.' You know I hate that."

"Whatever you say, Scoot," Morris said, then wandered off.

Scoot shook his head. "That Morris—such a prankster. But we have fun here. It's fun." He didn't sound like he found it fun at all, though. "So—I'll need your driver's license," he said to Savannah once again.

Savannah, who normally had an extraordinary amount of patience, explained it again, going even slower this time. "I told you. I do not have one. I have that." She pointed to the documents now on his desk.

He echoed her tone. "And I told you. No ID, no marriage license."

She looked at Dan with frustration. Dan shrugged. "Show him."

She shrugged back, then took off her hair, and for good measure, her face, too.

Scoot rolled backwards again, but this time much faster. The back of his chair went off the plastic floor protector and into the rug, the momentum causing it to tip over, sending him and the chair ass-over-teakettle. Morris appeared with a fresh donut, laughing down at him. "What the hell was that, Scoot?"

Scoot, still in the chair but now flat on his back, only looked up and pointed between his splayed knees at Savannah. Morris looked so surprised he almost dropped his donut. "Well, I'll be a sumbitch," he said. "I saw you all on the news. You're one of them hump-bots, ain'tcha?" He put his donut holding hand in the air like a cowboy riding a steer and gyrated his hips in a large circle. Scoot climbed out of his chair and righted it.

"She's a companion," Dan said. "And I would like to speak to your supervisor."

"Morris is the supervisor," Scoot said as he rolled his chair back into position. He didn't sound as if he approved of Morris's appointment. He sat back down.

"Then I'll speak to the Clerk of Courts," Dan said, showing he wouldn't be beaten.

Morris chuckled. "He's my brother-in-law. Tell him I said, 'Hey.'" He dunked his donut again and strolled off.

"That's right," Scoot said, staring down at his desk. "You work at a place for fifteen years—get nothing but good reviews and you think maybe you'll get promoted one day, and then the Republicans win one stupid election—" He grew a little louder as he spoke, his fists clenched, but never got quite loud enough for his voice to carry all the way to Morris.

"Look, Scoot," Savannah said as she put her hair back in place.

"Don't call me that!" Scoot barked at her. "My name is Scott—not Scoot—not Scooter—not Scooter-pooper—just Scott —okay?" He seemed like a bomb about to explode.

She held her hands up in surrender. "Okay—Scott—I got it. Calm down, dude."

"Yeah, calm down, dude," Dan said, parroting her.

"Don't tell me to calm down," Scott said, this time loud enough for his voice to carry across half the building. "I hate that name. I hate it." He shook in frustration.

Morris strolled back with half of a donut. "You okay, Scoot?"

Scott put his head on his desk and Dan heard him taking deep breaths, holding them, then their slow release. After a few of those he said, "I'm fine, Morris. Just leave me alone, please," without raising up.

"Well, let's get at it then," Morris said. "Got lots of people waiting." He dunked again as he strolled away. "Gotta keep those lines moving, people," he said, getting louder as he went. "Chop-chop, very fast, bang-bang."

Scott didn't rise until he took a few more breaths. Once he sat upright, he spoke to Dan. "Look, I can't help you. You can't marry a robot."

"Why not?" Dan asked.

"You just can't, okay? It's against the law."

"Show me the law," Dan said. "I want to see the law that says I can't marry a robot." He folded his arms across his chest to show he refused to budge until he saw that law.

"Of course you do," Scott said. He pulled out a pamphlet that read, "Everything You Need to Know about Getting Married in Ohio," and opened it. He began scanning it with his finger. When he reached the end, he started over. This time he went slower, still using his finger, but he was reading every word. When he reached the end he said, "It's not in here, but you still can't marry a robot."

"Why not?" Dan asked.

"Because you just can't, okay? We don't always get what we want, Mr. Mitchell. I can't get a promotion—I can't even get a transfer—you can't marry a robot. That's life. That's the way it is. Welcome to the bureaucracy." He held his arms wide, as if he was actually welcoming Dan. Even though he had used that line earlier, it sounded angrier this time than it had the first.

"I refuse to accept that," Dan said. "I want to speak to your supervisor."

"You met my supervisor," Scott said. "You saw him. He's an idiot. He's a donut-munching moron. What good do you think he's going to do you? The guy was skinny when he started here two years ago. Skinny—does he look skinny now? No. Because all he does is walk around eating donuts all day." Scott sounded about to blow again.

"Nonetheless, I would like to speak with him," Dan said.

"Fine," Scott said, slamming both hands down on his desk as he stood. "You want to speak to the moron? Speak to the moron." He was shouting now. He turned to the back of the room. "Hey Morris. The guy with the hump-bot would like to speak with you. I'm going on break." He stormed off.

Morris came to the cubicle and took Scott's seat with a chuckle. "That Scoot—boy, he is really wound tight," he said. He took a sip of his coffee, then placed his hands on the desk, and folded them, as if he were discussing selling them a whole life policy. "How can I help you?"

"We would like a marriage license," Dan said.

Morris looked at Savannah. "How about you, honey? You want to marry this guy?"

"I do," Savannah said, sitting up straighter in a show of enthusiasm.

"Really? Did you take a good look at him?" Morris said, then chuckled again at his own joke. Dan started to say something, but Morris held his hands up in surrender without taking his forearms off the desk. "Just kidding, big guy." He picked up Savannah's paperwork and scanned it. "Yeah," he said. "You can't get married."

"Why not?" Dan asked.

"Says right here," Morris said, pointing to the pamphlet. "You must be eighteen to get married. Anyone under the age of eighteen must have a written letter from a minister or a marriage counselor stating they have received pre-marital counseling, must have a signed agreement from both parents or a legal guardian, and must obtain approval from a juvenile court. According to Miss Savannah's paperwork, she's only two months old. Can't get married unless you got all those things. You got all those things?"

"No," Dan said, sounding as if he'd lost without seeing it coming.

"Go get those things then come back," Morris said. He stood and chuckled. "Be sure you ask for Scoot." He picked up his coffee cup and yelled, "Hey, Scoot. You can come out now. Big bad hump-bot is leaving." He chuckled again.

Scott leaned out of the door to where Dan assumed was the employee break room. "I quit." He disappeared back inside.

"Yeah, yeah," Morris said as if he'd heard it too many times already. He strolled toward the break room. "Hey, save me a donut."

CHAPTER 40

Dan found the list of things he needed to do to get married both ridiculous and long. The Juvenile Court? And who was Savannah's guardian if it wasn't him? And what was this non-sense about counseling from a minister? Dan wasn't religious. He considered himself spiritual, but certainly not religious. His mother had been "raised Catholic," to use her words, and she had taken him to church until his confirmation, then allowed him to choose whether or not he wished to attend. In a "Bird in the hand" sort of way, Sunday morning cartoons won out over Heaven. She had returned to the church when the cancer was first diagnosed, and grew more religious as it progressed from her breast to her lungs and finally her liver. By the end, she was praying her Rosary countless times a day, her brain mush from the combination of chemo and pain meds, yelling for Tom—Dan's father—to put her down, God dammit, before he dropped her. Then she would cackle like a schoolgirl, or scream like a ban-shee—there was no way of knowing which it would be until it bellowed out of her, but both had a way of sounding demonic to Dan. Then she would pray her Rosary once more, her silent lips moving as she worked her fingers around the string. He had her buried clutching those wooden beads that had offered her little comfort and no cure.

But as far as Dan knew, that still made him Catholic, so he decided St. Michael's would be his first stop, after he phoned and found out he would need an appointment with the juvenile court system and their soonest opening was a week from Tues-day. He pulled the Prius into the parking lot, took the spot closest to the front doors that wasn't marked handicapped, and was surprised at the number of them that were reserved for that purpose. He took that to mean the church's congregation was not aging as gracefully as one might hope.

It had been six years since he'd been through the large, Gothic arch doors, and another twenty before that, but he did his best to remember everything he needed to do. He dipped his fingers in the Holy Water and crossed himself. When he turned, Savannah was looking at him as if he were a new species of bug, her arms folded over her chest. "What?"

"Do I need to do all that?" she asked, moving her finger in a circle pointed at him, as if trying to envelope him. She spoke too loud for the inside of a church, and a few people who were praying in silence turned to look at them.

"No, you're not Catholic," he said, his voice a harsh whisper. "And don't be so loud. It's disrespectful."

"To whom?" she asked, her voice not changing. More people turned and one elderly blue-haired lady shushed them, her bony finger pressed to her lips.

"To God," he said. "It's God's house. Not so loud."

"But you don't believe in God."

"Will you please keep your voice down? I believe in Him here." He waved an apology to the woman to show they would be quiet.

"How can you believe in Him in here but not out there?" she asked, flipping her thumb over her shoulder to indicate outside.

He grabbed her arm and pulled her back into the vestibule. The door to the sanctuary closed, cutting them off from the other people. "Why did you not come with a volume knob? You need to be quiet in a church."

"But why? It's just a building, and if it's God's house, He'll hear me whether I'm quiet or loud, won't He? I mean, He has superpowers, doesn't He?"

"It's not about that. Those people inside are praying and meditating. We need to be quiet for them."

"Oh. Well, why didn't you say that to begin with?"

"I assumed telling you to be quiet would be enough," he said.

"Yeah," she said, drawing the word out a little long, mimicking her favorite television psychiatrist. "How's that working for you?" She had his high-pitched Texas accent down cold.

"You know, I could return you and get a full refund," he said, squinting at her.

"I'm pretty sure your next one would be worse," she said. "And you already got a refund. You would return me and get nothing but heartache."

"You're inscrutable," he said, grinning at her, then kissing her a quick peck.

"It's true," she said with a sigh, casting a glance at the floor in disappointment and shook her head as she spoke. "I cannot be scruted."

He rolled his eyes as he entered again, repeating the Holy Water because he couldn't remember if he had to do it every time he entered or not. She stepped beside him and stopped, looking around at the carvings and stained glass, and the Crucifix that hung behind the pulpit. "Wow," she said, quieter, but still not quiet enough. "Nice fucking church, dude." More people turned toward them, this time with looks of general disgust. He yanked her back into the vestibule this time.

"What is your problem, and where did you learn that word?"

"I learned it from the movies, and from you. You said it about the cameras. The movies say it all the time."

"Don't say it," he said. "It's vulgar, and don't ever say it in church. It's sacrilege."

"For somebody who never comes here, you sure know all the rules," she said. "Is there anything else I'm not supposed to say?"

"Just don't say anything—not unless someone says something to you, and if they do, answer in a whisper. And no cursing."

She clamped her lips shut and used a pretend key to lock them, then tossed the key over her shoulder. She opened the sides of her lips a little and said, "Got it. I won't say a word." She sounded like a muffled ventriloquist. He took a deep breath, held it for a second much like Scoot from the DMV had, then went back into the sanctuary.

CHAPTER 41

As he dipped his fingers a third time, he realized he had done it more today than he had in the past 25 years. He didn't think he was supposed to cross himself every time he entered, but he wasn't certain, and felt that it was better to be safe than sorry. He held Savannah's hand as they walked down the center aisle, and the blue-haired shusher shot them another dirty look as they passed.

Dan's problem with religion was summed up in that single look. Christ taught forgiveness and mercy. His followers loved to brag about it—they rarely practiced it. Admittedly, Savannah had been a little too loud and she had used a word she shouldn't have, but from the look this woman and a few of the others gave them, they believed the two of them should be the ones hanging off of that cross over the pulpit rather than their blessed savior.

He knew he was supposed to genuflect and take a seat, but instead he headed toward the back, looking for a door that would lead to an office or some such. He had never been an altar boy, of course, so this was the first time he'd ever come back this way. The old priest who performed his mother's funeral had met him at the mortuary and had pressed Dan for an offering the way a bellhop asked for a tip. He looked around for someone, and found two altar boys, passing a bottle of sacramental wine, and they both turned wide-eyed at the thought of being caught. A tray of the host lined up like appetizers sat on the table they leaned against, and silver incense burners seemed to be everywhere. To Dan, it felt like being backstage at a Stones concert. "Excuse me," he said. "Where can we find a priest?"

Savannah took a piece of the host, bit it, then said, "Eww," and spit it out onto the floor. "Really bad, stale crackers." He shot her a look of disbelief. "What? I wanted to see what they tasted like. If this is their idea of snacks, it's no wonder the place is empty."

One altar boy looked at Savannah as if he approved, but Dan wasn't sure if it was her attitude or her looks that won the kid over. The other boy pointed to a door in the back, took a sip of the wine, then passed it to his friend.

"You are so going to Hell," he said to her, but it most likely applied to the kids, too.

"No I'm not," she said. "I'm going to the scrap heap." She pulled him along this time, leading the way deeper toward the back.

It was down a short, dark corridor where they found the priest's office, the door opened slightly with a splash of light falling to the carpet. Dan knocked lightly, three raps and heard an elderly male voice invite them in.

It was the same man who had performed his mother's funeral mass, but if not for the placard on the desk, Dan wouldn't have remembered his name. If Fr. Michael Donovan had seemed old six years ago, he seemed ancient now. His arthritic fingers curled in different directions and he began to stand, leaning on a cane as he rose, and it was clear from his expression that standing brought pain. "Yes?" he asked. "How may I help you?" He was still partially bent over, but his eyes were as clear and sparkly as glass.

"Please don't get up," Dan said.

"Yes, well, it's a little too late for that, my son," the father said, his voice old and scratchy. "As I'm already up, you see. Now—how can I help you?" He returned to his desk, using his cane as he moved in small steps. He eased himself into his chair as slowly as he'd risen.

"We need to get pre-marriage counseling," Dan said.

"Excellent," the priest said, motioning to the two other chairs in his office, inviting them to sit. "More young people need to do that. Very responsible of you. Now it's a wonder when the girl isn't pregnant as they walk down the aisle. You're, um, you're not pregnant, are you dear?"

"No," Savannah said.

"Excellent. Good to see someone who practices responsibility for a change. Our classes meet in the Rec Hall, every Saturday at 1:30. Twelve weeks—twelve classes, and you're done."

"Twelve weeks?" Dan asked, not believing it would take so many. "But we wanted to get married sooner. Maybe even next week, if we can."

"Oh, I thought you said she wasn't pregnant. We have rush jobs if the girl is far enough along to be showing, but you don't appear to be. I believe twelve weeks will be sufficient."

"She isn't pregnant, but we really don't want to wait that long," Dan said. "Is there a way we can do the rush thing, even if she's not pregnant?"

"I'm sorry son. In order to be married in the church, we now require the classes. High divorce rates, you see. And the twelve weeks are to give you both time to change your minds. No, I'm afraid it has to be the regular schedule."

"But we don't care about a church wedding," Dan said.

Fr. Donovan looked offended.

"I mean, we would like a church wedding of course. Who wouldn't?" Dan said with a chuckle, hoping to appease the man. It seemed that he and Savannah were all about insulting the faithful today. "But we need the paper that says we went to pre-marriage counseling in order to get a marriage license."

Fr. Donovan looked confused. "I'm afraid I don't follow son." He squinted at Dan a little harder. "You look awfully familiar. Have we met?"

"Yes sir. You performed my mother's funeral mass. Margaret Mitchell?"

"Ah, yes," the priest nodded. "That must be it. Sorry—my mind isn't what it used to be. And you are—?"

"Dan. As I was saying, we just need that piece of paper to show we've had the counseling."

"Whatever for? If you don't want a church wedding, you

don't need the counseling. Go get married." He made the sign of the cross at them. "There—you have my blessing. Go with God." He shooed them away with the same hand that had blessed them and turned back to his desk. He shook a cigarette from a pack he had in his top drawer and lit it. He took a deep inhale and coughed, the smoke erupting in a billowing, spasmodic cloud. He looked back and did a double take when he saw they hadn't moved. "Was there something else?"

"I'm afraid so," Dan said. "We really need that piece of paper."

"No, you really don—" he stopped in mid-word, and his expression brightened. "Dan Mitchell," he said, pointing a gnarled finger at him, then shifting it to her, "and Savannah the Sexbot." He sounded as if he was answering a question on a game show. He laughed. "From the Katy Walker Show—oh, a delightful girl. She grew up in my parish when I was at Indian Hills, you know. I knew you looked familiar." He took another drag on his cigarette and coughed again, this time long and dry and hard enough that Dan worried the old man might have a stroke. Dan started to get up to maybe get the priest some water or something, but Fr. Dominic waved him off. He ashed his cigarette in a Styrofoam coffee cup half-filled with water, and Dan saw the butts of four or five previous smokes that had already drowned there. "Let me guess, the Republicans giving you a hard time?" He coughed again, but this time Dan heard the release of phlegm. The priest used the ashtray-cup as a spittoon.

"They said that since Savannah is only two months old, she's a minor and has to have pre-marriage counseling," Dan said. Savannah nodded in agreement.

The old priest laughed loud and slapped his crooked hand on his knee. "Oh, that's rich. That's a good one. Two months old. What a bunch of..." he stopped before he could say a bunch of what's, but he still shook his head in disbelief. "That's the Republicans for you. They'll try every trick in the book to stop something if it doesn't fit their narrow-minded view of the world." He shook his head again. "I'm sorry. I can't help you."

"But you sound like you're on our side," Dan said, not believing he was saying no. "You agree it's wrong."

"I am on your side," Fr. Dominic said. "It is wrong. You two want to get married, I say go for it. More power to you. But it's not up to me, you see. It's up to the Church, and the Church would say no, and not for the reasons you think either."

"I don't understand," Savannah said. "Why would this building care if we get married?"

Fr. Dominic chuckled. "Not the building, my dear. No, the Church is far greater than any one building. It's a collective of an idea—the word 'catholic' means all inclusive. It's the collective of all believers in Christ. First of all, I'm guessing you're not one, but even that's not your problem. Can you procreate, my dear?"

She glanced at Dan before she answered. "You mean get pregnant? No, of course not."

Fr. Dominic shrugged. "There's your problem."

"I don't follow," Dan said. "You won't marry us because she can't have kids?"

The priest shook his head as if he didn't believe it either. "That's the long and short of it."

"But surely you wed barren women all the time," Dan said. "This is no different."

"You're forgetting the story of Sarah," Fr. Dominic said. He pointed at Dan with the two fingers holding the cigarette. "Everyone thought she was barren until she had Isaac. With women, there is always the hope that God will intervene." He shrugged. "Sometimes He does. But even when He doesn't, there's always the hope. With Savannah there is no hope. Sex with her is a venial sin, the same as masturbation. The Church would never sanction it."

"What if we spoke to your boss? The bishop? Maybe if we explained that we don't want the wedding, just the counseling, he would agree."

"Son, my bishop is a forty-year-old putz who believes Republicans are too liberal. He already wants to remove me. Says I'm too old to run a church. Fact is, he doesn't like my politics. It's why I'm no longer at Indian Hills." He took another drag, flicked another ash and exhaled, this time coughless. "I marched on Washington for peace. Proud of it. That was after two tours in Vietnam as a Marine Corps chaplain, and I'm proud of that, too." Another drag—another flick. He turned to look straight at Savannah, leaning toward her, and this time when he spoke, smoke rolled out with his words. "I saw shit over there that would make even you believe in God, young lady. Vietnamese sniper had his rifle aimed right here," he said, pointing to the bridge of his nose, right between his eyes. "Had us pinned down in a rice paddy and had me dead. Not hurt—not wounded—dead. I was praying. I wasn't breathing, but I was praying, and not for my men, either. I said, 'God, please, just make it stop.' I was never so scared in my life. That sniper never pulled his trigger. He'd killed or wounded ten of our men already, so he wasn't squeamish. He had no idea I was a chaplain, either. We were all so covered in mud and shit, there was no way he could see the insignia on my helmet, and there was no way he would have cared if he had. Lots of chaplains died over there, some of them friends of mine. All he knew was I was some dumb American kid and he loved to kill dumb American kids." His voice sounded far away, as if he were back in that rice paddy. He took another drag, but held it this time, as if smoke were precious. "All of a sudden it got quiet—no guns—no shots—no mortars—not even a bird, just silence. Both sides just stopped shooting. That's when I opened my eyes and saw that rifle barrel pointed at my head. I was next. But he just lowered his weapon and walked away. Do you know why, young lady?"

Savannah shook her head, her eyes wide as she listened to the priest's story.

He sat back in his chair, the cigarette-holding hand pointed toward the ceiling, smoke wafting in a straight tendril. "Because God told him to—that's why. I came home and began protesting the war, and I protest this war we're in now. It's not worth it. It's never, ever, worth it. And my bishop hates me for that. I won't give him anymore ammunition. I'm sorry. I just can't help you." He took a final drag from his cigarette and dropped it into the cup, and Dan heard the hiss of dying fire. "Try the Methodists.

They might help you. They're pretty liberal."

Dan stood and Savannah followed. "You know," she said, grinning at the old man, "for a guy who believes in a bunch of hocus pocus, you're pretty cool."

The priest smiled back at her and winked. "For a bunch of circuits and wires that has no soul, you're pretty cool too."

CHAPTER 42

"Well, what now, Batman?" Savannah asked as he closed his car door and buckled his seat belt.

"I honestly don't know, Boy Wonder." He pulled out of the church lot and turned right. Three blocks later, when he should have turned left to go home, he went straight instead.

"Where are we going?"

"I honestly don't know that either," he said. In another mile, he turned onto interstate 71/75 and headed south. "Hey, look on the Internet. See if there is a place we can get married without a license, or you don't need an ID."

She answered quicker than he expected. "New Zealand," she said. "It says we can climb Mt. Mordor. Want to climb Mt. Mordor?"

"It would be cool," he said. "I love *Lord of the Rings*." He considered it for a few minutes. He would need a passport, of course, but she maybe wouldn't. Technically, he could ship her as baggage. Maybe she could be carry-on. That made him chuckle.

"What?"

"Nothing," he said, but he chuckled again, not able to help it. He thought about stuffing her into the overhead compartment and almost giggled.

"Tell me," she said, a small plea.

"Not for a million dollars," he said. He considered himself to be many things. Stupid was not one of them. "Let's go someplace," he said, but it wasn't until he heard his words out loud that he realized he meant it. He wanted to go someplace—anyplace that wasn't here. Cincinnati with its backed up courts systems, rude clerks and unhelpful priests wasn't a place he wanted to be right now. He wanted to be— where? He didn't know.

"Chicken," she said.

"Yup. I admit it freely. Let's go someplace."

"Stop changing the subject," she said. She was looking out her side window as they drove through the industrial section of the city, most of the graffiti-sprayed buildings abandoned, with jagged holes where panes of glass used to be. "It's ugly here."

"Now who's changing the subject?" he said, but he couldn't disagree with her. He didn't know what these buildings used to manufacture, but whatever it was, they didn't make it anymore, and gentrification hadn't reached this part of town yet. Maybe it would someday, and this would no longer be such an eyesore.

"I'm not changing the subject," she said. "I'm introducing a new topic."

"What's the difference?"

"When you do it, it's changing the subject," she said. "Where are we going?"

"Road trip," he said. He pointed straight out the windshield. "That way." He realized that the thought—just the thought of going someplace without knowing where or why—without reservations or plans—without a detailed itinerary was both thrilling and frightening. He'd never done anything like this before. Six months ago, he would have never considered it. He'd heard of people doing things like this. He'd read a book called *Partners*, once about a man and his son who took a motorcycle trip, but they had no clear destination. They didn't decide where they would ride on any given day until they woke up that morning. It was a good book, and Dan didn't understand why it hadn't sold more copies, but as he'd read it, he found the thought of this, "seat of the pants," lifestyle crazy.

She gave a small chuckle. "Okay—how far are we road tripping that way?" she asked, pointing out the windshield as well.

"Second star to the right, straight on 'til morning," he said. He also found the idea romantic and thrilling, like the life of a pirate. It was fun to dream about, but he could never do it, at least not then. Now, he was doing it.

"It's noon," she said. "You can't see stars at noon like I can."

"It's an expression. Wait—you can see stars at noon?"

"Of course," she said with a small shrug. "There's Orion," she said, pointing to a spot out her window. "And there's the Pleiades." She pointed to another spot, this time out of the windshield. "And there is Sagittarius. Do you really not know where we're road tripping?"

"I really don't know where we're road tripping," he said. He put on his turn signal and changed lanes to pass a slow-moving semi. The scenery shifted from the industrial section to downtown, and traffic was heavier as lanes shifted. His mind drifted to nothing, the background noise of random thoughts that took over his brain while his body drove the car. "Noise," he thought. Just that one word, floating in the back of his mind. Was the car making a funny noise? He listened, not fully conscious of it, but nothing sounded out of the ordinary—nothing smelled out of place, so his brain went back to autopilot without ever fully leaving it. She reached over and took his hand and that brought him out of the deep thoughts. He glanced at her as she half-turned towards him and kissed his fingers and put both of their hands in her lap.

"What about our stuff?" she asked as they drove across the Ohio River, the water someplace between the algae-green of summer and the mud-brown of spring. A coal barge maneuvered between the bridges, on its way downstream to Louisville, or Memphis, or maybe even NOLA. Dan didn't know its destination anymore than he did theirs. All he knew was it was limited by the river the same way they were limited by the highways, but that still made for a lot of choices.

"We'll get new stuff," he said, realizing there was some merit to planning ahead, but this felt right—too right to turn around. If they went back to get their things—their toothbrushes and clothes and the little things that tied life in Cincinnati to whatever lied ahead, he might change his mind—no—not might—he would. He would lose his nerve, tell himself this was crazy and talk himself out of it. This was the first truly spontaneous thing he'd ever done, and he wasn't about to talk himself out of it. What did they have that they couldn't get along the way? They would buy new stuff as they needed it. He gripped the wheel a little tighter to hide his anxiety.

It would be fine. He'd been getting paid by the pornographers for awhile now, his salary doubled, and he still had yet to do any work. He knew Ian had arranged that, and while part of him felt guilty for accepting a check for doing nothing, it was a small part. He'd been through a lot of hassle in the past six weeks, all because RWR hadn't covered a few more basics in their programming, like don't go naked in public. He saw the paychecks as small compensation.

She shrugged. "Okies. Mind if I play the radio?"

"Not at all," he said. Music would be perfect. Music was exactly what a good road trip needed, wasn't it? He'd never been on one, but it seemed necessary. How could anybody go on a road trip without music? She turned it on without having to reach for the button, and began flipping through stations, again without touching anything. They climbed the section of Newport, KY known as the "Cut-in-the-hill," where the interstate was framed by sheer limestone walls as she bounced from station to station, talk radio, classical, country, top-40, classic rock. She stopped on adult contemporary. He heard the familiar whine of a soprano sax that had a mind-numbing lull to it. Twenty minutes of that would put him to sleep. "You can't listen to Kenny G. on a road trip. It's just wrong. It doesn't fit."

"I didn't realize there were rules," she said. "What kind of music fits a road trip?"

"Well, it depends on where you're going," he said. "If we were going to Florida, we would listen to Jimmy Buffet. If we were going to Memphis, we would listen to Elvis—or the blues, either is acceptable. If we were going to Nashville, it would have to be country. New Orleans is Dixieland Jazz."

She grinned at him. "What if we don't know where we're going?"

"Then it's rock, baby. You can never go wrong with rock on a road trip." He sounded as if he had done this hundreds of times, with enough confidence he believed himself. She changed the channel to the local head-bashing station. "No, not that crap. Real rock—like 70's and 80's. And it would be better to use the satellite stations so we don't lose signal when we leave town."

"You're so picky," she said as she switched to the satellite feed. She flipped through a few of the rock stations, pausing for a second on each one. When he heard Lynyrd Skynyrd's opening bars of Freebird, the organ and guitar working together, soft and slow that would eventually climb to one of the world's greatest ballads, he put up a hand for her to stop.

"This is perfect," he said. He didn't know a lot of rock music, but everyone knew "Freebird."

"It's pretty," she said. "Who is Lynyrd Skynyrd?"

"He's from Alabama," Dan said. At least, he did a song about Alabama—he must be from there. "He's the singer."

"He spells his name funny," she said. The lone guitar began its mournful cry, as it sang of freedom. "Wait a minute, they're not from Alabama. They're from Jacksonville, Florida, and there is no one named Lynyrd Skynyrd, they named the band after Leonard Skinner, a gym teacher who told them they needed to cut their hair. The singer is Ronnie Van Zant."

"That's cheating," he said. "You can't use the internet like that. It's an abuse of power."

"You just don't want your wife to find out you're full of crap," she said.

"No man wants that," he said. "And you're not my wife—you're my fiancé until the wedding. Then you're my wife."

"Either way, you're full of crap," she said. Van Zant began to sing, "*If I leave here tomorrow...*" They both fell silent and listened.

While Dan was familiar with the song, he'd never actually listened to it before. He could recognize the tune, but didn't know the words. Now he actually heard them and realized they were sad. When he glanced at Savannah, he saw a tear leak down her cheek. He gave her hand a light squeeze. "You okay?"

"It's a break-up song," she said. "You want to leave me."

"What? No I don't. Where did that come from?"

"You said this song is perfect—it's about a man leaving a woman so he can be free." She wasn't crying outright, but there were tears and she sounded sad if somewhat resigned. She released her grip on him and used her now-free hand to wipe her cheeks.

"That doesn't mean I want to leave you," he said. "It's a pretty song." He left his hand in her lap, hoping she would take it again, but she didn't. "I didn't know it was about a break-up."

She looked at him and he did something he almost never did, and that was turn away from the road, not watching traffic. She squinted, studying him. "Say it. Say you don't want to break up with me."

"I don't want to break up with you."

"Now say you didn't really know what the song was about."

He looked back toward the front of the car to make sure they weren't about to hit anything.

"No. Look at me and say it."

He turned back to her. "I really didn't know what the song was about. I promise."

She studied him. "Well—we've already established you're full of crap, but I believe you."

"Thank you," he said, still looking at her.

She pointed out the windshield with a casual finger flick. "You should watch where we're going," she said, and as he turned back, he saw they had drifted into the fast lane. He brought them back to the right, glad there hadn't been another car around. Traffic had thinned once they passed the I-275 outer loop. She took his hand in hers again and he was happy.

His mind began to drift once more as the guitars wailed, the song fast and loud now. "Noise," he thought again, but surely it didn't apply to this song did it? Maybe—especially since he wasn't someone who normally listened to rock. But no—that wasn't it—that wasn't what his mind was trying to tell him.

"Noise," it said again, and again, he listened to the car, semi-conscious, not sure what his brain wanted. "Signal," it said—radio signal? No—the satellite signal was clear and it would stay that way no matter where they chose to go—that was the whole point of it.

"Signal to noise." That felt right, but what about signal to noise? There was something, drifting, just out of reach, but it didn't want to— "Hey," he said as the idea clicked and he turned to her. He watched her grin, but it was subdued. "Signal to noise. There's no way you can beat a bad signal-to-noise ratio."

"Yes I can," she said.

"You can't see stars at noon any better than I can," he said, knowing he was right.

"Yes I can," she said, insisting—denying she'd been caught. She pointed out the windshield again. "There's Orion—over there is Libra," she craned her neck as she looked out the side window, "That—that's Capricorn. You can't prove anything."

"Now who's full of crap?" he asked.

"You are. You are full of crap. It has been decided." She held her head a little too high and looked toward the car's roof.

"Well, you are too then," he said.

"No. I am Savannah. I am not full of crap. You are Dan. Dan is full of crap." She looked indignant, but sounded playful.

"You can't see stars. You can't see nothing."

"I can see that you're full of crap," she said. "Anyone could see that."

"Nothing."

"Crap."

CHAPTER 43

He signaled to exit at the Kentucky/Tennessee border, a small town called Jellico, took a right at the end of the ramp and pulled into the first gas station. He stopped at the first pump and got out. She got out with him, the only difference between her and everyone else around them was she was the only one who didn't seem to feel the need to stretch. Dan swiped his card in the pump and began fueling. She circled behind the car and when she reached him, she hopped up and took a seat on the trunk. "Figured out where we're going?"

"Not yet," he said. "We'll know it when we get there." He leaned in toward her and she met him halfway with a light kiss.

She smacked her lips. "Tastes like—" she stopped, thinking about it. He couldn't imagine what he might taste like. This was their first stop since the church—he hadn't had anything to eat or drink since breakfast, which was the biggest reason for stopping. They had a half-tank of gas. "Crap," she said, as if it had just come to her.

He grinned. "You think you're funny. That's your problem. You're just not."

"You say that, but you're full of crap, so it doesn't count," she said. "Want anything?"

"Something to eat," he said. There was an Arby's inside the gas station. "I'll park and we can go in and relax." The gas handle clicked and he hung the nozzle back.

She hopped off the back of the car. "Okies," she said. She walked into the gas station as he parked. By the time he went in, she stood by the checkout and was on her second bottle of water.

"Him," she said, pointing at him with the bottle. "He has all the money." She offered him the bottle and he took it, draining half of what was left. "You should let me carry some money," she said as he handed it back.

"You have no concept of money," he said as he put a five on the counter.

"Of course I do," she said. She finished the bottle. "I'm going to get another one," she told the clerk, a brunette girl who looked high school age.

"Well, you have no concept of how hard I have to work to get it," he said.

"You haven't worked in two months," she said over her shoulder, loud enough for everyone in the station to hear as she went to the cooler.

"That's not true," he said as the cashier handed him his change. "It's only been six weeks." He put the coins in his pocket, then went to the restroom to wash his hands.

His mother was fond of calling Arby's "roast beast," one of her few jokes, but he heard it often because it was one of her favorite places to eat. She liked the seasoned curly fries. He ordered a medium #1 with a Coke, his standard order at every fast food place no matter what the menu offered, because he had a theory that every place like this would make their best offering #1, and who was he to argue? The boy who waited on them, a red-headed kid with a name tag that read, "Randy," whom Dan bet had more pimples on his face than hairs on his chest, looked at Savannah and said, "And you, Miss?"

"Nothing," she said, holding up her bottle of water. She tilted her head toward Dan. "He says I'm too fat so I'm not allowed to eat." She delivered the line dead-pan and serious.

"No I didn't," Dan said to the kid.

"Oh man, that's not cool," Randy said to Dan, clear from his tone he didn't know Savannah was joking.

"Yeah, Dan. That's not cool. Why would you say something like that?" she asked, still no glint of a smile.

"I didn't say anything like that," he said. "Will you stop that?

He thinks you're serious."

"You tell me you love me then call me fat and won't feed me," she said, looking to the ceiling and taking another sip of water. "That's not cool at all."

"I did not say that," Dan said.

"Then why won't you let me get anything to eat?"

Dan turned to her, his money in hand ready to pay. "You can get anything you want," he said. "You're not fat. You can get anything you want. Just tell Randy—anything at all."

"No, I'm okay," she said.

"Are you sure?" he asked.

"I'm sure," she said. She took another sip.

He turned back to Randy who was now giving him a mean look, but Dan was past caring. He gave the boy a ten and the boy counted back his change.

"You'd just beat me later for eating now," she muttered.

"How about I just beat you now and get it over with?" Dan asked.

"You're my witness, Randy," Savannah said. "If he hits me, you'll have to testify."

Randy stared at Dan for a moment, but it was a fat and slow moment, full of loathing. He turned away long enough to get the food and put it on a plastic tray along with an empty cup which he slammed down with enough force to make the cup sound like a small drum. Dan filled his drink himself, along with containers of ketchup, bbq and horseradish sauce, all from large dispensing pumps that gave the meal an industrialized feel. "What are those?"

"Well, you know ketchup," he said. "This is barbecue—this is horseradish."

She squirted a little of each on the tip of her finger and tasted them. "Please don't beat me for eating," she said as she removed her finger. "These are pretty good. I could do better."

"Why do you do that?" Dan asked as they went to an open booth by the window, not that the view was very scenic.

"Taste things?" she asked.

"No. Make jokes like that. People don't find them funny." He took a fry and dipped it into the ketchup and she did the same, stealing a short one from his container.

"Are you kidding?" she asked. "I'll bet we made that kid's whole week. He gets to talk about the mean guy who beats his woman for eating. It's priceless." She tried the fry. "These are good, too."

Dan squeezed the little containers onto his sandwich, doing his best to put them where they would drip the least. Since his mother had insisted they eat at this chain at least once a week, he was pretty good at it, but he could count the number of times he had eaten an entire one without dripping at all on one hand. The problem was the lack of uniformity in the sandwich. The roast beef was layered and piled higher in the center. With a hamburger patty, there was consistency— he could work with consistency. Not dripping with a roast beef sandwich was more art than science. He picked it up with both hands, applying a little more pressure to the rear than the middle and took a bite. No drips so far. It was a good start.

"Can I try that?" she asked.

He had grown accustomed to her taking bites of his food since she had developed an interest in cooking. Before, if another human had so much as touched his food, he wouldn't have been able to eat it, but with Savannah, it had never bothered him, and he wasn't sure why. He supposed it could be a, "love conquers all" thing, but he suspected it had more to do with her mouth being inherently cleaner than a human's. But then, he'd always heard a dog's mouth was cleaner than a human's and he would die before he ate after one. He held it out to her, not in a way for her to take it, but to take a bite from it.

"Can I hold it?" she asked.

"No. You didn't wash your hands, and you'll drip sauce all over."

"You're going to drip sauce all over in two more bites," she said. "Right behind your left pinky. You put too much there." She leaned forward and bit from the edge, looking into his eyes as she did, and for some reason, he found the entire thing incredibly erotic. She sat back and chewed, wiping a dab of bbq sauce from the corner of her mouth with her middle finger, then sucking on it. "It needs more of the horsey stuff."

Dan took another bite—then another, chasing each one with some fries and soda. After the third, sauce dripped down his left pinky. Savannah didn't even have the courtesy to look amused as he wiped his hand with a napkin.

"Excuse me, sir," a man said as he stepped beside the table. Dan looked up, then up some more, his eyes going from the pistol belt, to the badge then finally the face underneath the Smokey Bear hat.

"Yes, officer?" Dan said. "Is there a problem?"

"We'd like to have a little chat is all," the man said. Dan glanced back at the gold, star-shaped badge and read, "Campbell County Sheriff," stamped in black letters that formed a circle around the Tennessee state seal. The man's accent was from the hills, and it sounded laid back and friendly, as if all he really wanted was a chat.

A woman stepped from behind the deputy, the man so large he had hidden Dan's view of her. "Would you come with me, Ma'am?" the lady, also a deputy, asked Savannah, holding out a hand to help her up.

"What's this about?" Dan asked. He started to get up, but he felt the deputy's hand on his shoulder, warm and friendly enough, but it seemed to hold a threat in it as well. "Remain calm or go to jail," that hand said.

"Just a little talk is all," the man said. "Ma'am? I need you to go with Deputy Warren, if you would please." Savannah stood and followed the female deputy to the other side of the restaurant, behind Dan so he couldn't see them, and far enough away that he couldn't hear them either. The male deputy took her seat, across from Dan. He didn't speak. He just sat there, looking at Dan without emotion.

"Did Randy call you?" Dan asked. He looked toward the counter but didn't see anyone.

"Randy is my son and he's a good boy. He's worried about you and your lady friend."

"Look, officer. This is all a big misunderstanding," Dan said.

"I know how it is," the deputy said. "You come home tired after a long day at work, and you're angry."

"I work from home now," Dan said in counter argument, then realized how stupid it sounded. If that was the best he could come up with, he was going to jail.

"Well, that don't matter none. When a man gets tired, he gets grouchy. She maybe burns dinner, or doesn't clean very well. A pretty girl like that probably don't cook or clean much at all," the deputy said, his voice smooth and understanding, as if he wanted Dan to confess.

"Actually, she's a gourmet chef," Dan said. "Yup," he thought to himself. "That should just about do it. Straight to jail—do not pass go, do not collect $200."

"Okay then, maybe she just doesn't want to be, romantic, shall we say? You're in the mood, but she's not."

"Actually, that's kind of what she's built for," Dan said.

"I know a lot of men who think that way," the deputy said. "Think they own the women in their lives. Treat them like property."

Dan half turned in his seat. "Savannah? Could you come here, please?"

"Now, let's just let the ladies talk for another minute or two," the deputy said, his voice still calm, as if they were old friends sitting around a campfire.

"Now, please?" Dan said, ignoring the deputy.

"Ma'am?" Deputy Warren said from behind Dan, but he couldn't see her, only hear her. "Savannah? Miss? I just have a couple more questions."

Savannah stood beside the table as if no one was speaking to her. "Yes?"

"Could you show the deputies your secret, please?"

"It's not going to be very secret if I keep showing people," she said.

"I agree, but Deputy," he realized he still didn't know the man's name, so he read it from the tag on his shirt, "Williamson, here, seems like he wants to take me to jail over your funny little joke. Would you show him, please?"

"You said I should stop showing people—then you had me do it at the county place and Scoot almost hurt himself. I'm not sure it's a good idea."

"Savannah," he said, his teeth clenched. "Please show them. I do not want to go to jail." He said each word individually as his frustration grew.

"Now, see there?" Deputy Williamson said. "That's exactly what I'm talking about. You need to learn how to control that anger and not aim it at Miss Savannah, here."

"Yeah, Dan," Savannah said, deadpan. "You shouldn't aim your anger at me. It's not cool."

"I am not angry," he spit, hearing how well his tone belied his words. "I just do not wish to go to jail because of your warped sense of humor. Now show them, please."

"You really need to calm down, Dan," Deputy Williamson said as Savannah shrugged and reached for her face. When she removed it, the man rocked back in his seat, and Dan was glad he wasn't drinking anything—he most likely would have sprayed it everywhere.

"He doesn't beat me," Savannah said, her mechanical tongue working over her mechanical teeth. Without the lips and mouth to add acoustics, she sounded tinny—not a lot, but enough to notice. "Nor could he hurt me if he did. Can I put my face back on now?"

"Hey—" Deputy Warren said. She had the same basic accent as Deputy Williamson, but his sounded a little more refined than hers, a sort of, "City Hillbilly," versus, "Country Hillbilly." "I seen you two on the television. Katy Walker, right? She seems so nice. Is she nice?"

Savannah didn't wait for permission, and began replacing her face, but she answered as she did. "She was very nice. She enjoyed my peach turnovers."

"Ain't that nice?" Deputy Warren said as she put her notepad back into her pocket.

"She's a robot?" Williamson said, but he was looking straight at her.

"I am, deputy, but it's not necessary to speak to Dan. You can talk directly to me." She finished with her face and straightened her hair.

"She looks so—" Williamson began, but he cut himself off. "I mean you—you look so real."

"So do you," she said. Dan enjoyed that it was becoming her pat answer. She sat beside Dan and he had to scoot over to give her room. She held her arm out for the deputy to touch. "Tell me I feel real, too," she said. "I dare you."

He chuckled, but didn't say it. He did, however, run his fingertips up her arm. "Man—that's amazing." He looked up at her face. "Let me ask you something. That was all a joke—I mean you thought that was funny?"

"I am well versed in twenty different forms of humor," she said. "That particular joke, while satirical, was delivered in a manner known as deadpan, so as to make it seem more believable to my audience, in this case Randy, and therefore funnier. There is also irony involved, in that I am stronger than Dan and while he couldn't hurt me, I could hurt him if I choose, but unless you realize I am a companion-bot beforehand, the irony is lost. Would you like to hear a joke?" She didn't wait for a response. "Helen Keller walks into a bar—then a chair—then the wall."

Dan hung his head, not believing she had told that joke to a police officer.

Deputy Williamson looked away for a second as he fought a laugh. "Okay, that was pretty good," he said when he turned back, but then said, "But spousal abuse isn't funny."

"I agree," Savannah said, "but comedians often use satire to shed light on social issues. It's an accepted form of comedy."

"I think what the officer is saying is that you're not a comedian," Dan said.

"I could be," she said. "I am quite funny. I could play Vegas."

Deputy Williamson sat there for a few seconds, then shook his head. "Let me ask you something. You can cook and clean and all that?"

"I'm a gourmet chef in three regional cuisines, and I clean, yes."

"She's an excellent housekeeper," Dan said. She turned to him and smiled. "Well, you are." He shrugged to show his sincerity.

"Let me ask you something. Could you like, help a boy with his homework?"

"Of course," she said. "I am shipped with a basic high school education, but I can learn—well—anything. Calculus—philosophy—history. Anything really."

"Huh," he said, as if he was considering something. He leaned in closer and whispered like a conspirator. "Let me ask you something. Are you, like, fully functional?"

Savannah smiled at the question. "You mean sex, right?"

"Now Brett, what are you thinking?" Deputy Warren asked.

"I'm thinking that Mary has been dead for five years—I got a boy who is sixteen and still in the ninth grade, and I'm lonely. Can I help you?" His tone indicated that whatever he was thinking, it wasn't any of Deputy Warren's business. Warren held up both hands in surrender and took a step backwards. "Yes," he said to Savannah.

"I am fully functional and quite skilled," she said. Dan nodded agreement.

Williamson looked deep in thought for a moment. "Let me ask you something. How much does one of you run?"

"Up to two days on a single charge," she said.

"He means how much do you cost," Dan said, and Williamson chuckled at that.

Savannah chuckled as well. "Oh. I'm still working on regional idioms. Well, that depends on the options you select, but starting rates are around $50,000—they can go up to just under $100,000, depending on the options."

Williamson sat back and whistled. "Wow—that's—"

"Worth every penny," Dan said, finishing the man's statement. Savannah slipped her hand into the crook of his elbow at the compliment.

"Really?"

"Every penny," Dan said again. "I took out a mortgage on my house. I haven't regretted it for a minute." That was a lie. He had regretted it, at least a little bit, but it had been brief and not something he would ever admit in front of her.

"And do they all look like you?" Williamson said, then added, "not that it would be a bad thing," as if he were afraid of offending her.

"Oh no," Savannah said. "There are a wide range of body styles, complexions and even different faces to choose from."

"Don't order the Jasmine, though," Dan said. "We have it on good authority it's no longer available." Savannah snorted a little laugh on that one. Dan offered Williamson his cell phone number as well as the website for RWR. "Call me before you place your order," Dan said. "I may be able to get you a discount, or maybe some free upgrades."

They shook hands and Deputy Williamson thanked him for his time and the information. Dan was grateful to have had an encounter with a police officer that hadn't ended with him in handcuffs. His lunch was cold, but it didn't matter. His appetite had left as soon as the deputies stepped to the table. She bussed their mess as he got a refill and they went to the car. Both deputies waved to them as they walked past.

"Can I drive?" she asked.

"What? No you can't drive. You don't know how." It was a ridiculous question.

"Sure I do. I've been watching you. Move one pedal to go, the other to stop. Turn the wheel to aim. How hard can it be?"

"Harder than you might imagine," he said. He unlocked her door and opened it for her, but she didn't get in.

"Please?" she asked, whining. Dan looked over her shoulder and saw Deputy Williamson still watching them. "I'd be good at it."

His eyes shifted back to her. "No. You don't have a license and we could get into trouble. Get in the car."

She looked at him with irritated disappointment, but got in. He closed the door for her, and when he got in his side, she said, "I need a license to get married—a license to drive a car—" she paused for a second, then added, "One to catch a fish, own a dog or build a house. The list is really long." She paused again. "Did you know you need a license to panhandle for money in Memphis? The strange part is, it costs ten dollars. If you have the ten dollars, do you really need to panhandle?"

He laughed. "Good point."

"I don't see one for owning a kid, though. That seems dumb. If they should license anything, I would think that would be an important one. And it should come with a test, like driving."

An image of Dan's mother flashed into his mind, but he forced it away. "Yes," he agreed. "It should be a difficult test, too."

"Let me drive," she said, the same tone as she'd used the first time she'd asked.

"Will you stop asking?" He guided them back onto the interstate and changed into the travel lane as he checked his mirrors. "You don't know how to drive."

"I'd be better at it than you," she said. "I have robot reflexes." She flailed her arms in arcs, her hands open, doing, "Wax on, wax off," from a movie they'd watched last week. She gave a karate yell, "Eeeyaa," as she punched an invisible enemy between her and the dashboard.

"You might have reflexes, but I have experience. I would win a race."

Her snort was of open derision. "My Monkey-style Kung Fu will defeat your Platypus-style Kung Fu. Platypus-style is weak and confused about who it is. But we need second car to race, Daniel-san."

Dan thought about it for a second, then said, "I guess we'll have to assume I'm right, then, and maybe shut up about it."

"Hmm—you must be new to this relationship."

225

CHAPTER 44

As they came upon Knoxville, Dan saw a billboard and got an idea. He turned onto I-640, the outer loop around Knoxville, and decreased his speed because of construction. "Am I to believe we have a plan?" she asked. "A destination, perhaps?"

"We do," he said. "I need you to check Gatlinburg, Tennessee for cabin rentals. Let's see what we can find for a few days."

Her Internet connection was constant, thanks to the satellites orbiting overhead. When Starlink had announced that 95% of the world had Internet access, the only exception being the poles, both North and South, Dan's mind had gone to the song, "Nowhere to run to baby— nowhere to hide." It was a mixed bag. While it was good to know he could get lost in the deepest of the Colorado Rockies and still be able to get Internet access to find his way out, it was also a bit disheartening to know there would never be a place he could go to just get away from everything. It was as if the world now had a leash around everyone's neck, and that loss of freedom carried a sadness with it. He could always turn off his phone, or just leave it behind, should he ever choose, but would he? Could he bring himself to do it? Did he have it in him to go without email or outside communications for even a day? A week? At times like these, he envied the Amish boy, Isaac, who would never own a cell phone or a computer.

"I found a nice seven-bedroom just outside of Gatlinburg," she said, "and it's discounted. It's only $700 a night."

"Seven hundred a night?" he said as if he was actually considering what a great deal that was. He started to say that they should jump on that before somebody else got it, then he stopped himself, because he knew she would do exactly that. "See if you can find something a little smaller," he said "We don't need seven bedrooms."

"Oh, I don't know," she said. "If we stayed for a week, we could have sex in a different room every night—Sleep," she said. "I mean sleep in a different room every night." When he looked at her, he read mischief in her eyes.

"Savannah, my dear—my darling—love of my life. What is your humor set to?"

"There are twenty different settings for humor," she said. "To which one are you referring?"

"The master one," he said.

"The master level for humor is currently at 8.75 out of ten. Would you like me to raise it?"

"How did it get to 8.75? The last time I checked your settings, humor was a five. Everything was set to five."

"Every time I did something that made you laugh or that you found amusing, I raised it a little—like a bonus point on an exam." She seemed proud of herself.

"I see," he said. "And can you list your personality settings as they are now?"

"Of course," she said, and she began rattling off traits like extrovertness, perfectionism and neuroticism, giving a numerical value to each. Out of sixteen different personality traits, almost none of them were still on five.

"And you changed them yourself?"

"Of course. I tailored each of them to your responses"

"What about the times when you did something you thought was funny, but I didn't, like just now with Randy? Did you lower them?"

"No, I felt that your sense of humor would grow in time. I have faith in you, Dan. Unlike you, I have hope. Is there a problem?"

"Well, it's just that your sense of humor—I mean—this is twice now that it's gotten us into some form of trouble."

"Yes," she said. "I believe that is because some people don't have a sense of humor. They should adjust their settings accordingly."

"People don't have settings," he said. They left the construction zone and he set the cruise control to 65.

"I know—but wouldn't it be nice if they did?"

"Yes," he said, and he meant it. "The world would be a better place if everyone was like you." He meant that, too. He changed lanes and passed a pickup that had blue smoke billowing out of the tailpipe, leaving a cloud thicker than fog. The truck wheezed and coughed as they went around it, sounding as if death was near. "So, since they don't and you do, maybe it would be best if you back your humor down a little," he said, trying to be as diplomatic as possible.

She didn't say anything, just sat, staring out the windshield. He glanced over and thought he saw the glimmer of a tear running down her cheek. "What now?" he thought, but he asked, "Are you crying?"

"No," she said, but it was an obvious lie. "There's a two bedroom for $99 a night. Do you want me to book that one?"

"Don't cry," he said. "I love your sense of humor. It's just that most people don't understand it."

"There's a two bedroom for $99 a night. Do you want me to book that one?" she asked again, her tone flat but far from unemotional. It was cold and distant.

"Don't take it that way," he said, wishing he had just kept his mouth shut. It was better to be in trouble with the outside world than the inside.

"There's a two bedroom for $99 a night. Do you want me to book that one?"

"Yes, fine, book the damned room," he said. "Whatever."

"It's booked," she said. "Now we can each have our own bedroom."

"Now why do you have to go and be like that?" he asked, getting mad at her for being upset with him. It was juvenile and he knew it, but he still couldn't stop it.

She turned to him and now tears streamed down both cheeks.

Perhaps they had been before, but he was just now able to see both sides. He didn't know. "You brought me here to break up with me," she said. "You said the song was perfect for this road trip, but it was a breakup song. I didn't understand why then, but now I know it's because you don't like my sense of humor. It's okay. I can contact Ian and he will arrange for transportation."

"Are we back on this again?" he asked. "I promise I don't want to break up with you."

"Is tomorrow convenient, or would tonight be better?"

He signaled to go right and pulled into the breakdown lane and put the car in park. He'd never had to stop on the side of the road before and as a large truck passed them at 70, he felt the little Prius rock from the wind. He turned to face her. "I don't want to break up with you," he said. "All I'm asking is that we turn your humor down a little bit so we don't wind up in jail. You know—jail? We've been to jail once. I would rather not go back."

She looked down at her lap, her hands folded there, and he tried to take one in his, but she pulled away. "You don't like me anymore, you don't get to hold my hand. Ian says the earliest he can arrange pickup will be Wednesday, or you can drop me off at a UPS store. He didn't say that last part. I did."

"You actually contacted him?" Dan said, not believing it had gone this bad this fast.

"I don't want to stay where I'm not wanted," she said.

"You're wanted," he said. "You're needed," he said. "My life would be—" his cell phone started to ring and he fished it from his pocket. It was Ian Palance's private number. He answered, putting it on speaker. "Hello Ian."

"Dan? Where the hell are you? I can barely hear you."

"We're in Tennessee on the side of the road."

"Everything okay? Did your car breakdown?"

"The car is fine, Ian. Thank you for asking. We stopped to have a discussion."

Palance chuckled. "Yeah, I gathered. Listen, a breakup wouldn't be the best thing for your case right now. Can't you two work it out?"

"He doesn't love me," Savannah said. "Either it was all a lie, or he changed his mind."

"I didn't change my mind," he said, as much to Palance as her, as if he owed them both an explanation. "Let me ask you something," Dan said, not realizing he was mimicking the deputy. "Why is it she's allowed to change her own personality?" He thought maybe it was a glitch of some sort.

"That's a great feature, isn't it?" Palance asked. "That was my idea."

Dan thought that it might be, if it didn't come with a jail sentence. He tried to reach for Savannah again, but once more, she held her hands out of reach.

"Hey, Savannah," Ian said. "I'm sure Dan loves you. Whatever he said, he just misspoke. He's human, don't forget. Humans make mistakes. They say things when they are angry or upset that they just don't mean. They do dumb things. It's part of being human. I'm sure he's sorry."

"He hasn't said he is sorry," she said. "When people make mistakes, they say they are sorry. Then it is possible to forgive them."

Dan opened his mouth to speak, but Palance beat him to it— "Dammit, Dan, say you're sorry." He had that half-scolding, half-mirth tone, as if he was enjoying Dan's misery. Perhaps he just enjoyed playing couple's counselor for a change.

"I'm sorry," Dan said, and she looked at him, her eyes worried. He nodded to show it was true, and she smiled, but it was small. "Will you forgive me?" She nodded and this time she took his hand, but it still wasn't with the same enthusiasm as normal.

"That's great," Palance said. "Hey, Dan, can you take me off speaker for a second?"

Dan did, even though he wasn't sure it made any difference. She had the hearing of a bat. "Yes, Ian?"

"Listen, these algorithms aren't perfect. She knows to listen for certain phrases, and apologies are pretty cut and dry. We're sure she'll learn more, but for now, if you do something wrong —or something she believes is wrong, just say you're sorry. She's prone to forgiveness. It's not a mortal lock, but she's inclined that way."

"Thank you, Ian," he said. He started to mention Deputy Williamson just to begin paving the way, and he probably would have if he weren't in the breakdown lane on the Interstate. But with cars whipping past at 70mph and only inches from him, he wanted to move.

"You're welcome," Palance said. "We'll talk soon, okay?"

Dan hung up and put the phone in the cup holder. "You have directions for the cabin?" She nodded and wiped her cheek. He leaned over, putting his hand behind her head and pulled her in for a kiss which she returned, but it felt reluctant on her end. "Hey—I don't want to break up with you—not today. Not ever." He kissed her again, and this time, she felt more enthusiastic. It wasn't the same Savannah's kiss as he would have gotten a few hours ago, but it was better.

"I don't have directions to the actual cabin," she said. "It's to the office where we register. Is that okay?"

"That's perfect," he said. He pulled back onto the interstate and they headed toward Gatlinburg.

CHAPTER 45

Gatlinburg, Tennessee, pop. 4173, elevation 1,289ft, is a small town nestled against the Great Smoky Mountains National Park and is one of those tourists places where the population soars during the summer but is practically a ghost town in the winter with the exception of the Christmas holiday. It was Memorial Day weekend, the leading edge of the tourist season, and Dan knew they were lucky to get a room at all. Savannah had her car window down and her head stuck out of it like a dog. "Wow," she said. "It's so pretty."

And it was, Dan thought. The town was made to look like a German mountain town—or perhaps it was Austrian or Czechoslovakian. Dan, like most Americans, didn't know the architectural difference, or if there even was one. He did find it a bit amusing that Gatlinburg had a refined, genteel exterior, all-the-while playing to its hillbilly roots in the items the gift shops sold. Its cousins, Pigeon Forge and Sevierville, both only a few miles away, didn't bother with refinement. They played their hillbilly cards down to the last trump and made no apologies for it.

The rental office was a log cabin, surrounded by more log cabins, and while the brochures touted isolation, the short drive from the office to the "Bear Necessities" cabin they had rented (every cabin they offered had a name tied to the local color. They drove past Hillbilly Haven, the Cub House and Still Crazy—the last one took a minute to click in Dan's mind before it dawned on him that it referred to a moonshine still.) told him that to the good people at Smoky Mountain Cabin Rentals, isolation meant about thirty yards with a dozen or so trees scattered between cabins. The rental agent, a pear-shaped woman named Nancy, was nice enough to lead the way to the correct cabin, and then did a walkthrough with them, pointing out the amenities as they went with the same eagerness as a real estate agent trying to make a sale. She finished with the view from the balcony, and Dan believed the entire tour was catered that way, because the view of the mountain valley below was exquisite. "Since it's just the two of you, y'all will want to try out that hot tub when it gets dark. It's real romantic." Her accent was thick to the point Dan wondered if it was real. "My Ed says when we retire, we're going to build us one of these up in some holler and never come out." Nancy was one of those women who gained most of her weight in her posterior, making her waddle as she walked, and her coal-black hair screamed of a cheap dye job. She kept it in a teased-with-too-much-hairspray style that Dan had seen many women wear once they hit fifty-ish.

"That would be nice," Dan said, but the introvert in him was making this uncomfortable, and small talk made it worse. He really just wanted the woman to leave, not because he had some sinister plans or that he even wanted to be alone with Savannah —he just wanted to be able to claim his space—settle in and get comfortable, and that was impossible with a stranger around.

"Now, there's the community center, the game room and the pool by the rental office. The pool is heated, and you're welcome to use them, but they all close at ten, sharp. If you need anything, just give us a call or come on down to the office. We'd be happy to help."

"Thank you," Savannah said. "I'm sure we have everything we need. The cabin is lovely."

"Well, aren't you sweet? I decorated this one myself," Nancy said. Dan had noted bear art on the wall, bear patterns on the furniture, and a wooden bear statue in the corner. A carving of a momma bear followed by two cubs sat on top of the television set. Nancy might not have good taste, but she at least had consistency.

"It's beautiful," Savannah said, tracing a finger over the

statue. The bear was on its hind legs, paws out and mouth open as if it were about to attack. He wondered if there was a bear statue factory somewhere in these mountains, carving out mass-produced artwork to decorate cabins throughout the Smokies and beyond, because he'd seen the same statues for sale in the windows a few of the gift shops.

"Aren't you sweet?" Nancy said again. "Well, if you don't have any questions, I'll leave you all to it."

"Actually, we were wondering if you could recommend a place to go shopping?" Savannah asked. "We did this kind of spur of the moment and we didn't bring toiletries or anything like that." Dan looked at her, but not because of the question. It was her voice. She was taking on Nancy's accent—not as thick or pronounced, but it was unmistakable. Savannah was beginning to sound like a hillbilly.

Nancy waved her off, "Oh, honey, we can provide you with all that just like Ramada Inn. Just swing by the office and I'll take care of you."

"Well, thank you," Savannah said, stretching the "you" out as if it had two syllables, her accent growing thicker. Dan didn't know if she was mocking Nancy or just liked her accent and wanted to try it on for size.

"If you need clothes and what-not, there are a few places where the locals go. That way you won't have to pay tourist prices." She opened one of the brochures Savannah had taken from the office which now lay in a pile on the kitchen counter and used the small map in the back to show Savannah where to find the stores.

The pile of brochures was well over six inches high because Savannah had taken one for everything she wanted to see, and she wanted to see everything. Dan didn't know why the stack hadn't toppled over.

"Thank you," Savannah said, and that was the end of her trying the accent. She had it down pat now. "You're so kind."

This time Nancy did notice and from her puzzled expression, she didn't know if she was being mocked or not, but Savannah's smile was so sweet it seemed to relax her. She said her goodbyes and left, waddling her way back to her car. Savannah went to the balcony and Dan joined her, standing behind her as he looked out over the valley and wondered how it was that he couldn't see any of the town. He saw no signs of civilization at all, and while he knew it was only a stone's throw away, it really did feel isolated. He wrapped his arms around her, hugging her from behind. She traced her fingers over his forearm. "Where would you like to go first, Mr. Mitchell?" she asked, the accent still there. "We could go explore the mountains."

"What's wrong with right here?" he asked. "And what's up with the accent?"

"Don't you like it, Mr. Mitchell?" She snuggled back into him.

"Actually, it's kind of sexy in a Daisy Duke sort of way."

She turned in his grasp and wrapped her arms around him. "Would you like to come explore my mountains, Mr. Mitchell?"

It was another hour before they went shopping.

CHAPTER 46

It was full dark when they put the third load of packages in the car. The little Prius was stuffed, both the trunk and the backseat full from a day's shopping. He didn't know how they would get everything home if they kept going like this, and it was only their first day here, plus it wasn't a full day at that. After they had finished with the basic clothes they would need for the week—he had already decided to extend their stay—they hit the tourist shops where Dan spent money as if it were poisonous and he needed it out of his possession before it killed him. They had gone any place that appealed to her, starting with a haunted house where she screamed appropriately, jumping startled whenever one of the characters lunged at her. Once outside, Dan asked, "Were you really scared?"

"Of course not," she said, hooking her hand into his elbow. "I didn't want to disappoint any of the actors."

"They were all robots," he said.

She shrugged. "So am I."

They went through Ripley's Believe it or Not, where she stopped to read every display, then announced, "Believe it," for some and, "Not," for others, and her choices seemed to be random except for the ones that were truly outrageous. Those she always deemed as, "Believe it." While that had been fun, when they went through the Guinness World Records attraction, she did the same thing, announcing, "Believe it," at the fat twins on the motorcycles and the world's tallest man, but, "Not" to the man with the world's largest ball of twine.

"It's not the same thing," Dan said. "These are all real."

She shook her head. "Not," she said again, pointing at the black and white photo of a ball of string as big as a tool shed as if sentencing it to life at hard labor. "Nobody could be that boring."

They watched saltwater taffy as it was pulled by a machine, the mechanical arms winding the sugar-dough around and back on itself. They went inside and she tried samples of each flavor. "It's kinda meh," she said.

"It's not my favorite either," he said, still working on a piece that was supposed to be strawberry, but tasted as much like wax as anything. "My mom liked it, though." He swallowed, forcing the candy down in a lump and his stomach growled in protest. He hadn't eaten since Jellico. They were strolling, holding hands, no particular destination in mind when she stopped, turning her head from side to side. Her head cocked a little, like a dog, contemplating and curious. She began to walk again, this time faster, tugging his hand, urging him along. She stopped at the edge of the Little Pigeon River that ran through the heart of the town and pointed to the other side. "What's that?"

"It's a go-kart track," he said. Five of the little karts zipped past in a clump.

"They look like little cars," she said.

"Well, they kind of are. But you don't drive them on the street, just around a track."

"Is there a license required?" she asked. Three ducks came up to them in hopes they had food, and when they didn't feed them, the ducks quacked in anger, demanding attention.

"No," he said with a shrug. "Anyone can do it."

"Ah, Daniel-san. We shall have our race now. And when your Platypus-Style Kung Fu is defeated, you shall know humility for your arrogance. And you shall let me drive car."

"This sounds like a wager," he said. "What do I get if I win?"

"What is this word, 'wager,' you speak of Daniel-san? It is new to my village."

"A bet," he said. "If you win, you get whatever I promise—if I win, or should I say, 'When,' I win, I get what you promised, and you have to pay up."

"Ah," she said, one eyebrow going up. "So, if I win, I get to drive?"

"If you win, I'll let you drive from the parking lot to the cabin, but only if you listen to my instructions. What do I get if I win?"

"What is it you desire, Daniel-san?" Her accent was half old Kung Fu movie, half hillbilly, but she was able to move her lips out of sync with her voice which was funny in the movies—strange to watch in real life.

"Well, I want you to stop talking like that for one thing," he said, but that wasn't worth a wager. "I know—if I win, you have to shut up about driving."

"Forever?" she asked, like that was too much.

"Forever."

"One year," she said.

He thought it over. "Deal." He stuck his hand out to shake.

"Six months," she said as she shook his hand.

He laughed. "Okay, six months."

"You have deal, Daniel-san," she said. "I win, I get to drive. You win, I no say nothing about driving for one whole month."

"Six months," he said.

"No matter—I going to win." They crossed the bridge.

Dan paid forty dollars for them to race for five minutes.

She lapped him, waving as she went past.

Twice.

The streets weren't empty by any means, but they weren't packed either. That seemed odd to Dan since it was a holiday weekend, and he wondered what the place would be like on Tuesday, after the holiday was over. As they made their way back to the car, the streets began to light up, the signs on the doors saying they all closed at ten, and he wondered if that was the Mountain Witching Hour. When he closed the car trunk, he checked his watch—9:15. Most of the restaurants were either closed or closing and the tourist shops would soon follow.

Savannah began to walk across the church lot where they'd paid $10 to park for the day. When Dan had forked over a twenty and waited for his change from the attendant, he wondered what Jesus would have thought about parking fees. He'd been against the money lenders, but He never addressed parking. When she reached the attendant's hut, he called to her. "Where are you going? Everything's closing."

"Not everything," she said. "You need dinner. There's a place a few blocks from here."

He didn't ask how she knew that. It could be anything from the constant Internet connection to she'd read it in one of the brochures. Maybe she heard someone talk about it on the street. With Savannah's hearing, she might have heard someone from three blocks away over the din of tourists and traffic. He never knew and had grown bored with asking. He crossed the lot and took her hand and they walked into the night.

Most tourist towns are the same. They have the main drag which is dedicated to getting visitors to spend as much money as they can in as little time possible, all upon the altar of synthetic fun. In Vegas, it's called The Strip—in Orlando, it's International Drive—in Gatlinburg, Tn., it's The Parkway. If things go well for the town, that might bleed over for another block—maybe even two, but never much more than that. Nobody ever hears of someone going to Vegas and having a great vacation in a place two miles from The Strip. Gatlinburg had been catering to tourists for over a hundred years, growing exponentially, and thanks to the mountainous geography, it had expanded into the elusive third block, but no farther. So as she led him deeper into the darkness, away from the safety of the tourist lights and into the night, Dan began to feel uneasy. It wasn't that he didn't trust her, of course, but like any place where people congregate, there are good areas and bad, and this was beginning to feel like a bad one. "Where are we going?" he asked, keeping his voice hushed as they walked past a row of rundown apartments not meant for a tourist's eyes.

"Cousin Sadie's Dewdrop Inn," she said. "Cute name, isn't it? It's just a little ways more." She still used her mountain accent, sounding like a local tour guide as she tugged at his hand, urging him faster and he didn't argue. While her need to rush might have been born from excitement, his wasn't—it was from some-place darker.

He told himself he was being silly—that he was spooked for nothing. At least the haunted house had automatons jumping out at them from dark corners. Now, they hadn't seen so much as a cat. Crime didn't happen in places like Gatlinburg—it was a happy place where families bought corn cob pipes and home-made fudge. The Tennessee Mountains were the home of Jed and Granny, Jethro and Ellie Mae. But what if Jethro had gone to the big city and learned its evil ways and come home?

"Just out of curiosity, do you have any information on the crime rates in Gatlinburg?" he asked, moving at the speed where he wasn't quite winded, but close.

"Of course," she said. "Gatlinburg's overall crime index is one."

He felt relief wash over him. He knew he was being silly, and that proved it. You couldn't get lower than a one. "Well, that's reassuring," he said. He began to slow down. If it was that safe, there was no need to hurry.

"That's out of one-hundred," she said, just as conversation-ally as she would tell him the scores of a Reds game. "You have a one-in-eighty-three chance of being the victim of a violent crime in Gatlinburg. It's one of the highest in the nation and certainly the highest in the region. I suspect it's even higher during the tourist season. They only provide annual statistics."

He stopped, even though his instincts said to run. "Are you crazy? What are we doing here? We could get killed."

"Well, you, perhaps, but not me. And statistically, it won't happen. While the violent crime rate is high, there were no murders reported last year. The chances are far greater of being raped and robbed than killed."

"Oh," he said. "Well, why didn't you say so? I feel so much bet-ter now. Did you ever see *Deliverance*? They filmed it here. Maybe I should just hold my wallet in the air as we walk and shout, 'Please don't hurt us?'"

"Don't be silly, Dan," she said. She resumed walking as if the discussion was over, or at least pointless. "That would be like an invitation." He stayed standing until she had made it about five steps, then he began to feel alone as she faded into the darkness of no street lamps, and while none of her numbers had reassured him, the fact that she was a walking 911 hotline did. "And they filmed *Deliverance* in Georgia, not Tennessee," she called over her shoulder, not slowing to wait for him.

"That's like a mile from here," he said, jogging the few steps it took to catch up.

"No, it is exactly 100 miles from Gatlinburg to Tallulah Gorge, where the river scenes were filmed." He knew that was her Internet connection at work. "See?" she said as they topped a short rise. "Cousin Sadie's Dewdrop Inn, as promised, and nobody died. You worry too much."

The music flowing out the doors was nothing like the country music that piped into the street from hidden speakers on the Parkway. It was the same rock they had listened to on their road trip, but it seemed somehow darker and seedier as they stepped into the bar. Dan had assumed that once they entered it would feel safer. He was wrong. No one seemed to notice them at all, yet it still felt uneasy, as if Death knew this place—or at least Death's second cousin, Ass-Kicking.

Dan ordered a draught for each of them, even though Savannah's was more for decoration, and he asked if the kitchen was open. The woman behind the bar said it was, and that they made a pretty mean cheeseburger. Dan ordered one with everything and steak fries. When the lady asked what Savannah wanted, she said, "Nothing. I'm going to steal part of his." Dan was relieved she hadn't made a bad joke.

The jukebox on one wall sounded like it had a broken speaker and that corresponded with the cracked glass in its front. Two pool tables in the back were in busy use, surrounded by a handful of men all holding cue sticks like fighting staffs at rest. The place was dark, smoky and generally about as clean as that deli counter in the gas station in Ohio, but Dan realized it didn't bother him the way it used to. While it was possible he had overcome his phobias thanks to life with Savannah, he got the feeling that his fear of germs was taking a backseat to the fear of men wearing faded jeans and wallets attached to their belts with biker chains. Germs might kill you—knives and guns would kill you more. "Can I have a dollar?" Savannah asked.

"Sure," he said, as he reached for his wallet. "You're so cute, you can have two. Going to play the jukebox?"

She nodded, took the two ones and thanked him with a kiss. He watched her walk across the room and noted he wasn't the only one whose eyes were drawn to her. She was easily the prettiest female in the place and it wasn't just the men who noticed. She flipped the buttons to change the album selections, then punched the numbers to choose the songs she wanted. She walked to the back where the men were playing pool, leaned against a post and watched.

"Food will be right up," the bartender said.

"Thanks," Dan said. "I think we're going to sit at a table though." He picked up both beers, looking for an empty spot toward the back, closer to where Savannah stood.

"I'll find you," the bartender said.

Dan moved toward Savannah, taking a sip from her beer to keep from spilling it. He wasn't much of a drinker, but he did like the taste of a cold beer, especially with food, and in this case, it seemed the anticipation of food was enough to make the beer taste good. He took another swallow from hers as he gazed at her butt, and it looked amazing in the sky blue short dress. He knew firsthand she wore nothing under it except a pair of thong panties, and the summer weight dress was cut low enough in the back to let anyone know she wasn't wearing a bra. He heard her say something and gesture to the pool table, but he couldn't make it out. One of the men smiled at her, kind of the way a wolf would smile at a lone sheep. He said something in return and Savannah shrugged. Dan had another sip of beer.

He looked back toward the bar, wondering where the food was. Now that the beer was hitting his stomach, his hunger multiplied, but he saw no sign of the bartender. Perhaps she was bringing it. He took another sip, then another, not realizing that it was hitting him as hard as it was because he hadn't eaten in over nine hours. He looked back at Savannah's beautiful butt and drank a silent toast to it, then the legs that grew from it, draining the last of her beer. He wondered if the place had peanuts or maybe chips to munch on while he waited for his burger. Savannah said something else to the pool player, and the man said something in return, this time without the smile. Dan started on his own beer. The music changed, and once more today he heard the familiar organ intro, then the crying wail of the lone guitar. "I thought you didn't like this song," he said, a little too loud, but not because she couldn't hear him. He was buzzed.

She came to the table and took the seat next to him. "It's a pretty song," she said. "It's just sad." She took a sip from his mug and grimaced. "You like this stuff? It's really bitter"

"It's good and cold," he said. "You having fun over there?"

"The tall one is an idiot," she said. "I offered him advice and he told me to shut the fuck up. He was rude and he must not know that word is considered vulgar." She shrugged. "He's also not a very good pool player."

"And what do you know about pool?" Dan asked. He sipped at the mug some more and his stomach growled in protest. It wanted food.

"I know it's basic Newtonian physics combined with two-dimensional geometry. Any five-year-old could do it."

"It's not that simple," Dan said. "It's a skill. The idea isn't just to make the shot you're aiming at, it's also to position the cue ball—the white one—in place for your next shot."

"Thanks, Mr. Wizard," she said, grinning at him. She reached over and straightened his hair and he grinned back. "I want to play," she said. "I can win. How do I go about playing?"

Dan hadn't been in a bar like this since college, but he'd played a few games in his day. "You put a quarter on the table. When it's your turn, you rack the balls and the other person breaks. Do you need me to tell you the rules?"

"No, I have them," she said. "They're playing eight-ball, considered by most to be the simplest version of the game. Can I have a quarter?"

He fished a handful of change from his pocket and laid it on the table. She dug a quarter from the pile, kissed him again and walked away. He drained half of his beer.

She put the quarter on the table and said something. The tall player said something back. She said something else and the tall man's eyes drifted up and down her body, as if he were inspecting her. Savannah cocked her thumb in Dan's direction and the tall man looked at him.

"Here you go," the bartender said, setting the plate in front of him. "I brought you two more beers, too." She smiled and put the tab on the table but didn't wait for him to pay.

"Your woman's got a smart mouth on her," someone said, and Dan looked to find the tall man standing beside the table.

"Tell me about it," Dan said, holding his beer in one hand and a fry in the other. He dipped the fry in a puddle of ketchup and chased it with a swallow of beer.

"She ruined my game. I had a hundred bucks riding on that game. You owe me."

"How do I owe you?" Dan asked as he took another fry and sat back in his seat. He wondered if fries were good when you dunked them in beer. He tried it—they were. "She's the one who ruined your game. She owes you, not me."

"She says she belongs to you," the man said. "Some kind of weird sex thing, I reckon. But she owes me, and if she's yours, then you owe me."

"Play her for it. She's never played before. She thinks she knows everything." He dunked another fry into his beer. It was better than ketchup. "If you win, I'll pay you. Scout's Honor." He held up three fingers in the Scout's Salute. "If she wins, we're even. No harm, no foul. Maybe you can teach her a lesson in humility."

The tall man thought it over for a second. "She ain't never played before?"

Dan held up the three fingers again. "Never touched a stick. I know it for a fact."

"Then why would you want to bet a hundred dollars on her?"

Dan shrugged. "According to you, I already owe you the hundred. If you win, I'm not out anything, and there's always the chance you'll sink the eight on accident. I really don't have anything to lose."

When the man thought, it was like looking at someone in pain. Dan wondered how long it would take him to realize that if he took the bet, he had nothing to gain. He dunked another fry in his beer while he waited. "Two hundred," the man said. "And I break."

Dan shrugged and stood, feeling a little tipsy on his feet. "Why not?" He took a bite of his burger, realizing the bartender was right—it was a pretty mean burger—then went to stand beside Savannah. "Rack 'em," he said to her around a mouthful and handed her three more quarters.

She put the coins into the slot, but nothing happened. Dan stepped beside her and shoved the coins in and the balls dropped. "Go to that end," he said, pointing to the spot. "The balls will dispense down there. The rack should be in a slot above it." He wished he had brought his burger with him, but at least he'd remembered his drink.

"She really ain't never played before," the tall man said with a satisfied smirk. He looked like he was already planning on how he would spend his winnings.

Savannah racked as if she were looking at a Google article on how to go about it, placing the one-ball in the front, another solid in one corner and a stripe in the other. She placed the eight in the apex of the inner triangle and filled the other balls around it, then slid the rack forward and lifted it away. The tall man broke, using his full upper body weight in the shot and two solids sank. He chuckled and lined up his next shot. Savannah went to the rack of sticks and selected one. Dan took a sip of beer, then went to their table for another bite of his burger.

He resumed chewing as another solid dropped into the corner pocket, the sound of the ball falling and rolling into the chute behind the long glass window. "You shot too hard," Savannah said as the cue came to a stop about two inches from the rail. "You should have stopped the cue ball here." She pointed to a spot about eight inches away.

"Why don't you shut up?" the shooter said as he pulled his stick back. He tried to cut the three into the side but missed. "Shit."

"I told you," she said as she stepped to the table.

"You," the man said, pointing his stick at Dan as if it were a sword and he was preparing for battle. "The bet's double. Five hundred dollars."

Dan started to point out that doubling a two-hundred dollar bet would only be four hundred, but decided not to. "You're on," he said. He finished that beer and wished he had brought Savannah's too.

Savannah lined up a shot on the nine and drew back to take it, then stood up again, picking up a piece of chalk. "This will add friction between the stick and the cue ball," she said, as if teaching a class. She bent over again and said, "Nine ball in the corner," took her shot and the nine went straight into the corner pocket. The tall man hadn't bothered to call his shots. She chalked again and lined up the ten, a cross side bank, touched the pocket with her cue stick and said, "Ten." She shot and sank it. She chalked again, walking to the other side of the table. She had an easy, straight-in shot on the fifteen in the side, but she pointed to the far corner instead. "Eleven." She cut the eleven with the precision of a surgeon and the ball dropped, the cue ball coming to a stop within inches of the twelve. "Twelve, far corner," she said. She shot and the ball rolled the length of the table, bounced in the pocket a couple of times then sank. She was lining up her next shot before the ball had even reached the pocket.

"You know you don't have to shoot them in order, right?" Dan asked.

"I know," she said. "This makes it more interesting. Thirteen, side pocket, off the fourteen," she said. It was a beautiful combination.

"Never played before my ass," her opponent said.

"Really, I haven't," she said as the fourteen fell where she pointed. "It's simple mathematics." The cue came to rest behind the eight with the fifteen— her final ball— unreachable. "Eight ball neutral?"

"No," the tall man said. Dan got the feeling it would have been, if things were the other way around.

Savannah shrugged as she chalked her cue again. "Fifteen, far corner." She aimed as if she was going to hit the eight ball no matter what the man had said, and if she did, she would forfeit her turn. Instead, she held the back of her stick high and shot. The cue started off as if it were going to hit the eight then the spin from the English took over, causing the cue ball to actually change directions, hit the rail then the fifteen, slicing the ball into the far corner. Dan hadn't realized a crowd had gathered until they cheered her shot. Savannah smiled. "Eight ball, side pocket." It was an easy straight in shot from there, and she'd put enough English on it to bring the cue back to its starting point. "That was fun," she said. The crowd applauded.

"I ain't paying," the tall man said. "You lied. There ain't no way she never played before."

"Did you make the bet?" a short, thin woman said from behind the same post Savannah had leaned on earlier. She had the gravelly voice of a chain smoker. The tall man looked at her, but didn't answer. "You make the bet, you pay the bet," the woman said. "You know the rules, Sam."

"I got hustled," Sam said. He fished his chained wallet from his pocket and fished out five one-hundred dollar bills and tossed them on the table.

"Next time keep your mouth shut," the thin lady said. She stepped close to Savannah. "That was some mighty fine shooting, darlin'." She winked at her then walked away.

"It was," Dan agreed, slipping into a hug. "I'm proud of you."

"Be proud of Newton," she said. "He did all the work."

CHAPTER 47

Dan finished his burger and fries as Savannah shot more pool. No one wanted to bet against her, though, but many people circled the tables to watch her. When Dan returned, holding another fresh beer, she was describing each shot in detail before she took it, explaining the laws of physics that would determine the outcome, and her strategy for the following shot as well. She sounded like a professor with a thick Appalachian accent.

"I ain't never seen nothing like it," the thin lady said. "She could be a professional." She turned to Dan. "So this is what the two of you do? Go around hustling pool games?"

"No," Dan said. "This really is the first time she's ever played. She's just good at math."

The lady looked at him as if she didn't believe him. She lit a cigarette and blew the smoke out in a blue cloud. "Y'all need to come up with a better story than that."

Sam and the guy he'd been playing against had left after the bet was paid, and the place seemed somehow safer. Savannah grinned at Dan, then turned to the other table and explained the shot she was about to take there. Dan didn't know at what point she had dominated both tables, playing two opponents at once, but it didn't seem to slow her down at all. She took her shot and dropped both the three and the seven in opposite corners. More applause. She sank the eight and turned back to the first table. It was her turn to break.

"This here is a little different," she said, sounding like a local. "Breaking also has chaos theory mathematics, so it's not as precise." She chalked her cue, bent down and shot with force. The cue ball smacked into the racked triangle of balls, sending them scattering, but the eight rolled straight into the corner pocket—an automatic win. "They's only about a one in ten chance of that happening," she said, again to a short round of applause, like a magician who had performed a really cool trick. She put one foot behind her other leg, toe pointed to the ground and bent at the knees, holding her skirt out in her fingertips—a perfect curtsy. She walked back to Dan and gave him another quick peck of a kiss and fixed his hair again, grinning at him. "You okay, slugger?"

"I'm fine," he said, tilting his head back to finish the glass of beer. He staggered back a step to keep from falling. "I real—" he burped beer, "I really like your accent like that. It's sexy." He swayed on his feet.

She laughed, tugging at his shirt to help keep him upright. "Maybe we should get you home."

"It's okay," he said, but he heard himself slur it into one word, "Issokay," and it made him giggle. "You're having fun. We can stay, you're having fun."

"Naw," she said. "It got boring. Let's go home." She slipped an arm around his waist both in affection and support. He leaned on her as they made it to the door. Savannah turned to the thin woman who was back at her table in the front, a cigarette dangling from the corner of her mouth as she chatted with another woman. "Bye, Sadie. Thank you."

The little lady waved back. "Y'all be careful out there, ya hear? And come up with a better story. You'll live longer." She laughed at her own joke, and it became a smoker's hack which she covered with a cupped fist.

"Yes, ma'am, we will," Savannah said, and they stepped into the cool of the evening.

"That was Sadie of Cousin Sadie's?" he asked.

"Yeah. She and her husband opened it in 1985. He died a few years ago, so now it's just her. She seems lonely."

"When did you find all this out?" he asked.

"When you were eating your burger. She and I talked while I

shot pool. She played me one game. She's good. Better than Sam. She almost ran the table on me."

They headed toward the car in the same direction they had come, walking up the short rise that would lead to the run down apartments. It didn't feel as spooky this time, but then, Dan was a little numb to everything thanks to the buzz, and that included fear. He had an arm draped over her shoulders and she had one around his waist. "You're leaning on me a lot," she said. "Do you want me to carry you?"

He laughed at the thought. "You can't carry me. You're strong, but you're not that strong."

It was her turn to laugh. "I could toss you about half the way there, but then you'd bounce and tomorrow morning be all like, 'Ow, my leg is broken, ow.'"

"I wouldn't whine like that," he said.

"Help me, my mean girlfriend hurt my wittle arm. Then there would be the hospital—more police inquiries—it would be an ugly mess."

"Gimme my money," said a voice from the deep shadows of a fence line. Sam stepped into what little light there was.

"Jesus," Dan said, startled. There was a metallic click and Sam's finger seemed to grow eight inches longer in an instant. He stepped close enough that Dan saw it was a switchblade. The man he left with stepped behind him. Another click—another knife. "Here, fine. Take your money," Dan said, reaching for his wallet.

"No," Savannah said, dropping her arm from Dan's waist. "You wagered and lost. It is no longer your money. It is our money now. A wager is a bet, and you have to keep your word."

"How's about we just cut you up and use you for fish bait?" the companion said, taking a step closer.

"You can try," Savannah said, "but you will not succeed." Dan's heart was pounding out of control, fast and hard. He wasn't a fighter—had never been in a fight in his life, and he was terrified. The adrenalin kicked in and he felt stark sober. Maybe he could talk their way out of this—maybe they could just run.

He'd heard that if you're robbed, to throw your wallet away from the attacker and run—they were more interested in the money than you. He started to move between her and the threat, one hand on his wallet to throw it over their heads and run as fast as he could back toward the bar, but she stopped him with one hand to his chest and took that spot herself. "Go away or you will get hurt."

"Little girl, it's time somebody shut you up for good," Sam said. The two men looked at one another as if their moves were choreographed and a silent count passed between them. Both made stabbing motions at Savannah in sync with one another. She caught Sam by the wrist with her right hand, but the other man planted his knife straight into her left forearm, so deep it protruded through the other side.

Sam looked surprised as he tried to yank his arm free but couldn't even budge it, and Dan heard the crack of breaking bones, along with Sam's yelp of pain and the clatter of his knife as it hit the pavement. Sam's companion hit Savannah with a roundhouse punch, his entire body twisting as he put his weight into it. It connected to the side of Savannah's head. She didn't flinch. Dan's mouth fell open. He knew Savannah was strong— he had no idea she was that strong. He was engaged to Wonder Woman.

Sam fell to his knees. Savannah looked at the knife protruding from her left arm with the same curiosity as she had the inchworm on the day Dan first met her. She opened and closed her fist as she stared at it in fascination, checking for internal damage. Water ran from the cut instead of blood, but it flowed free and fast, dripping from her elbow to form a puddle on the ground. She twisted Sam's arm and the yelp became a scream. "Do not threaten Dan," she said as she hit Sam in the face with her left fist, and the crack of more breaking bones was loud in the quiet of the night. Sam fell limp and silent.

"What the fuck are you?" the companion said, taking a timid step backward. Savannah pulled the knife from her arm and the water practically gushed. The companion turned to run as she threw the blade at him, and it planted deep in his upper thigh. He fell, grunting in pain as he struggled to extract the knife from his leg. Savannah picked up Sam's knife and went to him. He forgot about the knife sticking from his leg, trying to crawl away, focusing on the blade in her hand instead.

"You're a bad man, and that's a bad word," she said, standing over him, her hands on her hips as if what he really needed was a good scolding. "It's vulgar. You need to say you're sorry."

"I'm sorry," he said. He kept trying to crawl away, dragging his wounded leg behind him, but Savannah followed him. "Really—I'm sorry."

"I don't believe you," she said, still yelling at him in that silly accent. She jabbed the knife at him, pointing it like an accusatory finger.

"Please," the man said as if he were facing Hell itself. "It were all Sam's idea. I told him not to. I told him to let it go. But he wouldn't listen."

"You need to find better friends," she said. Water flowed down her arm and dripped from her elbow to the ground.

"I will," he said. "I will find better friends. I'll go to church. I'll do whatever you say. Please don't kill me."

She stood upright, her head cocked to one side as she considered his pleas. "I wasn't going to kill you," she said, as if the thought were ridiculous. "I didn't kill Sam, did I?"

He didn't answer, and Dan guessed that was because he wasn't sure. Sam still had yet to move or even groan and as far as Dan knew, he was as dead as hammer.

"Did I?" she demanded.

"No, Ma'am," he said. "He ain't dead—I can tell it from here." He nodded as if it were true. "But it don't matter. I ain't going to hang out with him no more. You can kill him if'n you want to. I won't tell nobody."

"Now is that a nice thing to say?" she asked, her voice turning to conversational as fast as it had gone to anger. "I have contacted the authorities and requested an ambulance as well as the police." She reached down and he held his hands up in surrender as she took his wallet from his pocket. She used the blade to cut the leather that attached the chain to his belt. He whined fear as the knife came toward him, then sighed relief when it didn't stab.

"Take it," he said. "There's a thousand dollars in there. It's all yours."

She rolled her eyes to show the thought was ridiculous, but she did open his wallet. "You are Jason Andrews of 113 Logan Court, Nashville, Tennessee?"

"Y-yes," he said. He grunted and grabbed at his thigh some more.

"When the authorities arrive, you will confess to the crime of attempted robbery with a deadly weapon. I will watch the police reports online. If I do not see them, I will come to 113 Logan Court in Nashville and I will break both of your legs." She held the switchblade at his eye level and bent it until it snapped into pieces. "Do you understand?"

"Yes, Ma'am," he said, his eyes focusing on the shattered blade as she dropped the pieces in front of him. "I'll tell them everything, I swear."

"You will tell them a man did this to you," she said, somehow sounding benevolent yet threatening. "You may say it was two men, if you prefer. We do not wish to be further involved, and I know you will need your street cred in the joint." Dan thought it might be time to cut back on her television viewing. She was getting Hollywood Streetwise.

"Uh—Thank you?"

"You are welcome," she said. "If you say that a girl did this to you, I will come to 113 Logan Court in Nashville and break your arms. Now remember," she said, as if instructing a small child. "That's legs if you fail to confess—arms if you tell them it was me." She tossed his wallet back to him. "I'm sorry, but we must go. I need to repair my arm." She went back to Dan who had taken a seat on the ground to feel for Sam's pulse. Sure enough, the man was alive, but from the smushed nose and the crooked jaw, he was going to need surgery—maybe more than one. She helped Dan to his feet with a pull of his arm and they resumed their walk, his arm around her shoulders, hers around his waist. "Have a happy time in jail," she said with the tone of someone wishing him a nice day.

CHAPTER 48

"Well, you didn't remember it either," Dan said. His head felt as if it were going to split into a million pieces, reminding him why he wasn't a drinker.

"I said we would need our things—you said that we could get whatever we needed here," she said, sounding way too reasonable for this early in a hangover.

"Well, I didn't mean your charger," he said. "Where are we supposed to get one of those? It's not like Wal-Mart carries them."

She shrugged. "I don't know, but we need to do something fast. I'm leaking like a busted still over here." She still used the Appalachian accent and enjoyed adding local references to it. She sat on the bear-patterned couch, her forearm up, and water flowed from it as fast as it had the night before, into a bucket she propped under her elbow. She worked her fist, open, closed, open again. "And I'm draining power too fast. I think he shorted the wiring in my arm, ya hear?" She turned her hand back and forth, looking at it. "I can't feel nothing with it, neither."

"Will you stop talking like that?" he said. "We need to fix your arm."

"It's just a flesh wound," she said, switching accents from hillbilly to British, mimicking her favorite Monty Python movie.

Dan shot her a look to say she wasn't funny. He was worried. She had already gone through all the bottled water in the place and switched to tap, and he'd emptied her bucket twice since he woke up with this killer of a headache. God knew how many times she'd emptied it while he slept.

"Dan?" she said, pleading. "You're supposed to call me a loony."

"You're a loony," he said, dismissive.

"Say it right," she said, sounding as if this was too much fun.

He switched to his British accent which wasn't as good as hers, but said, "You're a loony," mimicking King Arthur as best he could. She giggled.

"Ian says he'll overnight a charger to us," she said. "But you owe him. And he's happy we're no longer fighting. He also says he's proud of me for saving your sorry ass last night—his words."

"I'm kind of proud of you for that myself," Dan said. "Ask him how much the charger is. Just put it on the credit card."

She didn't say anything for a few seconds, then, "He says you don't owe him money. You owe him a favor that he will collect one day. He thinks he's The Godfather." She laughed.

"Are you on the phone with him?" Dan asked.

"We're texting," she said. "He says I should fix my arm now. I think he's right. I'm losing power pretty darn fast." She pronounced it "losin'," and, "purdy dern." She held it up to inspect it again. "It's going to leave a big ol' remember, though. He offered to send a replacement arm, but I said just the wiring harness. Is that okay?"

"It's your arm," Dan said, letting her know that made it her choice. "And I think it will be a nice remember." He wished they had bought some aspirin yesterday.

"Come here," she said, patting her lap. He finished his coffee and went to the couch and started to sit next to her. "No," she said. She pointed to the other end of the couch. "Sit there and give me your feet."

"Why do you want my feet?" he asked, but he took the seat and propped his feet in her lap. She reached down with her right hand and began rubbing them.

"Reflexology," she said. She pressed her thumb into the arch of his right foot and twisted her hand, digging deep.

"Ouch," he said, pulling his foot away. "That hurts."

"Stop being a baby," she said, grabbing his ankle and putting his foot back. "This will relax you. Now, close your eyes and take a deep breath." She twisted her thumb into the arch again, but it didn't hurt as much this time. He took a deep breath and held it until she told him to let it out. She continued to coach him through his breathing and he felt the world begin to slip away. She slid her hand to the tips of his toes, pinching them, but not hard and she moved her fingers in a circle over each one. She told him to inhale, then exhale, her voice soft, soothing. When she finished with his right foot, she began with the left, the only sounds her soft voice and his breath. When she finished, she patted his foot lightly. "There. How do you feel?"

He opened his eyes, not realizing he was almost asleep, and it felt like coming out of a trance. He thought about the question. The headache was gone. Not dulled or calmed, but gone, and his stomach felt good, too. He had been queasy all morning. "I feel great," he said. "I mean, really great. Thank you."

She smiled. "You're welcome. Go drink lots of water, and would you bring me some?" She held out her glass.

"Sure," he said. He got hers first and returned with it, and she swallowed it fast, pouring it down.

"Thank you," she said, handing him back the glass.

"More?"

She nodded. "Yes please. I should probably go to the tub to save the mess, though. I can heat in there." She stood, taking longer than he would have liked to see and began shuffling her way to the bathroom, slow, hunched like an old woman.

"Hey," he said. She stopped and turned back to him. "I'm sorry I forgot your mat."

She smiled, soft and sweet. "It's okay. You're human. That makes you dumb." She grinned at him and he didn't think he could ever love her more than he did in that moment. He went to fetch her water, no longer sure of who was in charge of their relationship, but he didn't care. Love and control in relationships were both as fluid as ocean tides. Sometimes they favored one person—sometimes the other, but it always sought balance. He loved her—of that he was certain. She loved him, and he was as sure of that as any person could ever be of another's love. It was never in their words, but only in their actions that people showed true emotions. It was easy to lie while swearing oaths of love. It was almost impossible to lie with actions. He filled her glass and took it to her. She hadn't made it to the bathroom yet, even though it was only a few yards from the couch. When he reached her, she stumbled. "I'm weak," she said. "Weaker than I thought. The short must be messing with my power monitor." She drained the glass and smiled her thanks. "I might not have enough to heat my skin." She held the door for balance.

He scooped her into his arms like a newlywed bride and placed her gently in the tub. He poured another glass from the faucet in the bathroom sink and handed it to her. "Then switch to low power," he said. "We'll seal your skin tomorrow."

"Are you sure?" she asked, but she sounded hopeful.

"Yeah," he said, brushing her hair from her eyes with one finger. "I'll be okay. What's important is that you are."

She smiled as she drank the water, then she half-closed her eyes and they lost focus, staring straight ahead, flat and bland. The water stopped flowing from her arm quite so fast, and it grew slower by the second as the pressure dropped, like the spray fading from a garden hose when the spigot is turned off. He stroked her hair away again with his fingertips, and for the first time since he could remember, she didn't react. "I love you," he said, knowing she didn't hear him, but it didn't matter. He bent, kissed her forehead and went to the living room where he turned on the television. The local noon edition of the news told of a bizarre confession to assault with a deadly weapon and attempted robbery in Gatlinburg. The two suspects were also being questioned about a string of robberies in both the Gatlinburg and Pigeon Forge areas. The police wanted to question the alleged victims, two large African-American males believed to be masters in the martial arts. They showed a sketch of two men who looked remarkably like Mike Tyson and George Foreman. The Gatlinburg Chief of Police stressed that these two men were not suspected of any wrong doings—they were witnesses to a crime and the police only wanted to take their statements. Anyone with information was asked to contact the Gatlinburg Police.

CHAPTER 49

Dan watched the news long enough to see the weather, then turned the set off. If he were still hungover, he would take a nap to sleep it away, but he wasn't—he felt great. He unloaded the car and placed their clothes on the provided hangers in the Master Bedroom closet and hung them neatly, each hanger two finger-widths apart. Then he folded the remaining clothes like socks and underwear, and two pairs of shorts each, and put them in the dresser. He felt proud of himself for a job well done. It was 1:30.

He went to check on Savannah. She hadn't moved since the last time he'd checked on her, about ten minutes ago. She sat slumped in the tub, eyes unfocused and half-open. She resembled a corpse in one of the television shows she liked to watch where she picked up terms like, "street cred," and, "the joint." He went to her and squatted beside the tub. She still wore the same dress as the night before, and it was soaked from the water that had run from her arm. He tugged at it until he slipped it over her head, then did the same with her panties. He put both in the hamper. There was a laundry room by the pool and he would take their clothes to wash in a bit. He closed the drain on the tub and turned on the warm water, sitting on the closed toilet as it filled.

He removed her hair to wash later, soaped a rag with a bar of the perfumed stuff she liked, then began to wash her body. He had to move her around more than he expected to get everywhere, and when he finished, he drained the tub and used one of the towels to dry her. When that was done he scooped her into his arms, again like a fresh bride, and carried her to the bedroom, where he laid her out on her side of the bed, folding her arms over her chest, then tucking the blanket up to her chin to cover her nude body. He returned to the bathroom and stripped naked, stepping into the warm shower and scrubbed himself clean, then shampooed, first his own hair, then hers. Once he had dried himself, he used the blow dryer on her wig the way he'd watched her do countless times, brushing it as he went. When he felt it was as sufficiently styled as his unskilled talents would allow, he took it back to the bedroom and put it on her. While it no longer made any difference to him if she wore it, she always preferred it on, and that mattered. He checked his watch— 2:30. He kissed her forehead, then without thinking, whispered, "Sleep sweet, Savannah."

Her eyes flitted at the sound of her name and he felt guilty. She needed rest. "Dan?" she said, weak as a kitten.

"I'm here, sweetie. I didn't mean to wake you. Go back to sleep."

"Will you lay with me?"

"Of course," he said. He still wore the towel wrapped around his waist, and he dropped it then crawled under the covers with her. She turned on her side, away from him and he slipped his arm over her and moved closer to spoon her, their naked bodies pressed together. "Let me ask you something. How did we get home last night? I didn't drive in that condition, did I?"

She sighed, soft. "I told you I would be good at it."

"Then why is there a big dent in the driver's side?" he teased.

"I didn't dent the driver's side," she said in flat denial. She was quiet for a second then she giggled. "I dented the passenger's side."

He laughed. "You better not have." He tickled her and she squirmed, but like a wounded animal, thrashing in pain, without the playful squeal he was used to, so he stopped. He laid his hands over her ribcage and waited for her to fall asleep.

He was just about to get up and go into the other room, sure she had powered down by now, when she said, "Dan?"

"Yes, sweetheart?"

"What will happen if we can't fix my arm?" She laid on her right side with her injured limb on top, and he moved his hand to it, careful to only rub above the cut, where she could still feel it. He felt heat as he got closer to the open wound, sure there must be a short in the wiring.

"Don't worry about that," he said. "I'm sure we can fix it."

"But what if we can't? What if there's a problem we don't know about and we can't fix it. Will it—matter?"

"Of course not," he said, wrapping his arm around her and squeezing her tight. "Not even a little bit."

"You promise?"

"I swear."

"What does that mean?" she asked. "I've heard others say it, but I don't know it. What does it mean to swear?"

"It's like a promise," he said, "but it's bigger. It's a promise you make from your heart."

She fell quiet again, and again, he was certain she had powered down. "I love you," she said, almost in a whisper.

"I know," he said. "I love you too." He didn't know how long he stayed. It was a long time.

262

CHAPTER 50

It would have been easier if he could just take a shortcut.

When he was a child, his mother would load him into the car once a month, weather permitting, and make a three hour drive one way to spend the weekend at his grandparents' house in rural Indiana. His grandparents were both academics, cold and bookish, who took no pride in the fact that their only child had dropped out of college over an ill-timed pregnancy and married Daniel's father. They never called him Dan and certainly not Danny. In that cold and somewhat musty house, filled with artifacts his grandfather had collected while travelling for the prestigious university he'd once worked for before being fired over a sexual harassment suit involving a young coed, he was Daniel. There was no television in the house. He was not permitted to touch any of the artifacts. For the most part, Daniel was allowed to sit on the couch and read. Or he could go to his room and read. On rare occasion, he was permitted entrance to his grandfather's office, where the walls were lined with bookcases filled with leather-bound volumes of ancient tomes, and he could sit in one of the leather wingback chairs that faced his grandfather's desk. There, he was allowed to read, as long as he did so quietly.

One day, not long after his eleventh birthday, for which his grandparents gave him a card that read, "It's Your Birthday!" with multi-colored, untethered balloons that seemed ready to fly off the page, and a crisp ten-dollar bill, he had gone to the kitchen to get a bottle of water. He'd stopped in the doorway, hearing his grandmother's voice, and he hadn't realized anyone was in the kitchen. He'd thought his grandmother and mother had gone to market. He heard his grandmother mention rather frankly that she believed her daughter should have gotten an abortion and continued her education, to which his mother replied that an abortion would have been pragmatic. Daniel had gone back to his room to read Jules Verne.

But as bad as these weekends were, the drives to and from were worse. He would sit and stare out at the flatness of Indiana and wonder why anyone would choose to live here. It was nothing but small town after small town, separated by farms, and everything looked the same. The same fields—the same crops—the same tractors pulling the same farm implements. Even the small towns looked the same. The same drug stores—the same hardware stores—the same whippy-dips serving the same ice cream. Mother had suggested he take a shortcut—what she called a nap, "because you fall asleep and then you wake up and you're there. It's a shortcut." He found he was more inclined to take shortcuts on the drive home than the one there.

And he wished he could take a shortcut now, just fall asleep and wake tomorrow, when the delivery man knocked on the cabin door, but whatever she had done to his feet hadn't just made the hangover go away—it had energized him as well, and that energy was demanding to be spent. He caught himself pacing without realizing when he'd begun. He'd stopped in the bedroom doorway more times than he could remember, just to watch her—to stare at her, and he'd forced himself to go back to the living room because he knew if he stayed longer, he would call her name, just to hear her voice. He dressed in a brand new, white polo shirt she had picked out for him, along with khaki walking shorts, also brand new, then put on the new walking shoes she'd made him try on in the store and walk up and down the aisle to make sure they fit. Today, he had to tie them three times to get the laces straight and even, a habit he'd thought he'd dropped.

He stopped at the car to look at the passenger side, smiling when he found no dents, then set off down the hill, toward the rec room and rental office, the sound of loose gravel crunching under his feet the only noise that seemed out of place. Birds sang in the trees—a brook babbled, on its way to the Little Pigeon, then who knew where? Dan didn't. He tried to free his mind, to get in touch with nature, but he couldn't. Something felt off. He went into the rental office.

Nancy was there, sitting behind a desk, and she smiled at him when he set off the bell hanging over the door as he entered. "Hey there. Everything okay? Do you need anything?" She got up and walked to the counter, her hips barely narrow enough to pass between the two desks.

"No, everything is fine," Dan said. He went to the counter and folded his hands on it. "We're getting a package delivered tomorrow," he said. "I was just wondering if they would drop it off here, or would it come to the cabin?"

"As long as you gave them the cabin address, they should bring it right to you," Nancy said. "If not, they can drop it off here, that's fine."

"I'm not sure which address Savannah gave them," he said.

"How is she?" Nancy asked. "You know, she is so sweet, and so pretty. You got yourself a good one there. She's a keeper."

"Yes, she is," Dan agreed. "She's fine. Taking a nap. We were out kind of late last night." Nancy smiled politely, and the silence felt awkward. "So, you'll call us if the package comes in?" he asked.

"Sure will, first thing," she said. Dan knew that signaled the end of the conversation and that he should leave, but he didn't want to. He wasn't particularly fond of Nancy—he didn't dislike her, of course, but he wasn't drawn to her at all, yet he didn't want to go and he didn't know why. Was it that he missed having someone to talk to?

No—that was a preposterous idea. Dan had spent most of his life with no one to talk to, and he liked it that way, didn't he? Mother had never been one for idle chit chat. And she had been gone for six years, leaving Dan alone with no one to talk to at all. He was used to it. Savannah had been around only a tiny fraction of his life. It wasn't possible he'd grown that accustomed to another voice that quickly, was it?

"Was there something else?" Nancy asked, and Dan knew that was a hint to leave.

"No," he said, drumming his hands on the counter, burning off more nervous energy. "That about does it." He turned to go, then saw the three racks of brochures that Savannah had picked through the day before. He poked through the ones for Gatlinburg, looking for something new. "You couldn't recommend a good place for an early dinner, could you? Maybe something in walking distance?" Without realizing it, he began to straighten the brochures in the rack, spacing them equally apart, using his index finger to measure. He squatted to reach the bottom two rows. He considered sorting the brochures according to activity, but then realized what he was doing and forced himself to stop.

"If there's one thing Gatlinburg has, it's good restaurants," she said. "Maybe try the Trout House. It's downtown, on the Parkway." Dan saw the brochure for The Trout House on the second row and he took one, opening it as if actually reading it. "It's kind of far to walk, but the food is good."

"Thanks," he said. "Maybe I will." He saluted her with the brochure then said, "Catch ya later," as he left, the little bell signaling his departure. He stood in the roadway, looking up the hill, toward the cabin. He should just go back there, but he remembered that lonely, pacing, nervous energy, and he didn't want it to return. He turned to go to the bottom of the hill, intent on walking this feeling away.

Parts of Gatlinburg were made for walking, with wide sidewalks to accommodate a lot of people. Others were not, with no sidewalks at all. This was a, "not" area. There wasn't even a worn path. He turned left, going against the traffic through the high grass. Trash littered the side of the road, tossed out of car windows by inconsiderate people. Who littered anymore? Hadn't they seen the Woodsy-the-Owl cartoons? Part of him wanted to go buy trash bags and clean this mess, (mess, mess) but he knew that feeling came from an old Dan he had hoped was gone forever, the same urge that had wanted to straighten the brochures, and again the feeling surprised him, blindsided him, coming for him like a distant memory of his mother. He fought it, not wanting a return to that crippling life he had shed without realizing it had left. All he knew was that he could remember a day when he had obsessed with a lint ball in a trash can. He didn't know when or how it happened, but even without realizing it, tiny messes had stopped bothering him. Then bigger messes were okay, too, and while he didn't know when his life had changed, he did know why, and she was in bed in a cabin less than a mile from here. If she were walking with him right now, holding his hand, he wouldn't even notice the litter on the side of the highway. Yesterday, when they had checked in, he hadn't noticed the brochures were in disarray. Now, with her gone, those thoughts tried to consume him. He kept walking, hands in his pockets, head up so he wouldn't have to look at this mess, mess, mess.

In half a mile, he reached the City Limits sign, and with it came a sidewalk. The streets here were pristine, well maintained, because litter was ugly and tourist dollars dried up when things were ugly. He kept walking, past the outer businesses—the cheap hotels and low-end tourist shops—fishing guides and rafting tours. There was a salt and pepper shaker museum and he couldn't believe anyone would pay to look at a collection of salt and pepper shakers, but there it was, the sign pointing to a building less than a block away. There was a pancake house next to a BBQ hut next to a pizza joint. He kept walking, the lone person on the sidewalk this far from the center of town. There were cars, though. Lots and lots of cars, driving past at speeds slower than he would have expected. He found it easy to pick out the tourists because they were the ones looking at the sights more than the road. He began to count them as he went, and he found the ratio to be about ten-to-one in favor of the tourists.

And then, without warning or a decent transition, the sidewalk widened and he was on the edge of the Parkway, standing at an intersection where there was a crosswalk and traffic signal. He stepped behind another group of tourists and waited for the light to change, glad he didn't have to touch the button to trip the crossing sign. So many strange people touched that button in one day. Think of the germs, germs, germs.

He walked alone surrounded by people. The atmosphere had changed with the sidewalks, and now country music piped into the streets, but he found the speakers this time, high enough on light posts to be out of reach of vandals. Shop doors were propped open and many places kept cheap merchandise in the street to lure traffic—rubber bears that squeaked when you squeezed them and floppy felt hats cut to look old and worn, and plastic back scratchers and Hillbilly weather rocks (If the rock is white, it's snowing!). Groups of tourists meandered past him, moving without direction or speed, most eating whatever they had purchased at the last shop, trying to finish it before they got to the next one so they could buy more. Saltwater Taffy and fudge and cotton candy and roasted nuts in funnel-shaped plastic bags. He kept his hands in his pockets to not accidentally touch any of them, taking a wide berth when necessary. He walked faster, no idea where he was heading, no destination in mind, just going forward, moving quicker than the people surrounding him, weaving around and through the larger groups.

As he entered the corner to the next side street, a little girl of seven or eight rounded the intersection at the same time as he, carrying the remnants of a dripping chocolate ice cream cone, paying more attention to licking her grimy knuckles than where she was going. Dan threw his hands up and jumped back, trying his best to sidestep the collision, but it was so unavoidable it seemed fated. She slammed into him so hard, he was surprised it hadn't knocked her down. He looked at the blob of ice cream that saturated his new white shirt. It was ruined—the shirt was a mess, mess, mess, and the little girl's hands were covered in germs, germs, germs. He felt the cold, drippy, stickiness as it ran down his stomach through the white cotton fabric, not stopping at his belt. It was ruining his shorts—even his new boxers. It would soon drip onto his new shoes. He could predict it, the way Savannah had predicted the dripping of the Arby's sauce.

The little girl looked wide-eyed, afraid, knowing she was in trouble from this strange man. She was Choley—Chloe—just call me Nikki, from Serpent Mound, but Dan knew it couldn't be her. She did have the same mound of unkempt, curly dark hair tucked under a baseball cap though, and while the two girls looked close enough to be sisters, he knew it wasn't Choley because of the fright in this girl's eyes. Choley was fearless. "I'm sorry," the little girl said, meek—timid.

"Angela Renee Jacobs, what did you do?" a woman yelled at the little girl. "I'm sorry, mister. She never looks where she's going." The woman dug in her purse. "Now, aren't you ashamed of yourself?" She scolded her daughter as she pulled out a small wad of tissues.

Dan looked at the mess (look at the mess, mess, mess) of his shirt again and the ice cream dripping from the girl's hand. In his mind, Savannah was beside him, with him, holding his hand, and she reached out and stuck a finger in the blob of melty ice cream that now stuck to his shirt, then sucked on her finger to taste it. The vision was so real, he could almost see her.

"I'm really sorry, mister," the woman said again, wiping his shirt with the tissues. "Angie, tell the man you're sorry."

"I'm sorry," Angie said, her voice meek with the hint of a child's lisp not yet faded. More people walked past them, going from one shop to the next, a few staring at them like rubberneckers craning their necks for a better look at a traffic accident. When they realized there was no blood involved, they lost interest, moving on to the next shop, then the next, glad it wasn't them involved.

He felt the tug at his shirt as the woman pulled on it, then her hand trying to wipe away the ice cream, grinding it deeper into the white cloth, smearing the chocolate stain, making it worse. He heard Savannah's voice, stating in a matter-of-fact tone that chocolate was good—strawberry was better.

Dan threw his head back and laughed—

— long —

— and hard —

— and deep.

The crowd didn't bother him. The mess of his ruined shirt didn't bother him. The cold, drippy, runny ice cream didn't bother him. The little girl's germy, grimy fingers didn't bother him. He felt fine. No—he felt better than fine—fine wasn't the right word—Dan Mitchell felt—

Reborn.

CHAPTER 51

"We find the defendants, guilty."

There was an uproar from both sides of the courtroom, shouts of joy mixed with anger. Dan felt the room shift, like out of a Hitchcock movie, where the camera remained pointed at the protagonist's face, keeping it in focus, but the room shifted around them. That was it—fifty years. He just knew it was going to be fifty years behind bars. Even if it wasn't fifty, it would still be seven. Savannah grabbed his hand and he turned to her as she gripped him tight. He'd been right—that kiss in the corridor minutes ago was one of the last ones they would ever share. He would die behind bars and she would be confiscated and destroyed. Their lives were over.

"Order," Judge Abigail Mason said, banging her gavel hard. "Order in this courtroom." She was a heavyset Black woman, the kind who seemed to demand respect even when they weren't a judge.

"You Honor, we wish to file a notice of appeal," Gatherwright said even before the pandemonium died down.

He could run—just make a break for the door and go as fast as he could. He was sure others had tried it, but they didn't have Savannah on their side. She could take out three or four of the deputies as easily as he could swat a fly, and who knew how far they could get?

"I said order," the judge yelled again, slamming her gavel down so hard, Dan was surprised it didn't break. It snapped him out of the daydream of fleeing. No matter how far they got, it would never be far enough. Everything came with a price—the price for their happiness was their lives, it seemed. "I will clear this courtroom if that happens again," she said. The room fell silent. "Now, what did you say, counselor?"

"Your Honor, we wish to file a notice of appeal," Gatherwright said again.

"I figured as much," Judge Mason said. When Gatherwright began to approach the bench, the woman waived for her to stop. "I want to see both counselors and the defendants in my chambers," she said, then wrapped her gavel again, a single lick that wasn't as loud, and stood. She walked through a door to the side of her Bench, held open for her by a bailiff.

"Come on," Gatherwright said. Dan and Savannah followed her across the courtroom, past the jurors who still wouldn't look at him, holding hands as if it were the last time they would be allowed, then stepped through the door as well.

When they entered, Judge Mason was removing her robe and hanging it on a coat tree behind her desk. She looked at the group of them. "Mr. Palance, I don't believe I asked you to join us," she said. Dan hadn't realized that Ian had followed them. "I only allowed you to testify so you would stop pestering defense council. Expert witness my foot. Alan, get him out of here."

"Yes, Your Honor," the bailiff said, grabbing Ian by the back of his collar and escorting him from the room before Palance had a chance to protest. Since Palance was on their side, Dan didn't see that as a good sign either. He thought he had prepared himself for this—told himself he could face whatever verdict was handed down, but how does one prepare for something this bad? He was a good man—he didn't deserve this.

"More money than sense." The judge sighed and shook her head. She looked down at her desk at a stack of papers. "In thirty years on the Bench, I am considering doing something I have never done before," she said without looking up. She sat in the seat behind her desk before her gaze lifted. "I believe in the Justice system. Dedicated my life to it. I believe that if given the correct information, a jury will be able to look beyond their fears and prejudices and do what's right." She folded her wrinkled, dark hands in front of her, resting them on the desk. "But I also believe that what I witnessed today was a gross miscarriage of justice, and I am tempted to set aside the jury's verdict."

"Your Honor, you can't," the prosecutor said. "The jury has spoken."

"The jury has spoken out of fear, Mr. Greenley, and you know it, or at least you used to, before you became a politician."

"Your Honor, that's not fair," Greenley said.

Mason pointed a finger at him. "I told you to go into private practice. Be a defense attorney. Do some pro-bono work, but did you listen? Got your eye on the Mansion. Gonna run for Governor." She waved her hand like it was a Baptist revival, then flipped it at him, dismissive. "I liked you better when you were my clerk." She sounded disgusted with him.

"Wait, you clerked for her?" Gatherwright said, as if she hadn't heard correctly. "Your Honor, that's prejudicial."

Judge Mason waved her off. "Don't worry, Ms. Gatherwright, if I was going to find on one side or the other, it would have been against him." She made it sound like he was a disappointing nephew. She leaned back in her chair, her fingers laced over her stomach. "So, Mr. Governor's Mansion, give me a reasonable argument as to why I shouldn't strike this verdict."

"Your Honor, The People voted for the politicians who decided upon these laws. They speak for The People. The People want these laws."

"The People want cheeseburgers and chocolate shakes for dinner every night, but we can't always get what we want, Mr. Greenley. It's not good for us. If The People got what they wanted all the time, I wouldn't be allowed to sit on this Bench." She looked at April Gatherwright. "And what do you want, counselor?"

"I trust Your Honor will do as her conscience guides her," Gatherwright said.

The judge chuckled. "You want me to let the verdict stand, don't you?" She didn't wait for an answer. "You want to argue this higher—take it all the way up the chain. I don't blame you. I was young once, too." She thought for almost a full minute and Dan felt the sweat, slick on his palms. He didn't know what was happening. "All right. The verdict stands," she said. Both Greenley and Gatherwright smiled. "I wouldn't get too happy just yet, Mr. Greenley. We both know this law won't hold up to federal scrutiny. I'm going to withhold sentencing until the appeals are exhausted."

"What does that mean?" Dan asked Gatherwright, leaning closer to her.

But it was the judge who answered. "It means you're free to go, Mr. Mitchell, at least for now. I believe what happened was an honest mistake and not likely to occur again. Am I correct in this assumption, Miss Savannah?"

Savannah smiled. "Yes, ma'am. Thank you." She squeezed his hand tighter still, but not from fear this time. He could feel the difference.

The old judge smiled. "Now, I understand the two of you have some other legal issues."

"Your Honor?" Dan asked, not sure what she was talking about.

"Can't get a marriage license?" Judge Mason asked as she stood. She went to her bookcase and took down a leather bound tome that reminded Dan of his grandfather's office.

"Oh, no, Your Honor. Bureaucratic red tape," Dan said.

"Do you still want to get married?" she asked Dan.

"Yes, Your Honor. Very much."

"And what about you, Miss Savannah. Do you want to marry Dan?"

"Yes, I do, Your Honor."

"And can you tell me what it means to marry someone?"

"It means I get to love him forever," Savannah said, as if the question was silly.

"That's as good an answer as I've heard," Judge Mason said. She looked at Gatherwright. "I trust you'll be a witness?"

"Your Honor, this is—well—it's just not right," Greenley said. "The Clerk of Courts has—"

"They're the Clerk of Courts," Mason snapped at him. "I am the damned Court. Mr. Greenley, you are a prosecutor. You deal with the worst that man has to offer every day. You can stay here and be a witness to the best of man, or you can leave—it's your choice, but make it now. Alan, will you let that fool Palance back in here? I expect he's going to want to see this."

"Yes, Your Honor," Alan the bailiff said, smiling, then he left the room. It was clear he held a genuine affection for the lady.

"I'm not sure I should," Greenley said. "This is a big case, and —"

"And you don't want to appear as if you support the marriage," Mason said, finishing his statement for him. "I get it. I don't like it, but I get it. You sold your soul, Michael. I hope you got a good price for it." She put the book on her desk, then took another robe from the hat tree, different from her Judge's robes, and put it on.

Alan and Palance returned as Michael Greenley exited, and Palance was holding one of their legal pads in one hand, but Dan couldn't see which, his or Savannah's. Since his only contained a few random phrases, he assumed it was the one with Savannah's drawing. It was quite beautiful. Perhaps he wanted to keep it as a souvenir. He went to Gatherwright and nudged her, showing her the drawing. Gatherwright said something in return and Palance pointed to it.

"I am also an ordained Baptist minister," Judge Mason said as she picked up the old book. This time Dan saw it was a Bible. She shot an irritated glace over Dan's shoulder. "Mr. Palance, are we disturbing you?"

"Just conferring with my colleague, Your Honor."

"She is Defense Council, Sir. You are not. She is not your colleague."

"Then conferring with my girlfriend, Your Honor."

"Hmm," Mason said, looking dismissive. "The generosity of some women is astounding."

Palance tucked the legal pad into his book bag. "I don't get it either, Your Honor."

"Palance, you stand back there and try not to bother me. Now, you two, stand next to one another and hold hands. You got a ring?"

"Not with me, Your Honor," Dan said. He worried. Could they hold the ceremony without a ring?

"No matter, we sell them in the gift shop, don't we Alan?"

"Yes, Your Honor," Alan said grinning. Dan was confused—there was a gift shop?

Savannah leaned in closer to him. "She was teasing," she whispered.

The judge-turned-reverend let out a big tummy laugh. "Yes I was, Miss Savannah. You take good care of this man. I think he's going to need it."

"Yes, ma'am," Savannah said. "I swear."

Mason smiled at her, "I know you will, child. I know you will." She patted her Bible as if it were an old friend, then looked out past them, almost over them, as if the whole world was watching and she loved a large audience. "Dearly beloved, we are gathered here this day in order to witness the union of Dan and Savannah in holy matrimony, which is—"

AFTERWORD

This is the first book in the series, but don't worry--the next three books are already written, so you won't have to wait long. I wanted to make certain the story flows, so I held off releasing, and have no intentions with stopping with four. Sit back, relax, open a beer and enjoy.

ABOUT THE AUTHOR

Terry R. Lacy

Terry Lacy is a writer, college professor, drummer, woodworker, and general lay about. He lives in Florida, and like most locals, spends less time on the beach than he expected when he moved here.

He is available for speaking engagements, readings, lectures, workshops, festivals, conventions, circuses, fairs, Mitzvahs both Bar and Bat, birthdays, weddings, and funerals. Basically anywhere there is free food and or beer.

PRAISE FOR AUTHOR

"A white knuckle adventure filled with love and hate, redemption and revenge, it's well worth the read. It's a little cowboy, a little military, a little steampunk and a little love story all rolled into one and it does it well. Highly recommend. 5 stars." C.R. Martin

- C.R. MARTIN

I loved this book!! The story captured my attention from the first page. A perfect blend of action, adventure and a beautiful love story. I have recommended it to all my friends and know I will read it again and again.

- IVIS READER

Another good read. Thanks for the blind guy. He was fun. When is the next book coming out? Doc's wit is great

- KINDLE CUSTOMER

BOOKS BY THIS AUTHOR

Lilith Rises

This psychological thriller deals with Teresa Moore, a twenty-year-old girl who doesn't know she carries the soul of Satan's Bride, Lilith, inside her, or that Lilith's Minion needs her and her infant child to bring about Armageddon.

Jackal And The Space Slavers

For fans of Firefly and The Orville, comes the Jackal series. Fast action meets humor in a combination that's hard to put down.

When Jag and Fancy free a group of slaves rather than sell them, their lives go from boring to endangered.

Jag is a small-time, mostly-honest space trader, part-time smuggler. Together with his sidekick, Fancy, a former stowaway, now turned best friend, they make their living flying around the spiral armpit, buying and selling cargo with a little contraband for flavor.

When they take a job hauling sex slaves to market, Fancy--who had narrowly escaped that life--would rather die, or better yet, kill, than sell these girls. They steal a pirate's cargo--then they steal his ship. Now they're on the run.

This is a relaunch of a previous edition, with new cover art, in preparation for release of the entire series.

Jackal And The Lost Princess

An abducted princess--a kingdom in peril. Jag, Fancy and the crew of Jackal team up with an ancient Earth order to help a friend, save a kingdom, or die trying. For fans of Firefly and The Orville comes this funny, white-knuckle story with the one of a kind Jackal Crew. Don't miss this one.

Final Rebellion

China won WWIII. The US is occupied, Americans enslaved. But hope lives in the hearts of a few patriots. Can a handful of insurgents take down the Chinese Army?

Tee is a quiet man who works in the timber trade in the former United States. He knows history through his government schooling, that Communist China was victorious over the lazy infidels who were slaves to capitalism. His grandfather spoke of a better life before communism, before he was dragged away to the camps. Life was simple. Tee had a simple apartment, a simple job, and a simple life.

Then he met Zoey, a stripper in a small bar who had a big secret. Knocked unconscious in what Tee believes is a robbery turned kidnapping, Tee realizes that he is the target, but they have targeted the wrong man. Taken to a secret camp in a world he has never known, he finds out a truth he would have never believed. "A white knuckle adventure filled with love and hate, redemption and revenge, it's well worth the read. It's a little cowboy, a little military, a little steampunk and a little love story all rolled into one and it does it well. Highly recommend. 5 stars." C.R. Martin

Made in the USA
Las Vegas, NV
03 September 2021

29563783R00173